A LINE IN THE SAND

A JESSE JAMES DAWSON NOVEL

K.A. STEWART

Also From K.A. Stewart

The Jesse James Dawson Series
A Devil in the Details
A Shot in the Dark
A Wolf at the Door
A Snake in the Grass

The Arcane West Trilogy
Peacemaker

Second Olympus

Because now is all we get...

<u>Acknowledgements</u>

As always, this book would not be what it is without a group of very hard-working people who get no payment and never as much credit as they deserve. So, without further ado, I give you my beta-slaves, Alice Loweecey, Lori Diederich, Will Sisco, Dr. Gita Bransteitter, Jenn Wolfe, Janet Yantes and Caron Woods. In addition to that kickass team, I have my own support group, consisting of the Purgatorians, without whom I would not be so sane, and Scott and Aislynn Stewart, without whom I would not be so crazy. Thanks to everyone for sticking with me all these years.

1

Once upon a time…

If there is one thing I've learned from television and movies, it's that everybody has an origin story. Be you hero or villain, there is a moment, one shining moment where you are bitten by a radioactive spider, or splashed with toxic chemicals, or maybe just slapped down one too many times. Something changes in you from that point on, something that makes you into the person you will be for the rest of your life.

For me, most people would think that it was the moment I chose to challenge a demon over my little brother's soul. They would be wrong. I mean sure, that was a momentous event. But my feet had been set on that path years before by three people who could not have been more different from each other.

The first was a man named Thaddeus Carter. He was a county court judge who just happened to preside over the jurisdiction where my youthful indiscretions got me arrested and hauled before his bench.

The cops were done with me. The school was done with me. It was even possible that my father, dressed in the only nice suit he owned and standing beside me with a stoic look on his face, was as done with me as a parent can get.

I hadn't been an easy child. Full of anger and energy with no way to burn it off in our little one-horse town. Like so many of my friends, I looked to drugs for some escape from the ungodly monotony of our daily existence. At fifteen, I'd tried pretty much everything we small-town boys could get our hands on, and it was only a miracle of fate that I hadn't come to harm in the process. We skipped school, we drank and smoked and occasionally borrowed an unattended vehicle without permission. Once, I crashed a stolen riding lawn mower. True story. My only saving grace was that I hadn't been caught before.

Somehow, despite all of that, Judge Carter saw something in me worth saving. To this day, I don't know what or how. He perched honest-to-god pince-nez glasses on the end of his long beaky nose, and stared down at me, seeing a person who could be greater than what he'd shown so far.

The owner of the business I'd helped vandalize was livid when the judge passed down his sentence. Probation until I was eighteen, and mandatory martial arts classes at the only dojo in town. He made it very clear that if I stepped out of line even once, the only thing that waited for me was time in the juvenile detention center the next county over.

He retired not long after handing down my punishment, and it was years later that I realized that I was the reason he'd been encouraged to step down. Alternative sentences weren't big in that big little town back then, and not everyone agreed with his assessment of me.

Regardless of small town politics, to which I was oblivious at that age, I was bundled up and appropriately delivered to my first karate class the very next week. I'd never been to the run-down building where someone had started a tenacious little dojo. I knew that at one time, the building had been a pharmacy, sometime back in nineteen-dickety-two, and that the shadier side of our society had sometimes used the vacant building for their own ends.

Then, Carl Bledsoe had arrived and purchased the structure almost before he'd purchased his house. I remember what a stir the Bledsoes caused upon their arrival, the one and only African-American family in the whole town. Even more exotic, they had moved there from New York, Carl's wife Theresa taking on a job in Kansas City despite the hour commute each way. New York was far enough away back then that it may as well have been Mars, and we watched these new faces like they were celebrities, bound to display strange and disturbing big-city habits if we just kept an eye on them. I remember the oldest boy, a year or two younger than me, being challenged on the playground when we were both still young enough to care about things like recess. He dropped two bigger boys before the teachers intervened, and while he was the one who got sent to the office, no one bothered Noah Bledsoe again.

Somehow, my drug-baked brain had never connected that boy's fighting skills with the fact that his father was a martial arts instructor. I wasn't firing on all cylinders, back then.

So my father walked me to the door of the school, giving me a push inside with a stern look that promised all kinds of hell to pay if I screwed this up. He didn't even come inside with me, instead electing to sit in the car and read (and probably waiting to see if I was going to make a break for it out the back).

The building had been gutted down to the cement brick walls and exposed air ducts and pipes running across the ceiling. Everything had been painted a bright white, and words had been painstakingly stenciled on the walls in a variety of bright colors. I didn't even bother to read them, already writing them off as some kind of snobby nonsense, and I scowled at the sea of tiny faces that turned to face me. The class was taking up one set of red mats on the floor, their shoes neatly stored in little cubbies off to the side.

If those kids had come up to my waist, I'd have been amazed. Tiny little beings, all dressed up in their sharp white *gis* with their little white belts tied firmly around their waists. Six years old, the tallest of them, if that. There was another kid, closer to my age maybe, leading them through their exercises. He looked about as scrawny as I was, with fewer inches of height and more red in his hair than blond, and his wire-rimmed glasses were thick as Coke bottles. He wasn't anyone I knew from school, and I had to wonder what town they'd trucked him in from. His *gi* was also pure white, but his belt was brown, and when he demanded their attention again, the munchkins all turned back and set themselves to work again. A dozen little voices yelled "Kiyai!" in unison, punctuating their fierce little punches.

"You gotta be fucking kidding me," I muttered, but I kept it low, mindful that my continued freedom was dependent on this guy telling the judge that I was reporting as ordered.

"You must be Jesse." The deep voice startled me, and I stuffed my hands in my pockets and slouched harder to hide my flinch. I hadn't noticed the big man occupying the other set of empty mats, and I tried really hard to pretend that I wasn't intimidated by the sheer *size* of him.

Granted, I was a spindly thing myself, but Carl Bledsoe's thighs had to be as big around as my waist. He wore white *gi* pants and a black tank top, showing off the obscene amount of muscles across his chest and arms. He hadn't bothered with a belt to denote his rank. His black hair was cropped close, military style, and I could just make out the dark shades of some indistinct tattoo on his left biceps. His bare feet made no sound on the mat, and I couldn't help but think that he could stomp on my head and have room leftover. He gave me a smile, and I tried not to stare at how blindingly white his teeth were against his dark skin. (Hey, I hadn't been exposed to a lot of the world yet. And I was dumb.)

"I'm Carl Bledsoe. When you're here in this dojo, you can call me Sensei." He offered his massive hand, and I stubbornly kept mine in my pockets. After a moment, he gave me an amused quirk of his brow that only served to make my latent anger simmer hotter. I hated him already. "So, you're looking like you're pretty tough already. You probably don't need all of that foolishness, right?" He gestured toward the white-belt class.

I shrugged, keeping my eyes on something distant, and thought he should be happy he got that much out of me.

"Okay, fine. So how about you go a few rounds with me and we'll see where you're at."

That got me to look up, eyes going wide. "Are you out of your mind?!"

He grinned, expecting that reaction. "What, you don't think you can handle me? All right. How about Kevin there?" He nodded to the teenager currently instructing the little ones in a pattern for blocking. "He's more your size."

I eyed the brown-belted kid, and decided yeah, I could probably beat him. I'd scrapped with some pretty big kids in my time, and I never really *lost*, per se. "Sure. Okay. I don't have any clothes, though. Y'know, the uniform."

"You don't need one, if you don't want to have one. Though I'd recommend coming in sweats and a t-shirt from now on, instead of your jeans. Easier to move." Carl motioned for his student teacher to come over. The younger students, as if on cue, all melted down into cross-legged positions, their hands resting primly on their knees. A few of them grinned, turning in their seats so they could watch what was happening.

"Kevin, this is Jesse. He's going to be joining us as a new student. We need to test him to see what belt to start him at. Okay? He's not wearing a cup or headgear, so watch your shots."

"*Hai*, sensei." The bespectacled boy bowed from his hips, arms clapped firmly to his sides.

At Carl's gesture, I kicked my sneakers off and we found places facing each other on the empty mat, Kevin giving me the same bow he'd just given his teacher. After a moment, I bowed back, feeling like a world-class jackass, and hoping that no one outside this place had seen me. That formality exchanged, the smaller boy fell into what I would learn was a fighting stance, his weight balanced lightly on the balls of his feet. He held his fists up in front of his chest, and I had to smirk. The curled hands were tiny, his wrists skinny to the point of frail, and he gave me a smile behind his thick lenses that I didn't return. I was going to destroy this little nerd, and then maybe they'd leave me the fuck alone.

I waited for what seemed like forever for him to do *something*. Instead, he continued to bounce on his toes, still giving me that same friendly smile, and I finally lost my patience. With a snarl, I lunged forward, swinging with all my might for his face, only to find out too late that he wasn't there anymore. I pitched forward, my balance careening me across the mat, and I was lucky to keep my feet. Turning to look behind me, there stood Kevin, still smiling, still bouncing, and completely untouched. So what did I do, but go at him again.

Four times I charged the kid, never managing to make a single point of contact. Not once did he try to strike me back, always greeting me with his cheerful grin when I'd spin to locate him once again. "Stand still and fight, you little creep!"

Kevin glanced at his sensei, who gave a nod, and the kid shrugged his scrawny shoulders. "Okay."

My next charge ended with me again staggering for footing, only this time I was rewarded with two light taps to my ribs as I passed him by. There was no mistaking the message. If he'd wanted to hit me hard, he could have. It would have hurt. The lack of pain only seemed to make me angrier. The next time I went at him, he didn't dodge. Instead, he slapped my punch aside like it was an annoying mosquito, and jabbed me in the stomach. Again, it wasn't hard enough to hurt. Before I could round on him again, his foot lashed out and caught me on the thigh, shoving me off balance and sending me staggering in the opposite direction.

That brought me face to face with the grinning class of white belts, and I was sure there was mockery in those beaming little faces. My vision was a haze of red when I spun again, and I remember roaring as I dropped my shoulders and charged, intending to take my irritating opponent to the ground with me.

The next thing I knew, I was blinking up at the bare dojo ceiling, gasping for the air that had been forcefully evicted from my lungs. I had a vague memory of traveling through the air, at some point being totally upside down, but no real idea how I'd gotten into that position before I crashed down full force on the padded mat beneath me. Carl Bledsoe's dark face moved into my field of vision, and he looked me over for injuries for a moment before hauling me to my feet with one massive hand.

"I want you to take a few things away from this experience," he informed me, and I didn't have enough breath to argue about it. He held up one finger. "First, you cannot let anger rule your actions. It makes you sloppy, and it makes you stupid." The second finger went up. "Second, you must learn patience. Often times, simply waiting will force an opponent to do something dumb." He raised the third finger. "And third, remember that the size of your opponent has nothing to do with their ability to beat you, if you ignore the first two things."

I leaned my hands on my knees, bent over and wheezing, but managed a nod. From the corner of my eye, I caught a glimpse of a white shape, and it resolved itself into Kevin, the boy showing the first glimpses of uncertainty on his face. He offered his hand to me, to shake, to show there were no hard feelings, but I could see that he fully expected me to slap it away. I had to wonder if he had many friends, that he was so worried about what I, a total stranger, thought. I didn't shake his hand. I couldn't, that day. I wasn't yet the person that I would be later. But I did nod and give him a weak thumbs-up, which he seemed just as happy with.

It would be cool if that was my turning point, the point where I suddenly set my feet on the straight and narrow. It wasn't. I dutifully showed up at the dojo for my twice-weekly court-ordered lessons (in a white *gi*, with my white belt), but I wasn't just going to cave in and toe the line. Sensei

Bledsoe quickly learned to teach me one-on-one, with Kevin's occasional help. My propensity to spew foul language every time I turned around made my presence a bit too scandalous for the younger classes. So I spent Tuesday and Thursday evenings drilling forms and movements into my unbelievably thick skull.

On the nights when I was feeling particularly disruptive, either Kevin or Carl would let me take a run at them again. I never landed a punch, but there came a moment when I realized I was actually getting closer. It so startled me that I forgot my footwork and Kevin's counter strike landed squarely on my nose, bloodying it but good. Instead of lashing out at him in retaliation, I actually busted out laughing, doing my damnedest not to get blood all over our neat white uniforms. Sensei quickly appeared with a towel, and tended to my busted face with quiet efficiency, but I caught the hint of a smile at the corners of his mouth. That was the night, I think, that I first started to give a shit.

I took classes with Carl Bledsoe and Kevin for four years, well past the ending date of my probation. In fact, my last lesson was on the day I moved away for college, traveling all the way across the state (it was actually just an hour, but it seemed like another planet). My ribs still ached where Kevin had managed to tag me in our last good-natured bout. It was all right, though, because I'd nailed him too, and we'd laughed about it afterwards.

I was headed for the big city with college on

my mind but no real plan, and he was leaving in another week for some engineering program on the East Coast. In the time I'd spent learning with, and from, him, Kevin and I had become friends. We promised to email, but we didn't as often as we should have. I mean, we were nineteen year old boys. We were still mostly idiots.

Halfway through my freshman year, I got word that my friend and long-time sparring partner had been killed in a car accident – drunk driver coming out of nowhere. I made the interminable journey (still just an hour) back to my hometown, and Sensei and I stood next to each other at Kevin's funeral, both of us bowing solemnly to the casket before it was lowered into the giant hole in the ground. That was the day I learned that giving a shit hurt like hell. I'd never lost anyone before, especially not someone who was my age, who should have been going off to college himself and living life for decades to come.

I could feel myself wanting to slip into old habits, the siren song of oblivion calling to me. Anything was better than *this*, someone young and vibrant who was now just a bunch of nothing in the cold ground. I knew where my old crowd still hung out. Hell, most of them were probably still stoned off their asses in the same basements right where I'd left them years ago.

As we left the grave site, Carl's hand closed around my shoulder, still able to make me feel small even though I'd gained quite a few inches since our first meeting. "Tell me about college. Tell me about this girl."

It helped. Just the simple act of relating to him the new experiences, the new people I'd encountered so far away from my small hometown. The pretty dark-haired girl with flashing green eyes who'd actually agreed to go out to a movie with this scrawny little blond kid from Podunk, Missouri. Instead of seeking out drugs and drowning out painful feelings, we talked all night on the Bledsoes' front porch, despite the bitter cold of a winter that refused to let go. We talked about me, to start, just catching up on the months I'd been away, but then it became about Kevin. Things we remembered, things we regretted. Things we'd do in the future, just so that we wouldn't forget the painfully skinny kid with the big smile and outrageously thick glasses.

"I want to hit something," I confessed. "I want to find the guy who did it and beat the ever living shit out of him."

Carl nodded, sipping the one and only beer I'd ever seen him drink. "He'll be dealing with his own demons. I doubt there is anything you could do to him that would hurt more than his own guilt."

"Yeah, but it would make me feel better."

"No it wouldn't." He gave me a small, fond smile. "And it wouldn't change anything."

"But it *should*. There should be something to do, somebody we could go to and say, 'hey, you made a mistake, he's a good guy, can we please have him back now?' I mean, Kevin was going places. He was smart, and decent to people, and I'm kinda pissed off at God for just yanking him out of here before he got to *do* anything." I knew I was sulking, at this point, babbling nonsense. But the part of me that felt like a petulant child had the need to be heard, that night.

The older man outright laughed at that. "I have no doubts that you would storm the Pearly Gates themselves if you thought you were helping someone you cared about. That's who you are." He sighed, watching the darkness. "We can't change what happened before, but we can change what happens next. That's what you have to do, Jesse. You have to become that good man that you thought Kevin was destined to be. Do it for him, since he can't anymore."

I snorted softly, watching my breath curl in front of my eyes. "I'm barely clinging to 'just okay'. Good may be out of my reach, still."

"Try. It's the trying that's as important as the being." The big man shifted in his chair, turning to look at me seriously. "And remember that there's no one way to be good. Good can be as big as saving kids from burning buildings, or it can be as small as giving someone a smile when no one else will. The world has a shortage of good. Every little bit counts."

I went back to college, back to the city that seemed so very far away from where I'd started. I declared philosophy as my major, like that was somehow going to help me find some kind of sense in the senseless. I thought about what it meant to be a good man. I thought about Kevin, and Carl, and where I was and where I wanted to be.

I found a tattoo parlor and plunked down some of my hard-earned cash to get a line of kanji tattooed down each biceps. "The way that is spoken here is not the eternal way. The name that is spoken here is not the eternal name." The first two lines of the Tao Te Ching. I heard them in Carl's voice, every time I saw the dark lines inked on my pale skin. There was no one way to be good. I just had to find mine.

As the years went by, I thought about Kevin less often. Still, I would catch a glimpse of a kid down the street, sometimes, all gangly elbows and knees, and I would have a slight jolt of "hey, is that…?" It wasn't, of course, couldn't be, but the mind can be cruel. To this day, the sight of thick lenses on glasses just screams "Kevin" to me, though the reminder doesn't hurt anymore.

We were a lot alike, he and I, when you got right down to it. Two kids from small towns, skinnier than anyone had a right to be, learning to be bigger people than our bodies would reflect. On nights when I let my mind wander, I wonder if he would have been a champion, too. He could have fought with a katana, same as me. He could have found a girl, had some kids, saved the world maybe. But Kevin was gone, and that left just me, trying to do enough good for both of us combined.

Sometimes, I still wish I'd gotten a radioactive spider instead.

2

Now…

My son was born on a Tuesday. He came into the world without extraordinary drama, and we named him William Martin for my two best friends, even if one of them was no longer speaking to me. My father, the Wild West expert who'd named his sons Jesse James and Cole Younger, immediately dubbed the baby "Billy the Kid" and no matter how Mira and I objected, the name seemed likely to stick.

That night at the hospital, after the nurses finally let Mira sleep and the visitors had been politely hustled out, I sat in the darkness cradling that tiny new life in my arms. His head was almost completely bare under the blue knit cap they'd plopped on him, but I could already tell that what few wisps of hair he had promised to be strawberry blond just like his big sister, Annabelle. He seemed so tiny in my large hands, and I wracked my brain trying to remember if my daughter had been so small. I remembered being terrified when I first held Anna, a young father now responsible for another human being. I was still scared to death as I looked at my son, but for different reasons.

With the room illuminated only by the glow of the TV near the ceiling, it was easy to see the lines of white filigree as they crept down my hands to my fingertips. The souls riding in my skin ventured out to cautiously investigate this new curiosity. My sleeping son didn't stir, and I knew they weren't going to hurt him, so I allowed it. Even if one of the nurses had walked in at that moment, odds were they wouldn't be able to see anything unusual.

Those souls, two hundred and seventy-five sparks of life, didn't belong to me. Sure, we'd been sharing the same body for months, though it seemed like much longer. I'd inherited them from their previous…owner? Host? Vessel? But they weren't mine, and that meant that they could be taken from me. I was carrying the spiritual equivalent of a nuclear bomb, and there were many less than noble creatures in the world who wanted that power.

The bad guys were coming for me. I knew that as certainly as I knew the sun would come up in a few hours. They were taking their sweet time about it, obviously, but demons were, for all intents and purposes, immortal. They didn't usually get in a big hurry about things.

To put it in perspective, their leader, a fallen angel currently going by the name of Reina, had been waiting a literal millennium for her chance. What was a couple of more months or even years in the face of that?

Reina would come for me and these souls, and this late night moment with my newborn son might be all I'd get. I rocked the reclining chair back, lay the baby on my chest so he could hear my heart beating, and closed my eyes. The souls would wake me if something happened.

Only once during that night did they stir as the smell of cloves tickled my senses. I opened my eyes a crack to see Mira awake and watching us. With my magic-enhanced vision, I could see the tiny golden threads of magic drifting out from her fingers, wafting across the room on a non-existent breeze to weave a delicate gossamer blanket around the sleeping infant on my chest.

She was beautiful, my wife. From the first moment I'd laid eyes on her, with her wealth of dark curly hair and startlingly green eyes, I'd been lost, utterly and entirely. And then, I got the joy of realizing she was kind, and intelligent, and funny, and… In all the years we'd been together, I'd only grown more amazed that someone like her would pick a scrub like me.

It was only after I learned about demons, after I learned about all the terrible things that went bump in the night, that I also learned her magic was real. Some genetic quirk in the population, some unused part of our brains, I never knew why some people had the talent and some didn't. But a select few – I wasn't one of them – could draw upon the power of their own souls to work wonders, and my wife was one of them. Mira wasn't the strongest practitioner I'd ever seen, but she had a combination of power and precision that made her formidable. It was accurate to say that she'd kept me alive through sheer willpower, over the past few years.

While she was pregnant, Mira had been unable to cast the simplest spell, for fear of it harming our unborn child. Now, with the baby safely in the world, she whispered things I couldn't hear, and the room filled with the warm and soothing scents of her magic. The souls in my skin tingled and squirmed at the sensation, but even they seemed to know that this magic, this spell, was welcomed. I dozed again, for what was probably going to be the last peaceful night I'd have for a while.

The next few months went by in a kind of pleasant daze. We adjusted well to the new member of the family, and Billy turned out to be a very easy baby. Sure, he woke in the night like any infant, but between Mira and I, and the two bodyguards who still shared a roof with us, someone was always there to offer a bottle or midnight diaper change.

I will admit, the first time I woke to find Sveta singing softly to my son in Ukrainian, I was a little nervous. Sveta had the hollow-eyed look of someone who had seen combat and the scars to prove she'd survived it. After sleeping in just her T-shirt and underwear, we'd all gotten a good look at the marks that marred the smooth skin of her arms, traced patterns down her legs, carved a path across her ribs. Along with the physical wounds came the invisible ones, the touches on the mind that would never quite heal. I had it, Estéban had it, my brother had it. PTSD was just a fact of our lives. I couldn't say how much she might have changed since taking on the champion role, but she wasn't exactly known for her stability after.

But I watched them that night and saw a gentleness in the cold woman that I'd only glimpsed once before. On a recent trip to Mexico, I'd been soothed to sleep one night by the scarred warrior singing a soft lullaby to a group of adolescent boys.

I'd crossed it off as an oddity at the time, but now I realized that Sveta genuinely liked children. And they liked her, apparently. My son gazed intently at her face as she sang, as if he understood every word. Who knows? Maybe he did. Maybe babies aren't limited to just one language until we teach them to be.

I turned to sneak back to my room and nearly walked into Estéban. My protégé-turned-bodyguard offered me a small smile, and we both returned to our rooms. We didn't worry about Sveta and the baby after that.

Life was working, for a change, and I did my best not to dwell on the moment when it would stop working. Anna took to being a big sister like a duck to water, doting on "her Billy" and scolding us when we didn't care for him just so. Even our big lummox of an English mastiff, Chunk, seemed to understand that he was large enough to hurt the tiny baby, and while he would curl up at the edge of the blanket when we laid Billy on the floor, he never tried to get close, never got too rowdy.

I still had nightmares, of course, but I was getting better at coming out of them without rousing the entire household. The tunnel dream returned time and time again, where I would step from a mysterious opening into a flat empty area. Some kind of arena, I'd decided, and far across the dirt expanse, I would search to see if the dark figure was standing there. Sometimes he was, sometimes he wasn't. Then the dream would hiccup, and I'd be back in the tunnel, stepping out all over again. Frustrating, yes, but not frightening.

Mira started back at her shop, Seventh Sense, part time. The store was a labor of love for her, carrying new age and occult supplies for the greater Kansas City area, and she hated to be away from it for very long. I returned to my job at It, selling band T-shirts, ripped jeans, and over-sized piercing accessories to the masses. I was often accompanied by Estéban who decided to pick up a few hours himself. I couldn't begrudge him that, a kid needs spending cash. On the days he didn't work with me, Sveta would lurk nearby, but it increasingly seemed like a waste of time. Things were good. Things were real good. It couldn't last.

"Hey, Old Dude!" I glanced up from restocking the juniors t-shirt rack in time to see something small rocketing at my head. Without thought, I snatched it out of the air, revealing a soft foam novelty football. Raising a brow, I looked at my assailant across the store.

Kaden, a gangly teen with a shock of bleach blond hair crowning his otherwise brunet head, gave me a grin. I rolled my eyes and threw the missile back at him, smirking when he nearly fumbled and dropped it. "Cat-like reflexes, son!" Behind me, Estéban snorted, so I turned to glare up at him, too. "And where were you, Mister Bodyguard?"

The young man shook his head, gazing down at me from atop the high ladder where he was precariously changing light bulbs. "If a foam football takes you out, you deserved it."

"If I see that football fly through the air one more time, it's going up someone's ass!" Kristyn, my green-haired-for-today boss, fixed us all with the Look of Doom™ from her place behind the cash wrap. We all pretended to be suitably chastised, and Kaden dumped the offending weapon back into the bin with the rest of its cronies.

Kristyn wasn't really mad, of course, and we would probably last about half an hour before we found some other irritating way of spending our time. The store was overstaffed for the minimal customer traffic we were having, and it left us with nothing to do but busy work. Not that I minded. Work was work, and it kept my mind off other things. The younger dudes, though, it took more to occupy them. Estéban wasn't so bad anymore, his time training with me instilling a modicum of discipline, but Kaden was new, and young, and like a puppy, prone to chewing on things when he was bored. And I fully admit, I instigated about half of it. I mean sure, I had quite soundly aged out of Its target demographic, but at heart, I would never grow up. I mean, I was wearing a shirt that said "0 Days Without an Accident."

As I turned to resume my task, a subtle vibration came from my back pocket. Glancing to make sure Kaden wasn't looking, I slipped my cell out to see who was calling. We weren't technically supposed to have our phones on the floor, but as the only other person who had been at the store as long as Kristyn, and having a history of emergency calls I couldn't miss, my boss elected to overlook the rule so long as I didn't flaunt it in front of the kids.

Seeing that it was Mira, I swiped to answer automatically. "Hey, darlin'."

"Hey, sweetheart. You have a minute to

talk?"

I glanced around the store, seeing a distinct lack of customers, and shrugged. "Sure, what's up?" Estéban mouthed "tell her I said hi" at me as I made my way back to the break room. "Kid says hi."

"Tell him I said hi, too." In the background, I could hear my daughter's voice chattering away, punctuated occasionally by Sveta's quieter tones. "Listen, I was talking to Dee today about my hours at the shop."

I perched my butt on the corner of our decrepit card table and nodded, like she could actually see me. "You wanting to go back full time?"

Mira sighed quietly. "I…yeah, I do. I think I'm ready. But I wasn't sure how you'd feel about it. We don't really have enough to put both kids in daycare, and I wasn't sure…"

"Mir, we will make it work. Okay? If you're ready to go back to the shop full time, I'll talk to Kristyn about reworking my hours here, and maybe we can get away with daycare only a couple days a week."

"Are y—" Whatever Mira was about to ask was cut off as our infant son let out a piercing howl in the background. "What the hell?" Simultaneously, the deep roaring bark of our Mastiff rang through the phone line.

I frowned. "Everything okay there?"

"Not sure. Gimme a second." She carried the phone with her as she walked through the house, the sounds getting louder. The baby crying, the dog baying, and Sveta cursing not so softly in her native language.

"Mira?"

"What do *you* want?" The question wasn't directed at me, and I instantly recognized the sound of fury in my wife's voice. "You're not welcome here! Get out!"

"Mira! What's going on?" Either she didn't hear me, or she had to ignore me to deal with whatever was happening at the house.

For a heartbeat, I thought I heard the sound of a muffled male voice under all the cacophony. The next sound was exploding glass, and Mira's phone went dead. Instantly, the souls in my skin surged to the surface, alarmed by my sudden adrenaline rush. I dialed her back, and it went straight to voice mail. I didn't try a second time.

"Kid, we gotta move!" I dashed through the store without even saying goodbye to Kristyn, barely noticing the sound of Estéban's boots hitting the ground running behind me.

Piling into my ancient Mazda pickup truck, I threw the phone at the kid. "Keep dialing Mira, let me know if she picks up." He set about his task without question, and held on for dear life as I peeled rubber out of the parking lot.

It was a fifteen minute drive from Sierra Vista Mall to my home, and we made it in nine, breaking multiple traffic regulations and several laws of physics. I didn't even bother with the driveway, plowing to a halt in my own front yard and catching my sword as Estéban retrieved it from behind the seat. I could already see the line of smoke rising from the open front door, and my heart nearly stopped.

"Mira!" With the kid on my heels, I bolted through the front door, the jamb of it charred black and smoking mournfully. The door itself wasn't just open, it had been blasted off the hinges, and was currently in a pile of kindling in my kitchen floor. Only then did I realize that there had been no tingle of magic as I crossed the threshold of my house. The wards were down. "MIRA!"

Nothing. No response. The only sound I could hear was my own heartbeat thundering in my ears and Estéban's ragged breathing behind me. No voices, no dog, just dead silence.

"Sweep the house." I was amazed that I even came up with words, let alone coherent ones.

Estéban moved past me into the kitchen, his own stained machete in hand, and his boots crunched on broken glass. The sliding glass door in the kitchen had been destroyed, though it looked like more glass had gone out than come in. Turning, I started down the long hallway.

The first room to my left was Estéban's, and it was dark and empty, not a thing out of place. Even the computer, glowing cheerfully, was still in sleep mode. Whatever had happened, it hadn't been enough to jostle the machine. The bathroom was likewise vacant, and I swallowed a half-ton rock in my throat as my steps took me toward Anna's room.

My daughter's room held no answers. Her stuffed animals were still scattered about the floor, and in the back of my mind I could hear Mira telling her to pick them up over and over. Her little sneakers were at the corner of her bed, and an absurd part of my mind was upset that she'd obviously left without them.

The last place I could look was my own bedroom, and I was disappointed there as well. Nothing. No sign of my wife or my children, my dog, or my other bodyguard. Even knowing it was futile, I raised my voice again. "Mira! Anna! Billy!"

Nonononono... I was drowning. There wasn't enough air in the world, and I knew that my entire body was glowing like a beacon to heaven, my passengers ready to burn themselves to cinders to defend me, if they just had a target.

Estéban appeared in my doorway, shaking his head. "Checked the yard and the garage. They're not here. But Sveta's weapons are gone."

I grasped at that tiny fact like the last molecule of oxygen in the world. Sveta was with them, and she was armed. The kid moved out of my way as I stalked back down the hallway. "Try her phone again, maybe—"

"Jesse?" The voice came from the front of the house, maybe even outside, standing on my front porch. I didn't really care at that moment. It was Mira's voice.

"Mir??" Rounding the corner, I could see her standing in the wreckage of our living room, peering into the gloom of our darkened home. Dropping my sword, I crossed the space in an instant, yanking her into my arms and crushing her tightly against me.

"We're okay," was the first thing she said

after I released her, but the smile she offered was tremulous at best. "We're fine. The kids are across the street at Dixie's."

"What happened?" Glancing over, I saw that Estéban had collected my sword, and was keeping a watch on the backdoor as best he could. *Good boy.*

"Something came." Mira shook her head, her green eyes dark against her pale skin. "I didn't see what it was, but it was strong enough that it just blasted through the wards." Her hand stroked our burned door jamb and came away black with soot. "Thank the goddess we weren't here."

"I heard the door shatter, and you were still in the house."

Mira grimaced. "Uh, yeah… That might have been me. I was a little angry."

"Can we discuss this somewhere with lockable doors?" Estéban's frown reminded me that I still wasn't thinking clearly. I could feel the tremors starting in my fingers as the adrenaline rush faded, and the passenger souls receded back into their tattoos on my back.

"Come on over to Dixie's. We told her we thought we had a gas leak, and Sveta's trying to keep her from calling the fire department."

I took my sword back from the kid with one hand and held tightly to my wife's hand with my other. Estéban shadowed our steps as we crossed the street, holding his machete tight against his thigh to try to hide it from nosey neighbors. "Let her call them. The more people we get here, the less likely they are to come back, whoever or whatever it was."

As we stepped up on our neighbor's porch, the kid asked, "So, why weren't you in the house when it came?"

"We were warned."

Mira pushed the door open as I asked "By whom?"

A tall blond man stepped into the foyer as we entered, mumbling through a mouth full of something. "This is the best fucking cookie I've ever had." Even muffled under cookie crumbs, he sounded like me. *Exactly* like me. It was creepy.

"Language, Axel!" Mira snapped like chiding a demon was something she did every day, and Estéban and I just stared in amazement.

The lanky demon just blinked and looked back and forth between the three of us. "What? They're really good. I'm telling you, Jesse, I never would have screwed with her cat if I'd known." Not so long ago, Axel had come to visit me by possessing Dixie's over-sized orange tabby, dubbed Garfield. I'd persuaded the demon not to kill the animal, but Garfield hadn't been quite the same since.

"Deal with this," Mira muttered to me, managing to push past Axel without actually touching him.

The man-demon turned to watch her go for a moment, then shook his head. "You need to see about some anger management therapy for her. Did you see what she did to the door?"

"Shut up. Just…shut up." I grabbed him by one thin arm and dragged him into Dixie's living room. Suddenly, we were surrounded by lace doilies, decorative kitten plates, and more lilac perfume than a person should use in a year. Estéban took up a post in the doorway, watching down the hallway. "What the hell just happened?"

The man-demon calmly shoved another snickerdoodle into his mouth, whole, and munched thoughtfully. "Someone got ambitious. I heard about it in time to get your family out."

"Why?" Demons never did anything for free, and I'd paid dearly for the last favor I'd returned to this one.

He raised a pierced brow at me. "You'd rather I let them die?"

"I mean, what do you want?"

"Can't I just do something out of the goodness of my heart?" He did his best to give me an innocent look, but a smug grin twitched at the edges of his mouth.

"No. As far as I know, you don't actually have a heart." Demons had bodies on this side of the divide, but they were made up of a substance I called blight. No organs, no bones, just a solid mass of toxic black goo that would wisp away as you sliced bits off.

"Point." Another cookie went in his mouth, and he rolled his eyes in ecstasy. "I'd swear she sold her soul to learn to make these, but the old bat still has hers. It's crazy."

"I swear to god, I'm going to stab you in the face."

All hint of humor and human nature instantly drained out of the demon's face, and his eyes flared red for a heartbeat. "Be *careful*, Jesse. I saved them, and I've asked nothing. Don't try my patience." Something sinister crept in behind that voice, speaking of rancid oil slicks and foul, sulfurous fumes. A demon's voice, just in case I'd forgotten what this creature actually was.

"Don't."

Axel smirked. "That's better."

"I wasn't talking to you." I jerked my chin toward the doorway behind him, and he turned to see Mira and the kid both standing there, spells hovering at the tip of their tongues. To my eyes, they both blazed with light, Esteban's golden with tongues of red flame licking at the edges, while Mira's was pale green blending to soft yellow at the center where a knot of deep swirling magenta waited.

Axel was silent for a long moment, and I knew he was weighing his chances. He was the most powerful demon I'd ever seen, but the sight of my wife and protégé ready to blast him into the beyond gave him pause. "Well. I see how it is. See if I do you any favors again." With a poof of wispy blight fog, he vanished into thin air, taking the handful of cookies with him.

After a moment of tense silence, Estéban released the magic he was holding, and snorted. "I think we hurt his feelings."

"Like I give a fuck." Mira let her own spell go, and I swore I could feel a soft breeze as the magic went wafting by me.

"Language, Mira?" I raised a brow at her. She wasn't prone to cursing (not like me, who cussed every other word if I wasn't careful), and it spoke to how rattled the day's events had left her.

"Fuck you, too." I could see her shaking, though, and I moved to draw her into my arms again, tucking her head under my chin.

Estéban silently asked me a question, and I nodded him on into the house. "Go check on Sveta and the kids. Make sure Chunk isn't chewing through anything." I wasn't sure that the dog wouldn't try to eat his way into the house to get at Axel, even though the demon had departed. Dogs and demons were never the best of friends, which is why we had the giant Mastiff in the first place.

"On it." The young man vanished down the hallway.

Mira and I stood in stillness for a long time, both of us waiting for the shakes to subside. I buried my face in her wealth of curly chestnut hair, breathing in her scent of strawberries with a hint of the cloves that came from her magic, and she wrapped her arms around my waist and squeezed as tightly as she could manage.

Finally, she broke the silence first, her voice more than a little teary. "I can't do this anymore."

"Can't do what, baby?" Looking down, I tilted her head up so I could see her eyes.

"This. Any of this. The whole demons…souls…thing." Tears clung to her lashes, but her green eyes were clear, serious. "We can't go on like this. Our safety today depended on a creature that could just as easily been the one blasting through the front door."

"I know. I agree." I traced the line of her

jaw with my thumb, trying not to think about how I almost never got the chance to do that again. "I don't know how to fix this, Mir."

"Find it. Find a way. Before we lose everything."

Outside, I could hear the plaintive wail of an emergency siren drawing ever closer. Someone had finally called the fire department. This time, they'd show up with nothing to do but search for a nonexistent gas leak and make sure my door wasn't going to set the rest of the house on fire. The next time... There couldn't be a next time. I couldn't allow it.

I hugged her tightly to me again. "I'll figure it out. I swear."

3

The firemen clambered all over, under and through our house, and could find no evidence of a gas leak. We were strongly advised to call an inspector for a more thorough examination and stay elsewhere in the meantime, and of course I nodded and made all the appropriate noises until the nice men in their fancy red truck went away.

Leaving Sveta with the kids and our very nosy, but well-intentioned neighbor, Mira and I set about cleaning up the mess, aided by Estéban. He held up the massive sheet of plywood as I nailed it over the gaping back door, grunting each time my hammer hit, and Mira went about collecting the shards of glass.

"Maybe they're right. Maybe you should go stay somewhere else."

Mira raised a brow at me as she stood up straight, stretching her sore muscles. The spell backlash had held off until her body had decided it was safe, and then she'd been wracked with nasty muscle spasms. We'd hunkered down in Dixie's bathroom, my wife muffling her cries on a mouthful of bath towel while I tried to massage the worst of it out of her calves and feet. Given the sheer amount of power she had to have unleashed to shatter the door, we were lucky it hadn't been worse. I'd watched a man nearly die from something very similar.

"And where should we go?"

"Bridget's?" My wife's best friend was a

doctor, if nothing else. She didn't know about demons and souls and champions and magic, but she could take care of my wife and children for me. That much I knew.

"Bridget's house isn't warded."

"Neither is ours." I gestured around flippantly, but in truth, the sudden absence of the spells I'd become so accustomed to over the years made my skin itch. My home no longer felt right, no longer felt familiar. Even worse was the question of just what was so powerful that it could negate so much magic. Axel himself had never tested the protective boundaries of my home, and there was only one thing I knew to be as strong, or stronger, than him. *Reina.*

Only three months ago, I'd faced down with the fallen angel, absolutely willing to destroy the two hundred and seventy-five souls I carried with me just to save Estéban's life. She'd retreated then, not because she was afraid of me, but because she was afraid that I'd go through with my threat, and thereby destroy the source of power she was so desperate to claim. She needed the souls intact, and that was the only reason any of us were still alive. If she'd managed to grab Mira or the kids, though… There was nothing I wouldn't trade for them, and I had a feeling that everyone in the world knew it.

Wisely, Estéban stayed out of our discussion, just moving as needed so I could hammer more nails into place. After a few moments, my wife sighed. "You're probably right. At least until the doors get repaired. We can't have Chunk running loose in the neighborhood."

"Keep him with you. He'll be your first warning if something nasty shows up." I nodded for Estéban to step back, and we surveyed our handiwork. It'd do, for now. The kid took the broom and dustpan away from Mira and set about finishing the floor.

"I get the feeling you're not coming." She leaned her hip against the counter, fixing me with an unflinching gaze.

"You know I can't." I sighed, running a hand through my hair, absently noting how long it had gotten again. "I'm a danger to you all so long as I'm not alone in here." I gestured to my temple, as if she needed reminding.

Mira was quiet for a moment, then nodded. "So what are you going to do?"

I'd been thinking about it for a while, actually, and as much as I hated to do it, I didn't see another choice. "Ivan's on his way. The kid called him while we were talking to the fire chief. We're gonna go talk to Cameron, see what it'll take to get help from his people."

Cameron was also a champion, but not like me and the kid. Instead, he was a Catholic priest, belonging to their secret order of demons slayers, the Order of Saint Silvius, a saint that didn't really exist as far as most people knew. Sanctioned by the Vatican, they not only fought to retrieve souls from demon clutches, but they took it upon themselves to police the magic-using community too, removing the less-than-savory characters from the population.

I didn't have any proof of that last part, of course. It didn't seem like the kind of thing that an organization would advertise. But Ivan believed it, and he wasn't the only person I'd heard similar things from. Besides, what else would a super-secret team of holy warriors do in their spare time?

Cameron was currently living in sin with my wife's best friend, dear Doctor Bridget, and hey we were headed over there later anyway. How convenient.

"Do you think they can help you?" Mira tilted her head a bit.

"Carlotta and Terrence haven't made any progress. The Church is the next logical step." Estéban's mother and a former champion who was older than dirt had been trying to come up with a way to divest me of the souls I currently harbored. While we'd established that my passengers could be passed to another person (or demon), that wasn't an acceptable solution to me. We needed to free them, or at least put them where no one else could get at them.

In my mind, the question wasn't whether the Catholic Church *could* help me, it was whether they would. My only dealings with them had been through Cameron, and while he was a nice enough guy (don't you dare tell him I said that), the rest of the Order had always come across as snobby and rude. Appropriately, in a very mature and professional manner, I had dubbed them the Knights Stuckupidus. Like the demons I so often parlayed with, I was sure there'd be a price of some kind. "I don't see how I have another choice."

The young man with the broom cleared his throat a little, and both of us turned to look at him.

"I'll start packing bags for the little ones."

I nodded. "Pack one for yourself, too." That earned me an instant frown, and he opened his mouth to protest. I held up one hand to stop him. "I'll keep Sveta with me, and I want you to stay with Mir and the kids. At least until we figure out what the next part of the plan is." I wasn't ready to inflict Sveta on poor Doctor Bridget. The prickly Ukrainian champion could stay with me.

Estéban headed down the hallway, reluctance evident in the set of his lanky shoulders, and Mira shook her head at me. "He thinks you're trying to protect him."

"I'm not. You're used to working with him, magic-wise. If you have to, the two of you are better together." At one time, she'd have been right. It wasn't too long ago what I'd viewed him as just another one of my children, someone to shelter and keep out of harm's way. In the last few months, he'd proven that he could more than take care of himself, and while the occasional "kid" still slipped out when I was talking to him, I trusted him with my life. And now, with my family's lives.

Mira grimaced, shoving off the counter. "Well, I need to go feed my son, or I'm going to explode. I'll come back over and pack up my own stuff."

"Yeah, whatever you need to do. I'm gonna…work on the mess. Probably make some phone calls." I hadn't forgotten that I'd dashed out of work without so much as a "'kay bye" to my boss. And I had a feeling I'd be taking more time off in fairly short order, so I'd need to get that arranged. I needed to find out when Ivan's flight was going to arrive, and then maybe a trip to the home improvement store to get a new front door…

I stood in the middle of my trashed kitchen, spotting the remnants of Mira's phone poking out from under the fridge. Fishing it out, I saw that the screen had been reduced to so much glass dust, and the little device smelled of burned out electronics. No doubt a victim of the same magical blast that had exploded the sliding door.

Things had been good, for a little while at least. At least we had that.

The next few hours were lost to the simple administrative process of being an adult. There was an insurance company to call, my absence from my job to explain, lodgings to arrange for my wife and children. Sweet Dixie offered to let us stay with her until we could fix the doors, and we politely turned her down in unison. Neither Mira nor I wanted to think about what would happen if a demon came visiting our elderly neighbor. It was bad enough that Axel had invaded her home, and he was at least semi-friendly.

Ivan's flight was due in around seven, but before the kid and I could go fetch, I had one last thing to take care of. Making sure that my well-meaning bodyguards were preoccupied with Mira and the little ones, I escaped to my own back yard, noting how far the glass shards had flown. Mowing the grass was going to be perilous for a while, until we could find them all.

Standing near my little bonsai garden, I closed my eyes and stretched out my senses, testing for anything out of the ordinary. My ghostly passengers roused, curious, and it was their "eyes" I would use to see.

Around the boundaries of my lawn, a faint flicker or two of magic still lurked, left over from the protective wards that we had deliberately dismantled. I had to feel grateful for that decision, ultimately. It was how Axel had approached, leading my family out the backdoor as death came in through the front.

The wards on the house itself were so much ash to my magic-enhanced sight. It wasn't just the screen around the front door that had been annihilated, it was the entire protective fabric that had surrounded the house. Where once I would have seen a lacework web of gold, now there was only a dusting of black that was slowly blowing away as the chilly evening breeze drifted in. Almost like blight, I realized, and I shivered despite my warm hoodie.

I'd learned what I wanted to know, however, which was that I was alone. No demons lurked nearby, and the closest magic users were across the street and all familiar to me. Opening my eyes, I whispered one word.

"Henry."

For long moments, nothing stirred, the last summer birds chirping their goodbyes to the sun. Suddenly, like a switch had been thrown, silence fell, and a small branch of a nearby sapling dipped under added weight.

"James Dawson! Am here!" The creature that perched in the tree looked comical, at first. No taller than my knee, spindly arms and legs topped with a head that was entirely too large, with large moon-round eyes and ears that resembled bat wings. It was gangly and awkward, and hunched its thin shoulders like it expected to be kicked at any moment. Notice the vicious claws on its finger and toes, however, and the mouth full of jagged shark's teeth, and it wasn't so cute anymore.

I offered the tiny demon a small smile. "How you doing, Henry?"

My occasional minion hadn't yet mastered the art of small talk, and he ignored my question in favor of sniffing the evening air curiously. "What has come here, James Dawson? Why are magics gone?" He edged out toward the end of the branch, the limb bending alarmingly under even his slight weight.

"Well, that's what I want to talk to you about." I'd…acquired Henry on my trip to Mexico. The small demon was virtually powerless, as far as his kind went, and eager to make any deal he could to better his station. It had been easy to convince him to do me favors now and then, in exchange for some minor boons that I had yet to decide on. This was going to be the first time I'd actually exercised our new bond. I hoped it didn't come back to bite me in the ass.

Henry left off examining my magically decimated home, and spun himself around to hang from his branch, looking at me upside down. "What talks? What needs?"

I nodded toward my extinguished wards. "Something bad came here, Henry. It was powerful enough to blast right through every ward on this house. I need to know who it was."

The bat-wing ears drooped noticeably. "Henry does not have this information."

"I know. I didn't figure you did. But can you find out?" While I was ninety percent sure that Reina had visited my house today, there was still that little ten percent that said "Are you sure?" Just because Axel had never tested the protections on my home didn't mean that he wasn't fully capable of doing exactly this, and he had as much reason to want me rooted out of my safe little den as the next demon.

Did I think that Axel could have faked the whole thing to put me on the run, get me at a disadvantage? Hell yes I did.

The small demon's ears perked up. "Like a de-tek-tiv?"

I couldn't help but chuckle at the sudden enthusiasm on his ugly little face. "Yes, just like a detective. How do you know about detectives?"

Henry wrinkled his nose in puzzlement. "Not sure. See bugs on papers, only now they make words instead of squiggles."

"You're learning to read?" Tilting my head, I took a critical look at my odd companion.

Was he a little taller than when I first met him in Mexico? His hunchbacked stoop was harder to see, dangling from a tree as he was, but his knobby back looked a little straighter. And the cavernous mouth, still brimming with wickedly sharp fangs, looked a bit narrower, the jaw a bit more…human. His intelligence had increased, too, as I realized he'd spoken several complete sentences since arriving. Previously, his speech had been broken, childlike. Now, he was mostly understandable.

Henry was evolving.

This was my doing, I knew. However demons began their version of life, there was a definite power hierarchy they had to pass through. As their power grew, their forms would change to reflect that. I had names for the categories I'd encountered, everything from sentient oozes and insect-like critters that I called Snots and Scuttles, to furry mammalian creatures that would eventually grow to resemble humans as much as a demon could. I called those Skins and Shirts.

With just the little bit of power I'd given Henry, nothing more than two of my names, he'd grown. I had to wonder what the hell I was thinking, deliberately making deals with the demonic imp, knowing that I was really just breeding a bigger, badder demon in the long run.

"Will be de-tek-tiv for James Dawson. What will James Dawson give Henry?"

This was the tricky part. I couldn't give him my third and final name. That was too much, especially when he hadn't actually given me anything yet. But I'd known this day was coming, and with some help from Estéban on the sly, I thought I had it worked out.

"If – and I mean *only* if – you return to me with the true name of whatever it was that busted down my front door, I will give you this." I fished an object out of my hoodie pocket, and held it up in front of his moony eyes.

To anyone watching, it looked like just what it was. A ping-pong ball. White, plastic, fragile, bouncy. But to me, and to Henry, it glowed gold, with bits of red licking the edges like a flame that didn't burn. What I held in my hand contained a tiny, infinitesimal piece of Estéban's magic. Not enough to hurt the kid by donating, not enough to really cause anyone any harm if the power escaped.

I admit, I'd tricked the kid into making several of them under the pretext that we were trying to create a vessel that could house the souls I currently carted around. That pretty much put me in the category of "not nice person," but I hadn't been able to think of any other way to pay my debts. Mira, Sveta, the others, none of them knew about Henry, and for right now, the tiny demon was my ace in the hole, should I need it.

The ugly creature's pointed tongue darted out to lick his nonexistent lips, and he edged outward on the branch more, causing it to dip lower. "Where gets?"

"Don't you worry about where I got it. Do you want it?" I could see that he did. Henry had no poker face to speak of.

"Yesssss…." The big round eyes flared red, the color only dying back to its normal shimmery black in a slow fade. "Bring James Dawson the true name of the spell-breaker, and James Dawson will give Henry the treat."

"That's the deal." Something burned on inside of my left wrist, and I glanced down to see a crude black mark inked across the skin, the red searing edges cooling to nothing as I watched. It was done, then. My first official contract with Henry. Now all I had to do was keep the rest of my household from noticing the tell-tale mark. "And remember, Henry, if the Architect is nearby, you have to wait to reveal yourself until later. I don't want him to see you." I didn't know why the demons called Axel "the Architect", but the name served to sufficiently intimidate the smaller demon, so I invoked it when I could.

"Henry remembers. Henry will do." And with a poof of rapidly dispersing blight and the odor of sulfur, he was gone. The sapling branch sprang back into position, the entire tree shuddering as if glad to be rid of that toxic presence.

I pocketed the spell-ball again, then inspected my wrist. I'd been lucky. Most contract tattoos started on the back of the hand, which would have been harder to conceal. At least we were heading into autumn now, and long sleeves wouldn't be questioned.

Taking a deep breath, I closed my eyes and finally let myself be aware of my spiritual passengers. They weren't happy. They weren't happy at all, and once I allowed myself to feel it, the muscles in my back knotted and spasmed hard enough that my head was wrenched forcibly to the right. Gritting my teeth, I rode out the pain, and concentrated on bringing them back under control.

The souls, whoever they had once belonged to, recognized evil when it was nearby, and they hated all demons with the same passion. Even covered by my sleeve, I could see the tendrils of iridescent white as they crawled down my arm, inspecting the black mark burned into my skin. They would touch and recoil, and I could feel the horror and anger radiating from them.

"Sorry, guys. Sometimes, we have to do things we're not proud of." It took them a while to settle again, and I started to worry that Mira would come looking for me. There would be no hiding the agitated life force within me from her, and then I'd have some 'splainin' to do. And she'd probably punch me. I'd deserve it.

Organizing the family exodus was complicated by the fact that we needed to go get Ivan from the airport, and my trusty Mazda pickup only seated two. Sure, I could have gone alone, but even the mere suggestion of it had Estéban shouting and Sveta giving me the silent mercenary look of certain death, so that was a no go. In the end, it was decided that the kid would go, being the only other person I allowed to drive my truck, and I would go along to Dr. Bridget's with the rest of the menagerie.

I sat in the rear seat of my wife's Explorer with my two children, watching out the back glass as Estéban sped off in the other direction. My hand was draped over the seat back, fingers brushing the scabbard of my sword, The Way. My house receded into the growing twilight, and as we turned the corner to leave our neighborhood, I had the weird feeling that I wouldn't be seeing it again. Shivering, I buried my face in my infant son's hair, breathing in his comforting scent, and I tried not to think for a while.

4

Dr. Bridget Smith's house was a lovely split-level in a pretty housing addition neighborhood, surrounded by manicured lawns and literal white picket fences. Then, my family arrived, and everything descended into mass chaos. The moment the car door was open, Chunk bolted out of the vehicle and made a beeline for a cat across the street. The big oaf couldn't catch it, of course, and I don't know that he'd have any idea what to do if he did, but I still had to snatch his leash up and give chase. It was a game for the young dog, keeping his massive bulk just out of my reach with playful whuffs and a wagging tail, and it took me much longer to corral him than I'd hoped. All the while, Sveta leaned against the Explorer with her arms crossed, giving me an amused smirk, and my wife got the children and luggage inside with her usual quiet efficiency.

"No no, don't trouble yourself, I got this." I glared at Sveta as I hauled Chunk along behind me, the overgrown pup not the least bit repentant.

The dark-haired woman snorted. "It isn't my dog. And you could use the exercise. You are getting soft." She tried to jab me in the ribs, and I deflected the strike from sheer muscle memory. She chuckled. "Still fast, though."

I wasn't getting any softer than she was. We'd all taken to a strict workout regimen since returning from Mexico, all of us certain that we'd be fighting again in very short order. Sveta had even started teaching the kid to shoot, producing a disturbing assortment of firearms that she'd apparently had hidden around my home and her person.

Guns weren't really my thing. Most of them wouldn't do enough damage to a demon's physiology to help in a challenge, and the ones that would were likely to take out half a neighborhood block in the process.

But I also knew that there were other things in the world, things that had very real, very physical bodies. Sad, tortured creatures with no souls and no voices, their forms only desiccated shells of who they had originally been. Shapeshifting clay constructs that came on inexorably until the magic powering them could be severed. And men, some evil, some just misguided, who would do a demon's bidding in the hopes of coming out better than they'd been before. All of those things, you could hurt with a gun. So I let the kid learn, and I said nothing.

Bridget opened the front door to let us in, managing to give me a hug without getting tangled in the lumbering monstrosity's leash. The good doctor was lovely, as always, her deep brown hair piled on top of her head in a loose bun. Normally, I saw her in her office where she was always dressed in something stylish under her lab coat, but today, she had on yoga pants and a floppy football team sweatshirt that did *not* belong to our home town boys. I eyed the garment critically and raised a brow.

She rolled her eyes at me. "You can take

the girl out of Denver…" She closed the door as soon as Sveta entered, then lead the way toward her spacious kitchen. "Mir's getting Anna settled in the office upstairs. She was very excited about sleeping on an air mattress, once we told her it was like camping. You and Mir can take the spare bedroom with the baby, but I think Sveta and Estéban will have to make do with the couches down in the living room."

Sveta had been sleeping on our couch for months, I didn't think another one was going to upset her any. "Thanks, Bridge. This is just temporary, until we can get the house checked out and stuff." I let Chunk out into the backyard, hoping the fences would hold if he got too frisky in his new abode.

Bridget gave me a chiding smile. "Stay as long as you need to. You know that."

"So, uh…where's Cam?" I hadn't seen the other man yet, but we were going to need him sooner rather than later.

She nodded toward the door across the room. "Basement. He's working on that new model train display. You should check it out, Jesse, the detail is amazing!"

Yeah, model trains sounded just…fascinating. With a subtle jerk of my head to Sveta, we both went in search of the other champion.

We found him bent over a table that nearly filled the entirety of Bridget's basement. It was covered in minuscule trees, and even tinier shrubs, surrounding buildings that could have been shrunk down from real life. Plastic people went about their plastic lives amidst rather nice metal replicas of fifties-era cars, and through it all, the train tracks wound in lazy curves.

I couldn't quite make out what Cameron was doing to his intricate display, but the magnifying lens over one eye and the pair of tweezers he maneuvered with painstaking care gave him a bit of a mad scientist vibe. His dark hair, normally spiked with gel, was mashed into frantic shapes by the headgear he wore, and he obviously hadn't shaved in several days, judging by the stubble on his cheeks.

We stood and watched him in silence for long moments, until Sveta sneezed. Loudly. Given that I had never heard the woman sneeze in the six months she'd lived with us, I was certain it was deliberate. Cam startled, but managed to avoid damaging whatever tiny object he'd been working with. Flipping the monocle up, he gave Sveta a flat look. "*Et tu*, Brute?"

I have no idea what she said in return, since it was in Ukrainian, but the sweet smile on her face belied whatever foul words she had bestowed upon him. They'd only met a couple of times, the priest and the mercenary, but they hadn't tried very hard to become friends. I mean, I wasn't always real chummy with Cameron either, but I was at least civil. Most of the time.

In fact, when he removed his headgear and offered me his hand, I shook it quite congenially. "It's good to see you, Jess. I'm glad no one got hurt."

"Coulda been worse, that's for sure." And because it was right there, taking up the entire room, I was forced to comment on the train display. "This is…impressive."

Cameron chuckled. "Oh come on, this is the nerdiest thing you've ever seen anyone do. Don't lie." Well, yeah…pretty much. And I say that, fully admitting that I've done some pretty nerdy stuff myself. The tall man shrugged, his sheepish smile turning fond as he gazed over his pet project. "What can I say? I love it. Always have. Never really had a place to set up a good sized display before, y'know? This is the first place I've really…settled."

Cameron had come into our lives on a mission from the Church, one that should have involved him saving my life, then moving on. But he'd met Bridget in the course of his duties, and though their relationship was complicated in ways I didn't want to think about, they seemed to be genuinely in love. As far as I knew, Cam had managed to maintain his priestly vow of celibacy, despite living with the good doctor for the last year, and was obviously making plans to stay on a permanent basis. If Cam was conflicted about his commitments to the Church, I was about to throw that dilemma into sharp focus. I only felt a little bad. Okay, not really.

Cam blinked suddenly, and craned his neck to look back up the stairs. "Where's Estéban?"

"Airport. He had to go pick Ivan up."

That earned me another blink from the priest. "Zelenko is coming here?"

"This offends you?" Sveta took the last two steps down into the basement, her hand sliding toward the small of her back where she no doubt had some kind of weapon, and her voice almost dripping ice.

Feeling like I'd missed something somewhere, I moved two steps to the side. Sure, I probably should have stayed between them to head off whatever this was, but frankly, she scared me.

Cameron gave me a puzzled look, but I only shrugged in return. I had no idea what had flipped her switch. "Well, no… I was just surprised. I've never actually met the man."

She sneered. "You and your self-righteous sycophants, you are not worthy to lick his boots. A pack of puling cowards, hiding behind your Bibles…"

"Whoa, hey!" Okay, there was being mean to Cam for fun, and then there was downright insulting. And seeing as how I was going to be asking this man for a favor in the very near future, I figured this was the moment to step in. "Maybe take a deep breath or two, Sveta. Cam didn't do anything to deserve that."

Her frosty blue eyes wavered between the two of us for a moment, then she growled, "I will go help Mira with the little ones," and stalked back up the stairs.

Cam and I just stared at each other for long moments, before he whistled lowly. "What the hell?"

"Your guess is as good as mine." I peered up the staircase, but we didn't seem to be in danger of her returning. "I guess she has strong feelings about the Church."

The dark-haired man shook his head. "Don't we all?"

We spent the next few minutes in awkward silence, Cameron fiddling with his train diorama while I kept waiting to hear Sveta's boots on the stairs. I had no idea why Sveta had lashed out that way. The first time I'd ever seen her in Ivan's presence, I thought she was going to punch him, and they hadn't exactly been on warm terms in the times since. The display of loyalty was unexpected to say the least. Her venom toward the Knights Stuckupidus was startling, too. I mean sure, I bagged on them all the time, that was mostly because I was a jerk, not because they'd done anything particularly bad to me. I wondered what Sveta's story was. I wondered if I had the balls to ask.

"It wasn't a gas leak, was it?" Cameron looked at me from across the table, one eye magnified comically by the single lens.

"You know it wasn't." Cam knew about the souls I carried. He could see them plain as day, just like any other magic user. It wasn't hard to make the leap that someone, or some*thing*, had finally come calling for them. "Whatever it was, it blasted through every ward on the place. Just…wham, gone."

I saw his face pale a little at that. He knew the strength of the spells that had protected my home until today. "What are you going to do?"

"Not sure yet." I leaned my hip against the

table, careful not to jostle any of the tiny plastic people. "Carlotta and Terrence aren't making any headway, and if Axel knows how to get them out, he's not telling."

Cam's lips pressed tightly together at the mention of the demon, but he wisely left it unremarked. The priest and the demon had tangled once before, about a year ago, and neither was fond of the other. "Is it time for me to call Rome, then?"

I didn't believe for a moment that Cameron hadn't reported my situation to his superiors months ago, but I let it go. "Yeah, probably. Let's wait 'til Ivan gets here, though. We don't want to have to hash this out twice."

"Fair enough." He bent down to adjust something on the roof of a miniature drugstore. "If it's any comfort, Jess, I think they can help you. I really believe it."

"Glad one of us does."

It was another good hour before the kid got back with our new guest. To kill the time, Cameron regaled me with information about model trains and the keeping of such until I was almost ready to go up and face Sveta's wrath instead. It occurred to me, though, about halfway through the torture, that this was probably how people felt when I started going on about *bushido* and Japanese history, so I nodded when appropriate and pretended to be interested. Those of us with weird hobbies have to stick together.

We could hear the doorbell ring from the basement, and by the time we got upstairs, the greeting committee had already beaten us to the door. I couldn't help but smile as my feisty daughter flung herself at the large, silver-haired man, gleefully shouting "*Tjadko* Ivan!" Obediently, he caught her and hoisted her into the air, but I saw the faint grimace that crossed his face, and it made me look closer.

Ivan was a big man, topping me by several inches, and broader than two of me in the shoulders. (Come to think of it, with the kid's recent growth, I was now the shortest adult male in the house by at least an inch. That sucked.) Despite his age, which I put at anywhere between fifty and a hundred and twelve, he moved with the grace of a fighter, and held himself with the rigid posture of a soldier. At least, he had.

Beneath the black trench coat he always wore, those strong shoulders were stooped now, thinner somehow. His mane of pure white hair, always neatly groomed into a sharp crewcut, seemed yellowish. The hollows of his cheeks were more pronounced, and there were dark shadows under his piercing blue eyes that hadn't been there the last time I'd seen him, which was only a few months ago. When he moved to set Anna back on her feet, it obviously caused him pain, and he stood up again slowly.

Estéban, following behind with Ivan's duffel bag, caught my eye and gave me a small frown. He'd noticed too. I shook my head at him slightly. Now wasn't the time to mention it.

Mira presented herself next, hugging the old man gently, then introducing our newborn son. A smile split Ivan's craggy face, and he held Billy for a few moments, murmuring softly to him in Ukrainian. The baby gazed at the new face with rapt attention, and again I had to wonder if maybe he understood everything the old man was saying. Whatever the case, Billy only fussed a little when his mother took him back.

Mira also introduced Bridget. Ivan bowed over the doctor's hand, kissing it gallantly, and when he stood upright again, his eyes found me.

"Dawson." The voice, that thick, gravelly snarl, was the same, so deep I expected it to vibrate the windows. That was the Ivan I expected, and I started to wonder if I was overacting to his changes in appearance. I mean, the man was entitled to stress like any of us, right?

"Ivan." Stepping forward, we clasped arms like veteran warriors do. The hand the gripped mine was still strong, still vice-like, but the flesh had wasted away. I wouldn't quite call it skeletal, but the tendons and veins stood out in sharp relief. Pushing my worry to the back of my mind for the moment, I stepped aside and gestured toward Cameron.

"Ivan, this is Cameron. He's Doctor Bridget's boyfriend." Belatedly, I hoped that Estéban had briefed our esteemed leader on Cam's covert status. Bridget didn't know about champions and demons, much less that the love of her life was an incognito priest and warrior for the Catholic Church.

Regardless, Ivan didn't say anything that would blow Cam's cover. He shook the younger man's hand with a stiff nod, and Cam bowed his head respectfully. "Sir."

Ivan's eyes swept the foyer where we'd all crammed in, and a frown crossed his face. "Svetlana?"

I opened my mouth to make up some excuse for Sveta, when her voice responded from the behind us. "I am here." She'd obviously been watching us from the shadowed hallway, though why she hadn't come forward, I didn't know.

Her response was apparently sufficient for Ivan, because he nodded to her briefly. "I would like to be sitting, if possible. The flight was to being very long."

"Sure thing. Kid, go drop his bags in the spare bedroom." Sure, Mira and I were supposed to share that, but one look at Ivan told me that he shouldn't be sleeping on the couch. My wife and I could bunk on the air mattress with Anna, and when Mira shot me a small smile, I knew she agreed with me.

Ivan relinquished his coat, and I was startled by how much his impressive frame had shrunk in the last four months. That was more than stress. I caught Mira and Bridget exchanging looks too, and I made a mental note to pick the good doctor's brain later to see what her diagnosis might be.

Our strange group took up every inch of available space in Bridget's living room, even with Estéban and me occupying the floor with my kids and our enormous dog. Dinner was determined to be pizza, after much negotiating about sizes and crusts and toppings. Ivan ordered pineapple and arugula on his which just about floored me. He had never struck me as a pizza fan, let alone someone who had such particular tastes about the cuisine.

Sveta perched herself on the carpeted stairs, silently watching as we all exchanged small talk and caught up on our lives. She ate a few slices of pizza when it was offered to her, but she made no effort to join us, and her blue eyes rested on the big man at our center more often than not.

For a little bit, we were just normal people, doing normal people stuff. We ate, we talked, we laughed. Ivan told some outlandish stories of his travels, highly edited of course, in his unique version of English, and was generally the very picture of a charming houseguest. I watched him closely, but his energy level seemed good, as did his spirits. Maybe I was seeing nothing, flinching at shadows.

Eventually, the little ones started nodding, and Mira took her leave with that as an excuse. Bridget departed soon after, citing an early work meeting in the morning. Cam raised his face to receive a kiss, and promised to come along shortly. We all waited in silence for a few moments until we heard a door shut upstairs. Finally, we champions were alone. Almost immediately, the atmosphere of forced cheerfulness faded away, and the conversation grew somber.

"We are all to be knowing of the events of this day already, I assume." Ivan leaned forward, resting his elbows on his knees, and fixed me with a look that should have drilled a hole right through my skull. "So I must ask… The creature you are to be dealing with. It prevented harm to your wife and the little ones. What is it to be asking in return?" I'd been dealing with Axel for years, but Ivan had only found out recently. To say he was unthrilled was a grossly exaggerated understatement.

"He hasn't asked for anything, yet. In fact, he seemed offended when I mentioned it." The demon had disappeared almost immediately, without calling in the favor. I found that both oddly out of character, and disconcerting. I hadn't been able to parse his angle yet, and it was worrying me.

Ivan made some sort of disapproving growl in his throat. "It will. They are not to be doing good deeds for the sake of it."

"Can they?" All eyes turned toward Estéban, and his dark skin grew ruddy with his blush. "Stop, I mean. Can they choose to stop being evil?"

There was a long silence after that, and I finally sighed. "The thing is, kid, I don't think they think of themselves as evil. You gotta remember, every villain is the hero of their own story. To them, they're just doing what they have to, to survive in their own world. Just like any parasite."

Ivan snorted at that, but nodded slightly. "Nothing is so terrible as a man who is to be doing the wrong things for what is to being believed the right reasons."

Inwardly, I flinched at that and moved my hand to make sure my hoodie sleeve hadn't ridden up to reveal my demon contract mark to the world. It was still covered, and while I didn't think that Ivan's remark had been meant specifically for me, it stung. A lot.

The old man sat back on the couch then, and his gaze went next to Cameron. "You are to being in contact with Cardinal Giordano?"

"Um, not him directly, no. I'm a bit lower on the totem pole than that. But I can pass a message through the regular channels, if need be."

"And how long will that to be taking?"

"If I flag it urgent, I should hear something back in a few hours. It can depend on the time difference."

"Tell them the situation has changed. They will to be answering sooner, I think." Ivan also assumed that Cameron had already told them all about me. "Everyone here is to be having their traveling papers, yes?"

We all answered to the affirmative, but I shook my head when Estéban opened his mouth. "You're not coming."

Anger flared into his dark eyes, proving that he hadn't quite outgrown his adolescent temper just yet. "Why? Because I'm just a kid?"

I turned to look him square in the face, because that is what men do. "You stopped being a kid a long time ago. Long before Mexico, even if I didn't see it yet. Now listen very carefully to what I'm going to say next.

"You're not coming, because I need you here, protecting the three most important things in my life. You've worked with Mira's magic before, you guys blend well together, but more than that, I know you love Mira and my kids as much as I do. Even if we weren't leaving for Italy soon, you know I can't stay here with them anymore. Today proved that. And so you're all I have, Estéban. I'm putting my entire life in your hands." I held my hand out to him, waiting.

The kid – I had to quit thinking of him like that – held my gaze for long moments, then nodded and grasped my arm tightly. "*Sí*. I will stay, then. And I will protect them with my life."

I smiled a little, holding on when he would have pulled away. "Don't forget to take care of yourself, kid. I'd be pretty torn up if something happened to you, too."

He blushed again, and rolled his eyes at me in typical teenage fashion, yanking his hand back. Despite the show, I knew my faith in him had pleased him.

Ivan cleared his throat, the abrupt noise making us all jump a little. "Brother Cameron, if you would to be making your phone call. The rest of us should be getting what rest will come. We may to be having little notice before our flight."

Sveta and Esteban made to bed down on the couches, and it didn't escape my notice that the woman hadn't said a single word since Ivan's arrival. While she wasn't exactly prone to excessive chatter, I'd never known her to *not* have an opinion on things, and her continued silence puzzled me.

Cam showed Ivan to his room, and I continued on down the hallway to where my family was sleeping, curled up on an air mattress in Bridget's office. I opened and closed the door quickly, not wanting the light to wake the baby, but the brief glimpse showed me Mira, curled up protectively around Annabelle, with her other hand outstretched to touch the side of Billy's portable bassinette.

What I'd told Estéban was true. No matter how many souls I carried with me at the moment, *my* soul, the only one I would ever own, was there on that air mattress. If something happened to them, I'd die. Simple as that.

5

Unsurprisingly, my nightmares followed me into my sleep. They seemed evenly split between reliving old horrors and dreaming up new terrors to plague my night. Over and over again, my wife and children were torn away from me, screaming, and I would jolt awake with my heart pounding, ears straining for the sounds of an incoming threat that didn't exist.

The glowing digital clock on Bridget's desk ticked away an hour in ten minute increments, before I finally gave up for fear of waking Mira and the kids. Chunk, who had flopped down by our feet, raised his square head curiously as I rose, but I gave him the hand signal for "stay" and he lay his chin back down on his paws with a soft sigh.

I made it to the stairs before I heard soft bare feet padding behind me, a sound I automatically recognized as my wife. She slipped her hand into mine, and we made our way into the dark kitchen, mindful of the pair of jumpy champions sleeping below us in the living room. For a long time, we just stood there by the sink, me watching out the window while she wrapped her arms around my waist and tucked her head under my chin where it belonged.

"You know we can't keep doing this." Her quiet voice broke the stillness, and her breath tickled my bare chest. "*I* can't keep doing this."

"I know." I buried my face in her wealth of curls for a moment, then leaned back so I could see her face. It was impossible to tell that her eyes were green in the darkness, but I knew they were. Knew exactly what shade of emerald they turned when she was serious.

Her fingers traced my jaw, reminding me that I hadn't shaved in a couple of days. "I'm sorry, Jesse. You're doing the right thing. You know I believe that. But…when it threatens my children, it's too much. I just… It's bad enough, not knowing if you're coming home, but…"

Tears welled in her eyes, and I hugged her tightly to me again. "Shh. I know, baby. You're right. You're so right. You never signed up for any of this, and I just keep getting in deeper when I keep meaning to dig out." God, I was an asshole. All of this, everything that had happened to us for the last six years, was my fault. Every close call, every sleepless night, every near-death encounter. A man shouldn't do that to the woman he loved.

"They'll fix it. We have to believe that Cam's people can fix it," I murmured into her hair.

"And if they can't?"

I hesitated for a long moment before answering. "Baby, I can't come home. So long as these souls are in me, I can't come back and put you and the kids in danger."

A deep breath escaped her, like she'd been holding it, and it felt like she shrank in my arms. "What are you going to do?"

"I don't know yet. I'll jump off that bridge when we get to it, I guess. Estéban's staying with you, though. Between the two of you, you can ward the house again, and he can help out with the kids when you have to work."

"Does he know?"

"Yeah. He understands." Looking down, I tilted her head up to make very sure she was watching me. "You and the kids are my entire world. Protecting you has to come before anything else. The second – and I mean the *very second* – these things are gone, I'm out. No more challenges, no more demons. I'm done."

A ghost of a smile flitted across her face, but the sadness never left her eyes. "You say that now."

"I mean it."

"Jess." She silenced me with her fingers against my lips. "I know you. I know that you couldn't turn someone away if they were in trouble. And you shouldn't. You wouldn't be you, if you did. I wouldn't ask that of you."

"You shouldn't have to ask it of me. I should have done this a long time ago." I pressed my forehead against hers, just breathing in her strawberry scent. "I'm sorry, Mir. I'm so damn sorry, about all of this."

And now it was her turn to soothe me, her small hands stroking my hair. "Shh. I know."

We stood there for a long time, silently comforting each other, until a tiny, plaintive cry came from upstairs. Mira left me alone with a gentle kiss, and shortly after she disappeared, the house fell into deep silence again.

I stayed at the kitchen sink and watched the sky go from black, to midnight blue, to a faint tinge of gray emanating from somewhere beyond the housing addition. Dawn is a sneaky thing. One moment you're staring out at the dark sky. The next, it's blossomed into this pale gray with streamers of pink, and you're never quite sure just when that happened.

One more sleepless night to add to my count. I still had no answers.

Ivan was the first to appear, though I was fairly certain that Sveta had been awake just as long as I had. The old man shuffled down the stairs and straight to the coffee maker that had switched itself on a few minutes before.

Without his intimidating black coat shrouding him, wearing only a thin T-shirt and paisley pajama pants, he looked even more wasted than before. There was a slight tremor in his right hand as he went about making his coffee.

"So." I leaned against the sink, crossing my arms over my chest. "You gonna tell me what's going on, or are we gonna keep pretending I don't see it?"

"It is not to being your concern." Despite his obvious physical ailments, the big Ukrainian could still fix me with a look that made my insides turn to water. Not unlike Sveta, come to think of it. Must be a Ukrainian thing.

"Man, if something's wrong, you know we'll do anything we can to help, right?" I got the feeling that maybe Ivan didn't have a lot of actual friends.

A ghost of a smile crossed his craggy face. "I am to be knowing this. Thank you."

"Daddy!" That shriek was all the warning I

got before I was hit by a flying soon-to-be-seven-year-old. I hoisted my daughter up for a tight good morning hug.

"Hush, kiddo. Sveta and Estéban are still sleeping."

"No we aren't." Esteban's dark head appeared first, sleep-spiked like a startled porcupine, and Sveta followed close behind him as they ascended the stairs from the living room below. Both helped themselves to the coffee, clutching it like it was the last lifeline in the universe.

"What are we going to do today, Daddy?" Anna tilted her curly red head at me in a manner that reminded me so much of her mother.

"Not sure, Button. Depends on what Cam has to say when he gets up." It was barely past dawn, I didn't expect to see the priest until Doctor Bridget got up to go to work.

The feisty child frowned and squirmed to get down. "You're going away again."

What can I say, my child is perceptive. "Probably. Just for a few days. How did you know?"

"Mommy cried last night." Anna fixed me with a glare. "When you go away, she cries when you can't see."

Great. Now I felt about two inches tall. Glancing around the kitchen, the other adults were very studiously looking everywhere but at me and my tiny, but fierce, daughter. Sighing, I crouched down to look her in the eyes. "Button, I always come home. You know that, right?" Solemnly, she nodded her curly head. "And I'm hoping, after this trip, I won't have to go away anymore.

She wrinkled her pert little nose for a moment, processing that. "If you don't have to go away again, does that mean that Sveta and Estéban won't live with us anymore?"

Again, I glanced at the other grownups in the room. Dear god, someone save me from having to adult on my own. I'm not good at it! Estéban was the only one who would meet my gaze, and he just raised one dark brow at me. "We haven't gotten that far in our planning yet, Button. Let's see how this trip goes first, okay?"

After a moment, she nodded. "Okay. But you better bring Mommy something nice. And me too. And Billy."

"As you wish." I kissed her on the forehead, and my nearly worthless protégé-slash-bodyguard finally stepped forward to offer his hand to Annabelle.

"Come, Bellita. Let's go see that Señor Chunk has his morning outing before he makes a mess in Miss Bridget's house."

I watched Estéban lead her off to tend to her dog, and ran a hand through my long hair with a sigh. It had been easier, when she was younger. She didn't understand about my abrupt absences or frequent hospital stays. Now…she was old enough to start asking questions, and I would soon have to make the decision whether or not to lie right to my child's face. It wasn't something I was looking forward to.

"Children are to being precious. You should

to be cherishing the time you have with her before she is to being grown, and gone." When I glanced up, Ivan wasn't watching me, but Sveta instead.

The dark-haired woman drained the last of her coffee in one gulp and stopped just short of slamming the mug down on the kitchen counter. Without a word, she trotted off after the kids. I gave Ivan a questioning look, which he completely ignored.

Somewhere deeper in the house, an alarm clock sounded for a few moments before being silenced, and shortly thereafter, a sleep-muddled Cameron appeared at the top of the stairs. He shuffled toward the coffee maker as if Ivan and I were both invisible, then stood there blinking when he discovered the pot nearly empty. Finally, he sighed, his shoulders slumping. "Aw, coffee, no…"

Ivan snorted softly into his own cup, but when Cam turned around, it was me he glared at. "You're evil, you know that?"

"What the hell did I do?" I held up my hands, the picture of innocence. "I didn't even have any."

Cam grumbled as he went about making a new batch, and I couldn't help but smirk a little. Getting the machine reassembled, he stared intently at it, like he could make it brew faster by sheer force of will. The priest wasn't a morning person. Who knew?

For a little bit, morning went on like a perfectly normal family. If that family consisted of an incognito priest, five demon slayers, a witch, a doctor, two small children and a dog the size of a pony. It's amazing what you can come to think of as normal.

All discussions of the impending European vacation were tabled until Bridget left for work. Though no one had ever expressly commanded me to keep my strange world a secret from her, it had become the unspoken rule of our lives, all of us guarding the good doctor's innocence with extreme prejudice. Like, if we could somehow keep her from knowing there were actual monsters out there, it would somehow make it all better.

I'm sure she wondered. I frequently turned up with bizarre injuries after sudden and inexplicable absences, and I kept company with some extremely odd characters. But she didn't ask, and none of us were about to tell.

Cameron, revived by a fresh pot of coffee, got her off to her office with a homemade lunch and a disgustingly sweet kiss at the door. When he turned to find us all giving him the smirk-and-brow, he at least had the good grace to blush. "Shut up."

"If we can to be focusing now?" Trust Ivan to rain on our parade. "Are we to be having a response from the Order?"

Cam nodded, then shrugged a little. "Sort of. It's being forwarded up the chain, but my direct superior believes that we can get you an audience with the Cardinal."

"When?"

"That's...trickier." He grimaced a little. "I don't know how long it'll take to go through typical church bureaucracy, but when the summons comes, you better be there on site. They won't give you much time."

"So, what I'm hearing is that we need to get our butts to Rome, where we will sit upon them until someone deigns to acknowledge our existence."

"More or less. Yes." There was something else bugging Cam, besides the idiocy of red tape, and his gaze finally landed on Mira. "And I'm being recalled."

My wife frowned, adjusting her hold on our infant son to soothingly pat the baby's back. "What does that mean?"

"That means we're out of here on the first flight we can get today. It means I won't get to say goodbye to Bridget before we go, and I don't know if I'll be coming back."

Though Mira's face remained calm, the extra souls in my back felt the flare of power from her. There were few things that would rile my beautiful wife, but hurting her best friend was one of them. "Jesse told you what would happen if you hurt her."

Cam glanced toward me, and I did my best to melt into the woodwork. Sure, I'd told Cam a long time ago that if he hurt Doctor Bridget, I'd kick his ass, but I didn't expect to actually have to follow through on it. "I don't want to hurt her. I love her. More than…" He left it unsaid, but we all heard the "more than the Church" hanging in the air.

"What am I supposed to tell her when she gets home tonight?" Mira's jaw was clenched, and Billy fussed a little, sensing his mother's ire.

Cam hung his head, and I realized that even if I did try to pummel him, he'd probably just stand there and let me. That wouldn't be any fun at all. "I don't know."

"You could to be telling her the truth." Ivan's blessing was all any of us needed, but Cameron shook his dark head.

"No. No, if she's going to hear the truth, it needs to come from me. I owe her that. But…when I come back. If I come back. I'll tell her everything, then. If I don't come back…it won't matter anyway."

Mira's power licked around her in a faint halo, then subsided. I had to wonder if any of the others had even seen it, since no one had reacted. "I'll tell her it was a family emergency. Call her when you get to Rome."

"Yes, ma'am." I think in that moment, she could have told him to cut off his own ear and mail it home, and he would have agreed.

I cleared my throat, drawing attention away from the cowed priest. "Okay, if we're moving out, we need to go back to the house and pack up anything we don't have with us, and we need flight arrangements."

Obtaining airline tickets was actually the easy part. As everyone scattered to dress and get ready for what promised to be an excruciatingly long day, I thumbed open an app on my phone, then pressed my pinky finger to the screen, letting it read my fingerprint. After a bit of buffering, a face appeared in the window, blinking owlishly.

"Jesse? What time is it there?" Viljo didn't

look like I'd woken him up. In fact, he looked like he might have been snorting energy drinks. His pale skin looked whiter than usual, his dyed-black hair seemed a bit lank, and there was a hit of red around his eyes behind his thick glasses.

Once upon a time, Viljo had sold his soul for the hack of all hacks, bringing down the Great Firewall of China. I didn't know what champion had fought for him, but ever since, he had been in charge of the technological system that kept all of Ivan's champions organized, catalogued, and safe. The app on my phone was the latest in his long line of creations, allowing us instantaneous access to Grapevine, our champion database. There, we had records of all champions, a catalogue of their past fights, and their current locations. Everyone logged in at set times, and if anyone missed a check-in, an alert would go out to all nearby champions. So far, we hadn't had to test that function.

"Morning, Viljo. When was the last time you slept?"

"Sleep is for the weak." The goth-geek snorted, then craned his neck like he was trying to look behind me. "Is Svetlana there?"

I rolled my eyes. "Dude, I'm not helping you stalk her."

Even on the tiny screen, he managed to look mortally offended. "I will have you know that my love is pure. Now, since you are obviously not going to help me win the love of my life, what can I do for you?"

"We need passage for four to Rome, soonest possible flight."

I could hear the click-clack of the keyboard as Viljo's fingers flew over the keys. "You, Svetlana, Estéban and Ivan?"

"Not Estéban."

The typing clatter paused, and Viljo blinked. "Who is your fourth, then?"

"Cameron."

"I do not have data on him." The hacker's brow furrowed, as if the simple lack of information had locked up all his neurological systems. Sometimes, I thought he was so accustomed to having the world's knowledge at his finger tips that he forgot there were other ways to get it.

"I'll put him on the phone in a second, you can get what you need."

"Oh. Okay." His fingers started up again. "Return flight?"

"Yes, but I'm not sure when, or for how many. We'll get with you when we're ready to come home."

"Done. Put Cameron on the line, and I will have the tickets waiting for you at the airport. One thirty departure."

"Before that..." I glanced around to make sure I was truly alone, and then for good measure, I stepped outside on Bridget's back deck. "Have you talked to Ivan lately?"

Viljo screwed his mouth into weird shapes as he tried to remember. "In person, or online?"

"Either."

"Well, he logged his trip to KC yesterday..."

"Has he said anything to you about health

problems?"

The geek shook his head. "No. Why?"

"His flight yesterday. Where did it originate?"

"Um…Bethesda. He checked in from there about a week ago, then flew out when Estéban called him. Do you want his itinerary? I can send it through the app."

"No. I believe you." There were no champions stationed in Bethesda, currently. Hell, there were no champions on the east coast at all, and hadn't been since I started my tenure. But there were hospitals in Bethesda, good ones. I wondered. "Look, if you happen to think of anything, Ivan's being kinda cagey and I'm worried. Let me know, okay?"

"You got it."

"Everything else all right? Everybody making their check-ins?" Ivan had made noises in the past about me taking over leadership of our loose organization. I hadn't really intended to go through with it, but now that Ivan's health seemed to be flagging, I felt like maybe I should start being a bit more responsible. At least until I could talk him into choosing someone else.

He nodded, a lock of lank black hair falling into his face. "Everything is green. No active challenges logged at this time."

"Flag me if anyone does. I have a feeling things may start getting a little wonky, real quick." If Reina had made a play for me, through my wife and kids, it was possible that she'd try the same thing going after the other champions. It wouldn't be the first time we'd been targeted.

"You got it."

"I'll go get Cam." I started back inside. "Hey, Vil? Start a file on him, just in case." Cameron wasn't one of ours, technically, but…just in case. Like I said.

"On it, boss."

"Don't call me that."

A one thirty international flight required that we be at the airport by at least noon, and that was pushing it. Sveta and Estéban disappeared briefly, returning with a rental van that could haul all of us and our gear, and we spent a few minutes loading up our locked and warded crates of weaponry and armor. Just when we thought we were done, Cameron came out of the house with another long box laid over one shoulder and added it to the collection. Sometimes, I forgot that Cam was a champion too, and that surely, he must have a weapon of some kind.

The important stuff was loaded into the van, along with our duffel bags, but there was still the stop we'd need to make at the house to pick up anything we hadn't grabbed in our exodus the previous day. That meant the hard part came up real quick.

Anna's eyes welled up with tears, and she buried her face in my chest. "I don't want you to go, Daddy. It feels bad."

I exchanged a glance with Mira over our daughter's head. While neither one of us truly believed in precognition, I'd always had my early warning system in place, and at least one prophetic dream that couldn't be ignored. So when Anna said that something felt bad, I tended to believe her. "Button, I'm gonna be just fine. See all these people going with me? They're not going to let anything happen to me. I'll be home, and I'll bring you something from Italy, all right?"

She sniffled, but nodded, and I stood up to gather Mira and my son into my arms. "Miss you."

"Miss you more." Her smile was fine, her eyes dry. We'd done this before. "Eat some gelato for me, and be good."

I gave her a cocky grin. "Darlin', I'm always good."

"You're incorrigible."

"I'm incredible." It was what we did, this banter. It kept me from breaking down in her arms and crushing her against me. It kept her from crying and begging me not to go. It kept it from being goodbye, and just left it at "until later."

I clasped arms with Estéban, giving him some last minute instructions that he totally didn't need, but again, it's what we did. There was a small kerfuffle when it appeared that Sveta was about to leave without saying goodbye to the dog, of all things, but once the Ukrainian indulgently patted the slobbering beast on the head, Annabelle was mollified and willing to let us go without a scene.

It was strange to realize that even Sveta, with her frosty, prickly ways, had become like family. Once this was all over, and she was free to go her merry way, she would be missed. Cam once again promised to call Bridget when we got to Rome, no matter what time it happened to be, and then we were on our way.

The house was just as we'd left it, front and back doors boarded up and awaiting my brother's handy touch when he finished his shift at the police station today. Remembering my feeling of foreboding as we'd left previously, I mocked myself silently. *See? You saw it again. Idiot.*

Really, all we needed was more of the daily necessities for a long trip. For me, that involved stuffing about ten snarky T-shirts and more pairs of boxers in my already straining suitcase. For Sveta, it meant scavenging every weapon she had stashed around the house and finding places to stick them where the TSA couldn't find them.

I ducked out to the back yard for a brief moment, waiting to see if Henry would appear with news, but the little demon was a no show. Axel too, and I had to wonder what he was up to now. Nothing that would bode well for me, I was sure.

Too soon, and not soon enough, it was time to go, and we all piled into the van to head for the airport.

6

Our tickets were waiting for us as promised, along with some paperwork that Ivan flashed at security to insure that our locked crates were not opened for inspection. When I asked to see the documents myself, I was amused to find out that Ivan had us traveling as antiquities dealers. I had always assumed that we'd be hiding the weapons we were transporting, but instead, Ivan got through security by detailing exactly what we had, and declaring them historical artifacts. Why lie when the truth would serve just as well?

We produced passports, got poked and prodded and scrutinized, then herded onto our plane. Ivan sat in first class while the rest of us were shoved into coach, and I made a mental note to kick Viljo in the shin the next time I saw him. Cameron and I had seats next to each other, but Sveta was farther back in the exit aisle where she had room to stretch her legs out. By the third time Cam and I jostled each other's elbows, trying to use the same armrest, I had already planned out my trip to Colorado to strangle Viljo with his own ponytail.

"He did this on purpose, you know," I groused to Cam. "We're getting screwed in favor of the little geek's love life."

Cameron chuckled. "It's cute, in a weird sort of way. And she obviously returns some of his feelings."

"How do you figure?"

"He's not dead yet."

Hunh. I hadn't thought of it that way, before. Cam had a good point. Sveta allowed Viljo more leeway than I had ever seen her bestow upon anyone. Maybe she did have a soft spot for the awkward little hacker. "Still, *I* may kill him, after this."

"You may as well just settle in. We're stuck like this for fourteen hours." Cam had made himself at home next to the window with the ease of a frequent international flier. "Nudge me when they come around with the drink cart, would you?" He leaned his head against the side of the plane, cushioned on the complimentary little wafer they called a pillow, and closed his eyes. Almost immediately, his breathing evened out and he slept.

I was going to kick him in the shin, too.

There wasn't much to say about a fourteen-hour plane ride. Takeoff was uneventful, and the safety lecture was equally boring and terrifying. I mean really, there is no water landing. There is a long plunge into the dark depths of the Atlantic, and no seat cushion is going to save you.

I confess, I always found it a bit disconcerting, flying east into the night that fell quicker than it should. Like I'd lost a day of my life, from the already precious few I had left. They rolled a movie I'd already seen, and darkened the lights in the plane for those who wanted to try to sleep. I allowed myself to doze, a little, trying to make up for my previous sleepless night, but it was hard to relax with so many strangers moving about in the space around me. Any of them could be a threat in a way that the TSA could never scan for.

I caught myself eyeing the four-year-old two rows ahead, to see if his eyes ever flashed red, and that's when I knew that I was a hairsbreadth away from a neat white jacket and a padded room. *Get a grip, Jess.*

"Sleep." I glanced over, realizing that Cameron was awake again. "I'll stay awake. I'll watch."

I studied him for long moments before sighing. "I look that bad, do I?"

"No. But I've seen others like you. Soldiers who never left the battlefield. I've kept watch for them too, so they could sleep." The priest gave me a small smile, and displayed the book he'd picked up at the airport. "I'll read, it'll be fine. I'm more used to this trip than you are anyway."

With mental apologies to the poor soul behind me, I reclined my seat back just enough that I could stretch out a little. "Do you go back often?"

"Couple times a year, usually. This year in Kansas City…this is the longest I've been away since… Since I joined."

"And when was that?" Cameron looked to be about the same age as me, and I was still on the younger side of thirty-five.

"I was eighteen when I went to seminary. Twenty when I was recruited into the Order. They liked my 'athletic potential'. So…fourteen years or so?" A small frown creased his brow. "Seems like a lifetime, already."

I snorted a little, trying to get comfortable. "At eighteen, I was just figuring out how to pick up girls and bluff my way into buying beer without an

ID.   Can't imagine knowing that I wanted to dedicate my life to the priesthood at that age."

Cameron's face was shadowed, lit only by the flickering movie screen at the front of our section. "It's all I ever wanted to do. From the time I was small. My mother would take me to church, and we would sit there with the stained glass throwing beautiful colors all around us, and I could just feel God looking at me, smiling. I knew that I wanted to not only feel that, always, but to help other people feel that as well. That total, all embracing love."

"Don't think I've ever felt that." God and I, we had a tenuous relationship at best. I was willing to reluctantly admit that He might exist, but if I ever met Him, we were going to have a stern discussion about how He was running the world.

The dark-haired man sighed quietly. "I still feel it. Moments when I know that He's there, and He's watching over us. But they're not during church anymore. I sit in the pews, and I pray, and I feel like my words are echoing up into the ceiling but there's no one there to receive them."

I sat quietly for a moment, trying to decide what to do with Cameron's confession. I finally settled on a noncommittal "Oh?"

He smirked a little, probably the only cynical look I'd ever seen on his face. "I know you're thinking it's because of Bridget. And it is, partly. I didn't expect that, with her. But it's not *only* that. The Order hands out these edicts and commands, and I'm just…not sure I agree with them anymore. They're playing games with people's lives. *Your* people's lives, other lives, it doesn't matter. And if we're all serving the same cause, that seems a little…wrong."

"You can always quit, y'know. Come over to the dark side. We have cookies."

He rolled his eyes at me, but smiled. "I don't know if quitting is something I can do. Hoping this trip will help me figure it all out. But, regardless of my own mid-life crisis I have going on, I truly think they can help you, Jesse. We'll get this worked out. I believe that."

I hate to admit it, but with Cam on watch, I fell into a coma pretty quickly. I think it was my body's way of reminding me that I wasn't sixteen anymore and that a missed night's sleep must be repaid threefold. No dreams, no mysterious visions, just boom, I was out cold. Reina herself could have handed out the peanuts, and I'd never have known. The next thing I knew, a nice lady was prompting me to return my seat to its upright position, and we were landing in Rome.

"What the hell time is it here?"

Sveta smirked as she shouldered her way past me. "Day."

"Oh bite me, you had leg room." So, maybe I don't wake up well.

Once off the plane, Cameron pointed us toward the luggage claim. "Go wait for our stuff. I'll be back in a minute." Hefting his carryon over one shoulder, he disappeared into the bathroom.

I shuffled along behind Ivan and Sveta, doing my best to appear abused and tormented, but no one cared, and I soon gave up. With my brain still sleep-fuddled, I turned to bark a command at Estéban, only to remember just in time that he wasn't with us for this trek. It was strange, not having my junior shadow beside me. The kid had been on my hip for almost two years. I missed him.

As my head cleared, I started to pay more attention to the world around me. Ivan was speaking to a uniformed personage in Italian, and I had to wonder if he spoke that any better than he spoke English. Sveta had found a good vantage point against the wall, her icy blue eyes scanning the people around me with a predatory air. Trusting her eyes to find danger before mine would, I took a few deep breaths and turned my attention inward, feeling along the whispery lines of connections to the souls in my skin.

They were quiet, at the moment, which I found a bit strange. Normally, a crowd would rouse them to at least watchfulness, a tiny thread of tension humming along just above my range of hearing. I realized after a moment that they felt sleepy, and I wondered if their humans, the people they actually belonged to, were dreaming just then. It would be sometime in the wee hours of dark back home, and it stood to reason that most of those souls were U.S.-based at one point in their existences.

Sleep well. There were times when I was forcefully reminded that the bits of energy riding around in my body were actually people. They were living, breathing creatures with lives and hopes and dreams. They'd made some dumb decisions, obviously, but that didn't mean they were bad. And I was their last line of defense.

"Have they brought the crates up yet?" I glanced up at the sound of Cam's voice, and blinked a few times. Then I rubbed my eyes, and looked again.

He'd combed his short hair neatly, and looked about twenty times more refreshed than I did after the long flight, but that wasn't what was throwing me for a loop. Gone were the khakis and casual polo shirt. Instead, he'd donned black slacks and an even blacker shirt, if possible, which made the glimpse of white at his throat stand out like a beacon.

Cameron smirked at my expression. "What, did you forget I was a priest?"

"Did you?" I'd never seen Cam in his priestly garb before. It was strange. Like seeing Sveta in a frilly pink dress. It just didn't belong.

Ivan interrupted us with his deep gravelly growl. "They are to be bringing a vehicle around for our use." A long cart had magically appeared beside him with our luggage, and Sveta was checking over the locks and wards to be sure that nothing had been tampered with.

"Listen, I need to go check in, so I'll catch up to you guys later, all right?" Cameron moved to pull his own weapons case off the pile, propping it up on its little plastic wheels. "Viljo sent the hotel arrangements to my phone. I'll join you in a little while." Without really waiting for an answer, he trundled off, wending his way through the crowded terminal like he lived there.

After a moment with no response from anyone else, I muttered, "Well fine then, but you're at the back of the line for the shower."

I will preface this next bit of the tale by saying, if you value any of your life at all, never drive in Italy. And if your sanity is also a thing that you'd like to hang onto, *do not*, for the love of all that is good in this universe, let Sveta drive you around Italy.

I'm sure that the surroundings from the airport into Rome itself were very lovely, if seen at normal, mandated-by-law-and-common-sense speeds. We passed businesses, railroad tracks, and what looked to be farmland all within a few miles of each other. Residential houses butted up against new commercial developments, and in between gripping the seat in front of me (I'd wound up in the middle section of a rather generic van), I found myself wondering if an It store would do well here, and if I could talk the company into letting me transfer. Italy didn't seem so bad, provided that I didn't die smeared all over one of its scenic roadways.

Sveta, for her part, took absolutely sadistic glee in scaring the crap out of Ivan and me. Though, come to think of it, the white haired giant seemed rather stoic in the front seat, and I even caught a glimpse of a faint smile at the corner of his mouth. So maybe it was just me that spent the trip terrified, seeing all my past sins flashing before my eyes.

Getting into the city itself wasn't any better, and there seemed to be a rather large number of questionable drivers with whom we were now sharing the narrow city streets. Horns blared around tight corners, we jounced over genuine cobblestones, and when we finally pulled up in front of the lovely little bed and breakfast Viljo had found for us, it took everything I had not to fall to my knees and kiss the ground under my feet.

"Never again," I told Sveta, and she just grinned at me. "Y'know, the speed limit is in kilometers, not miles."

That only made her grin larger, and more evil. "Was it? It has been so long since I have been in Europe, I have forgotten." She even whistled as she shouldered her bag and dragged her weapons crate inside.

Ivan gave me a raised silver brow at my grumbling, and sauntered inside after her, smirking all the way.

"No one appreciates me, that's what it is," I groused to myself, since no one else was listening. Or, maybe someone was, because my statement was greeted with a soft, if eerily familiar, chuckle.

Glancing up, I caught sight of a tall, lanky figure strolling down the street, a block away. His back was turned, but there was no mistaking the distinctive blond mohawk, nor the glint of the sun off the many piercings in his ears. As he turned to round the corner at the end of the block, Axel glanced back over his shoulder and shot me a smirk before vanishing.

So. He was here, too. This was going to be interesting.

Our lodgings were quite lovely, just a quaint little bed and breakfast with only four bedrooms, which meant that we were occupying the entire establishment. The proprietress was a stunningly beautiful woman who might have been in her forties, but looked like her twenties. Her name was Lorena, and she was most effusive in her excitement at having us as her guests for the foreseeable future. Dressed in a pale blue sun dress that bared her shoulders and (I admit) rather shapely legs, she made a point of tossing her flowing mane of raven hair about when she laughed, casting sly smiles my way until I waggled my ring finger at her, displaying my wedding ring. That only got me a small shrug, and a not-so-sheepish grin in return.

The building itself was a single story little villa-type thing (you know better than to ask me about architecture), with each bedroom opening out into a common walled garden where a fountain tinkled away merrily. With shared wicked smirks, Sveta and I quickly claimed our preferred rooms, leaving Cam with whatever was left. Apparently, the time honored tradition of calling dibs was a universal constant.

Making note of the convenient dresser that I could push across the door – to keep out demons and amorous innkeepers, of course – I tossed my luggage in a corner and flopped down on the bed. The mattress had to be actual down, because I sank into it like it was full of whipped cream. The quilt looked to be handmade, a riot of colors from a random assortment of fabrics, and all I wanted to do was drag it over myself and fall into a coma. Instead, I allowed myself a few relaxing breaths, knowing that if I closed my eyes even for a moment, jet lag would take over and that'd be all she wrote. Reluctantly, I pried myself up off the cushy mattress and went to explore our temporary dwellings.

Sveta had taken the room to my immediate left, leaving the one farthest away for Cameron. Ivan was on my right, and I poked my head into his room just to scope it out. It looked the same as mine, though the quilt sported different patchwork hues, and he had a small writing desk tucked into one corner that my room lacked. His bags were there, but there was no sign of the man himself. Frowning a little in puzzlement, I continued on, finding a small, but functional kitchen, and then the single bathroom, which had the door partly propped open.

Normally, I'm not the kind of person that tries to peep on someone while they're doing their private business, but the door *was* open, and the sound of wet coughing from inside sounded horrendous. Leaning on the door jamb, I calmly pushed it the rest of the way open and crossed my arms over my chest, raising a brow at Ivan.

He was bent over the sink, his once-broad shoulders now shrunken and shaking with the force of every cough he tried to bite back. Though he tried to hide it from my view, I could clearly see that the plain cotton handkerchief in his hand was spotted with bright red blood.

Inwardly, I felt a deep, cold chill. That was so not good. On the outside, however, I reverted to my first instinct, which was to be a pain in the ass. "Still gonna pretend I don't see anything?"

"Go away." He couldn't even get the words

out without another bout of coughing wracking his once-impressive frame.

"I'm really not going to do that."

"You will to be doing what I tell you."

I snorted. "Yeah, no. You're sick, man. Like, really sick. Do you need to see a doctor? Or a hospital?"

"No. There is nothing to being done." He wiped pink stains from his lips, then turned the water on to rinse the spots of crimson from the white porcelain sink. "You will not speak of this to the others."

I pressed my lips together as I weighed the pros and cons of that. "All right. For now, it's just between you and me. But if I find you collapsed on the floor at any point in this trip, I'm damn sure telling *some*body."

"This is to being fair." He straightened up, doing his best to stand tall and imposing as he always had, and failing miserably. Whatever it was, it was eating him alive, I could tell. Just decimating him from the inside out. He held my gaze with his piercing blue eyes, and for the first time in ever, he was the first one to look down. "Thank you, Jesse."

"Psh. No thanking me. Pretty sure you need your ass kicked for this, and in your condition, I might even be able to take you."

That earned me a small, weary chuckle from him, which was the best I could hope for under the circumstances. "If you are to being very fortunate." He clapped me on the shoulder as he squeezed past me into the hallway, gripping just hard enough to prove that he could still draw a wince out of me. "I will to be resting until Cameron returns. That is all I will to be needing.”

"If you say so.” I had my doubts, but Ivan was well past eighteen and perfectly entitled to make his own decisions. “I’ll knock when he gets here, or when we figure out a meal.” I had no idea if it would be lunch, or dinner, or what. Where the hell was a clock?

Ivan nodded and vanished into his room, leaving me to watch his closed door for a few moments, listening for any more of those wracking coughs. After a long bit of silence, I shrugged and went to gather my things for a nice, long shower since I’d been so clever as to discover where the bathroom was.

7

Of course, Sveta beat me to it. There was a brief scuffle in the hallway as we both tried to shoulder our way through the narrow door first, and all I'll say is that Sveta fights dirty. She got the shower and I retained my ability to father children in the future.

By the time we both felt human again, we'd cycled through every bit of warm water in the country, it seemed, and were seated around the table out in the garden having a light dinner, lovingly prepared by our hostess. And by light dinner, I mean I ate four helpings of everything in sight. Ivan made no appearance at all, though Lorena assured us that she'd taken him a plate. Sveta frowned at that, more than her usual expression of universal disapproval, but she made no move to go check on him.

Darkness was falling, but unlike home where the autumn chill had started to set in, the weather was still fairly decent here in Rome. The garden was lit with strings of twinkling lights, and we could hear faint violin music a few houses over, which might have been cheesy if it wasn't so pretty. If you ignored the fact that Sveta had spent a good hour warding all the doors and windows, and was currently slumped over her plate like she might pass out face first into her pasta, it would have been the start of an amazing vacation.

Cameron appeared from inside, having dropped his gear off presumably, and eyed the idyllic scene. "How on earth can you eat that much and still be so skinny?"

"I'm wiry," I informed him, and made a show of licking the remnants of my dinner off my fork. "And it takes a lot of food to power this much awesome."

"Did you leave any, Mr. Awesome?" Cam took a seat between the pair of us, tilting his head at Sveta in concern. "Is she all right?"

"She's fine," I said, just as she growled something at him in Ukrainian without raising her head. "The wards drained her."

"I saw. They're impressive."

Cam was right. Sveta had laid down the protections extra thick, and if I left my eyes unfocused, I could see the ice blue layer of spellwork across the narrow doorway in the garden wall directly across from us. Of course, the wall was only about ten feet tall, so if something truly bad wanted at us, it wasn't going to bother with the door. In the interest of my own personal safety and child-fathering capabilities, I hadn't pointed this out to Sveta.

"You might wanna go over it, too. Can't be too careful." The more magic users involved, the harder it was to bust through the wards. Of course, that hadn't done a thing to protect my house.

Cam nodded, helping himself to dinner, which was in truth enough to feed an army, not just the four of us. "I'll do that after I eat. I haven't had anything since the flight."

Hunh. I hadn't either, I realized, which probably explained the sudden onset of gluttony.

"So, how was your meeting with your bigwigs, or whatever? Any word on when they'll see us?"

The priest shook his head until he could swallow his mouthful of food. "No. It's still being passed up through the channels. You wouldn't believe the amount of paperwork and bureaucracy involved."

"Yeah, not like this is an actual emergency or anything." I ran my hand over my face, scratching at the reddish stubble on my cheeks, and Sveta grunted something that might have been an agreement.

"They'll come through, Jesse. I promise. Just…give them time."

"So what do we do in the meantime? Sit here with our thumbs up our butts?" Cam gave me a chiding look at my crude language, but I didn't particularly care.

"Well, I thought maybe you'd want to do some sightseeing tomorrow. You've never been to Rome, right?"

I raised a brow at him. "You seriously want us to go play tourist?"

He shrugged, shoveling in another fork full of food. "You want to sit here all day and brood? I have a friend who lives here, and she said she'd meet us in the morning, show us around a little."

Sveta mumbled something again, that sounded vaguely like "Can we carry weapons?"

"What she said."

"Well, no. Swords tend to draw the same attention here that they do in the States." Despite the fact that she was barely conscious, Sveta managed a smirk, and Cam nodded a little to concede her silent point. "So no *visible* weapons."

"We should find a place here to hide the crates. Don't want anyone getting nosey while we're out." I hated leaving my gear behind, but chain mail armor and a katana didn't exactly blend. "Let's gather them up, see if we can find a place large enough for three cases."

"Two cases. I left mine at the chapter house." Sveta raised her head and we both looked at him like he'd lost his damn mind. Bad things were coming for me, and he left his sword behind? Cam hunched his shoulders under our gazes. "It's required. I have to turn it in when I'm here. It's not like it's *mine*, after all."

"Whoa, wait, explain that. Your sword isn't yours?" I leaned forward, resting my arms on the table. My swords were a part of me, like my arm or my leg. It had broken my heart when I'd shattered my first one, and if I lost The Way now, I'd be devastated. Or at least really pissed off.

"It belongs to the Church, to the Order. Most of the weapons that we use are hundreds of years old, passed from brother to brother. We don't get to keep them."

"So you just like, check them out? Like at the library?"

"Something like that, yes. We are assigned equipment, based on our level of experience and the duty which we are about to perform. For example, I'm assigned a basic, utilitarian sword. Someone who has been with the Order longer might be assigned one of the true holy artifacts that we have,

something with actual power forged into the blade."
When we kept staring at him, he hunched his
shoulders a little defensively. "They claim that they
have one with a nail from Christ's cross forged into
the hilt, but I haven't seen it myself. It could just be
something they tell novices, for fun."

Sveta snorted, managing to sit upright
finally. "So you are saying that they do not
consider you to be worthy of a valuable weapon."

"Well...sort of."

I couldn't help but chuckle. "A year ago,
when they told you all to come out and watch over
Ivan's champions, they sent a rookie to protect my
ass. Great."

The priest shot me a small frown. "That's
not true. I have combat experience. Just not as
much as some others. A sword with true power can
do so much more in the hands of an experienced
wielder. It's not that I'm not worthy, it's just that
there are others who are greater..." He paused,
glancing between Sveta and me. "What?"

"You are not worthy." Sveta smirked.

I nodded my agreement with her. "Totally
not worthy."

"I didn't say that." Cam's dark brows drew
together in annoyance.

"Say what?" Sveta gave him a sweet grin,
so he didn't even see it until he'd walked into it.

"I'm not worthy." The dark haired woman
smirked at him in satisfaction, and he sighed.
"That's not... I didn't say it..."

"You're supposed to bow when you say
that," I informed him, demonstrating the universal

motion for unworthiness.

Sveta's snort turned into a snicker, which made me chuckle, which made her giggle, and then we were both laughing helplessly. I couldn't even explain now why it was so funny, except maybe to blame it on the jet lag. Even Cam joined in a little at the end, when we'd almost gotten ourselves back under control.

"I'm totally getting you a shirt that says that." There, Christmas shopping done for Cam. I felt accomplished already. It also occurred to me that I was treating the priest like I would any of my other buddies. Insults were the same as terms of endearment to us. If I didn't insult you, I probably didn't like you. Hunh. When I had I started liking Cameron?

Perhaps having the same realization I'd just come to, Cameron only rolled his eyes at our jibes and continued to tuck into the amazing food. Sveta finally pushed her chair back and staggered off toward her room, and I wasn't sure if that counted as conceding defeat, or an epic triumph just for being mobile. Soon, the priest followed along behind her, saying something about starting with the front door. That left me all alone in the pretty little garden, surrounded by the songs of night birds and the scent of some kind of late-blooming flower.

It was beautiful, and I found myself wishing that Mira could have come with me. A nice Italian getaway, maybe, when this was all over. Something for just the two of us.

Relaxed and weary as I was, I should have been expecting the soul-sight to wash over my eyes, should have been on guard against it. But the enhanced vision sprang up into my senses without warning, and suddenly the entire garden was awash in star-spangles of light.

My own arms were wrapped in lacy tendrils of gold, delicate and iron-strong at the same time, and for a moment, I smelled strawberries. *Mira...* I was never alone, not really. My wife's touch followed me across continents.

Once I was able to drag my eyes away from the magic woven around my person, Sveta's wards on the rear gate were the brightest source of light, fresh and new and almost pulsing with a heartbeat I couldn't explain. I could see the very fabric of her spells, pick out the razor sharp edges she'd woven into their making. Any person with ill-intent who crossed that barrier was going to be damn sorry. It was a vicious piece of art, lethal and blindingly beautiful all at once. Part of me registered that one corner had frayed, just slightly near the top, and I reached out a hand to smooth the magic down before I remembered that I shouldn't. The magic in me wasn't mine to spend, and I forcefully sat on my own hands to keep it from happening again.

Still, it didn't stop my eyes from wandering, drinking in every texture, every miniscule waft of night air, every breath of every plant that surrounded me. And as I examined the rock walls that enclosed this sanctuary, I realized that I was seeing magic, embedded deep within the stone itself. That had me on my feet again, and I pressed both hands to the wall, soaking in the sensation of crystalized rock beneath my fingertips.

It was in everything. The rock of the wall, the paving tiles beneath my boots, the cobblestones outside in the street, the very pillars and posts of every house around us. Magic, so old and so faded as to make its origin an unsolvable mystery. Power that had simply soaked into the environment over decades, centuries, more.

And why shouldn't it? Rome had been the place of miracles, of religious faith and pagan magics for millennia. No doubt, the land itself was charged with the remnants of so many spells, so many lives and souls, and the moment I had that thought, I was spiraling down through the rock wall, senses seeking, searching for—

"Jesse?"

At a very great distance, I heard someone say my name. I ignored it, faintly annoyed that someone was trying to distract me from my journey.

"Jesse!" It came again, closer, and this time I was vaguely aware that something was touching…my shoulder? For a moment, I struggled to remember what a shoulder was, or why I knew what being touched there felt like.

"Slap him." A woman's voice. I knew that voice. It was ice blue, like the floodlight of magic off to my right.

"Jess, c'mon man." Something patted my face, not a slap exactly, but it stung a little.

It was the pain that brought me back. I found myself blinking, nose nearly pressed against the garden wall that was nothing but rock and mortar after all. Strong hands gripped both my shoulders, and those proved to belong to Cameron.

Sensing that I was perhaps more aware now, he gently tugged me back from the wall.

"Easy…" I wanted to scoff at his concern, but my knees had other plans. They buckled beneath me as I tried to take my first step, and if not for the priest's quick reaction, I would have hit the ground in an undignified heap. "Bring a chair."

There was a gawd-awful clatter as one of the dining chairs was dragged over and I was unceremoniously dumped into it.   Cameron crouched down, peering up in to my eyes closely. "You in there?"

"Yeah."   My voice sounded gravelly, and my throat felt dry. "What happened?"

Cam glanced over my shoulder to the person behind me – Sveta, I realized, the source of the frosty blue voice – then sighed, rubbing his face with one hand. "Thought you could tell us. I don't know how long you were there before I found you, but you've been standing at that wall for at least forty-five minutes."

How long?   I frowned, glancing back at Sveta. "What time is it?"

"Ten thirty."

I frowned. That couldn't be right. I'd stood up to look at the wall, right after Cam left the dinner table, and that had been around seven. "Shit. Three hours. I lost three hours." What if Cameron hadn't found me? What if he'd gone to bed, after warding the front of the property, and I'd continued to just stand, lost in the pretty sparkles within the garden wall?

What if Reina had come, while I was

spelunking through ancient magic?

I raked my hand through my long hair, relieved when it stayed just hair and didn't devolve into an in-depth study of each individual strand. Damn, that had been a bad one. I hadn't had an episode that bad since the beginning, when the souls were all still fresh in my skin.

"How many fingers?" Cameron held up three in front of my eyes, and I gave him a glare.

"One less, if you don't get them out of my face." I shoved his hand away and leaned forward, focusing my eyes on the tiles beneath my feet, taking a few deep breaths. "I'm fine, really. Just…need to sleep, I think." That was it. It was just the jet lag catching up to me, bringing my defenses down.

"Help me," Cam said, and with no more warning than that, I was hauled to my feet, Cam under one arm and Sveta under the other. I tried to protest that I could walk just fine on my own, thank you very much, but once again my legs betrayed me, and left me to be half carried to my room.

The bed was still as sinfully fluffy and welcoming as it had been earlier, and my eyes closed the moment I was horizontal. "You!" I managed to point in Cam's general direction, even without sight. "Call Doctor Bridget, or I'll kick your ass."

I heard him snort. "In your condition?"

I had to concede that point. "Call Doctor Bridget or Sveta will kick your ass."

"I will."

"Sveta!" For a moment, I wasn't sure I'd

managed to actually speak – things were getting a little gray around the edges – but then the bed sagged near my head as she sat next to me.

"Yes?"

"The garden door…spell is frayed at the corner…fix it." I was inordinately proud of myself for recalling that, salvaging at least one good thing out of my lost hours. "And kick Cam's ass."

"I will see to it. Sleep." The bed rocked a little, and I assumed she was gone.

I heard a brief discussion at my door, knew that Sveta or Cam would be coming to check on me every few hours, and I simply didn't care. Darkness came, and it was blessedly free of magical stars.

The problem is, the darkness never stayed dark for me anymore. Things waited for me there, with glowing red eyes and sharp fangs. Claws raked over my body, spilling my blood in a hot flood, ripping out my guts to land with disturbingly realistic plopping noises at my feet. Hordes of tiny scrap demons swarmed over me, devouring me cell by cell. A gaunt figure bounded from somewhere above me, missing one entire arm and her opposite hand, but blunt teeth closing around my throat all the same. A grotesque, mutated thing lumbered through my vision, madness and murder in its once-human eyes. And the looming white-furred Yeti howled just out of my sight, promising that its turn was coming.

Exhausted as I was, I couldn't pull myself out of my night terrors, and so they went on and on and on for what seemed like eons. At least it was just me, and not my family. My pain I could stand, but theirs…I think it might have driven me insane to be trapped like that, watching them die in front of me.

When the tunnel dream arrived, it was almost a relief. At least there, I knew I wasn't going to be torn to shreds every time the cycle reset.

As always, I stepped out of the tunnel, the ground beneath my feet changing from concrete to hard packed earth. Behind me, the air reeked of desperation and despair. Before me, the field – or whatever it was – spread out, empty and barren. There was no light, no moon or stars that I could find, and yet I could see with startling clarity. At the far end of the expanse, there was nothing. I was alone.

And I stepped out of the tunnel, walking a few feet forward, and the other end of the arena – Arena? When did I know it was an arena? – was occupied by a lone figure, tall and slender but swathed in shadows. I'd known it would be there, or that it wouldn't, and couldn't tell if this was good, or bad. Behind me, the air stank of pain and fear.

And I stepped out of the tunnel, onto an empty plain of solid earth, the tip of my sword scratching a tiny furrow because I was simply too tired to hold it up any longer. The sky overhead was black in a way that I had never in my life seen, and the silence pressed on my ears until it hurt. There was no one waiting at the other end of the field, and while I wasn't surprised, I was disappointed.

And I stepped out of the tunnel again. And

again and again and again, as if someone kept hitting the "back" button and playing the clip over. Sometimes, the mysterious figure was there, more often, it wasn't, and neither outcome seemed to offer any better result than the other. I could never see well enough to tell who or what it was, and I was never able to turn around to see what was behind me that drove me from my place of shelter, time and again.

Dawn came, the sun crested the horizon, and my eyes snapped open like I'd had an alarm set. The room glowed with a white light that emanated from my own skin, my bare chest covered in white soul tattoos. (*When did someone take my shirt off, and why don't I remember that?*) By that light, I surveyed my surroundings, finding them unfamiliar, but safe. Gradually, my mind recalled the bed and breakfast in Rome, the weapons case stashed under my bed, the suitcase in the corner. Italy. I was in Italy. I took a few deep breaths, calming my racing heart by sheer force of will, and the protective souls slowly receded back to their proper places on my back. Bit by bit, the light dimmed, until I was left with just the faint traces of morning sun, creeping like mist through my single window.

Raising a hand, I rubbed at my face, partly to reassure myself that it was still there. Narrow nose, slightly lumpy from a long-ago break? Check. Beard-stubbly jaw? Check. Rock hard skull? Got it.

What a gawd-awful night. If anything, I felt worse now than before. Nothing like running marathons in your dreams to start your day off on every single wrong note.

Mira was right. We couldn't keep doing this. *I* couldn't keep doing this. If nothing else, the PTSD was going to have me lashing out with magic in my sleep, and not only would someone near and dear to me get hurt, but one of the souls within my body would get burned up, killing whoever it belonged to. Two hundred and seventy-five souls could cause a metric fuck-ton of damage, as I'd been given to understand, not to mention that it was a helluva lot of murder. I was a ticking bomb, just waiting for the right detonator. These things had to go, and sooner rather than later. For everyone's safety.

8

Needless to say, when Cameron knocked on my door at eight in the morning, I wasn't exactly the happiest camper. The heavenly cup of coffee that Lorena pressed into my hands, though, went a long way toward cheering me up. Normally, I was a take-it-or-leave-it coffee guy, but after the night I'd had, it was the nectar of the gods.

Ivan, on the other hand, looked markedly better than he had the day before. Some color had come back into his cheeks, and the hollows under his eyes weren't quite so dark. He grinned and flirted with our hostess in Italian, and while I couldn't understand a word of it, the old guy seemed to be pretty smooth.

Sveta did not appear to be so amused by our leader's skills, and at one point, she stalked from the table, muttering to herself in Ukrainian. Ivan's gaze followed her, sadness drifting into his blue eyes, but when he caught me watching him, he quickly turned his attention back to our lovely hostess.

"So, our guide is going to meet us a few blocks that way," Cam pointed somewhere vaguely west, as he sat down with his coffee and some kind of gooey pastry. "Thought we could walk around, check out some of the lesser-known sights, then have a nice lunch at this little place she knows."

"On foot?" He nodded at me, and I glanced at Ivan. "You want to sit this one out? Just spend the day here being pampered?"

The old man's glare could have frosted over Lake Michigan. "I am to be fully capable of spending a pleasant day walking and seeing the sights."

I held up my hands in surrender. "Of course you are. Just…offering."

In honor of our team-building exercise, or whatever the hell this was going to be, I donned a gray t-shirt that said "Auto correct can go duck itself", and glanced longingly at the sword case underneath my bed. I'd feel a lot better with that bone hilt riding at my hip. *It's just a day out, like normal people do. Not everything is a fight to the death.* I said it several times, but I never quite convinced myself.

My one comfort was knowing that Sveta would be armed to the teeth, possibly literally. I might not see whatever it was she was carrying, but it would be there, and she of all of us had the least compunction about using lethal force.

Like good little ducklings, we formed up just outside the front door, bidding a cheerful farewell to Lorena, and then we headed out, following Cameron through the streets of Rome. We weren't alone by any means, life in the city beginning bright and early, but it didn't take long to figure out that we were moving against most of the foot traffic.

"So, what do they know that we don't?" When Cam looked at me questioningly, I nodded toward the obvious herd of tourists heading the opposite direction. "Is there some grand attraction we're missing?"

"Oh, well… Vatican City is about three blocks that way," he gestured, "so they're probably all heading to get in line for the tours. The lines form early, there."

I gave him a skeptical look. "We're going on a tour of Rome, but not visiting the kinda major thing that's just a few blocks from our hotel?"

Cameron rolled his eyes at me. "Everyone goes to see the Vatican, Jesse. The Sistine Chapel, all that? We can hit that later once we get our audience. Thought maybe we'd visit some of the less well-known venues."

"Worst. Tour. Ever." I gave him a look of annoyance until we both broke into smirks.

All in all, it was probably a good thing we weren't trying to join the throng of camera-wielding tour enthusiasts. We definitely didn't fit in with the eager, wide-eyed groups that went out of their way to skirt around us on the sidewalks.

Cam, in his stark black priestly garb, had point, being the only one of us who knew where we were going, but it didn't escape my notice that Ivan and Sveta had deliberately chosen to bring up the rear and flanking positions, respectively. All without a word, they'd formed a protective wall around me, leaving my right side to be protected by whatever building we were passing. Every time we crossed a street, leaving that side exposed, I felt Sveta tense up, and her frosty gaze swept the drivers of any cars, staring until they would drop their eyes under the sheer force of her personality.

While I was fairly certain that her sense of caution was maybe a bit over-pronounced, I found myself watching her left as she watched my right, waiting to see something big and nasty jump out of the café we just passed or the group of elderly women who went tottering along under the direction of a handsome young tour guide.

As it was, I nearly walked up the back of Cameron's leg when he stopped abruptly in front of me, waving to someone on the next corner. "Mary Alice! Over here!" I heard the abrupt screech of car tires, a man and woman yelling at each other in Italian, and then Cameron swooped a small figure up in his arms and spun her around in a circle, laughing. Only when he sat her down did I realize that she was wearing a nun's veil. I was *not* expecting that.

She was young, for starters, and if she'd seen thirty yet, I'd eat my hat. Her clothing didn't immediately denote "nun," either. Her plain khaki slacks and navy sweater didn't really stand out, nor did her scuffed sneakers, which did attest to how much time she spent on her feet. A tiny thing, forced to crane her neck to look up at Cameron, she smiled brightly, babbling at him fondly in Italian. He answered her, though it was plain he wasn't as comfortable in the language as she was, then he turned to present her to the rest of us.

"Everyone, this is Sister Mary Alice, one of my dearest friends. Mary Alice, this is Jesse Dawson, and Svetlana, and Ivan Zelenko."

"It's a pleasure to meet you all! Brother Cameron has told me so much about you!" Her English was flawless. Or rather, it wasn't flawless at all, proving that it was her first language, not one she'd learned later.

"You're American?" I asked as we made our introductions.

"Born and bred in Buffalo, New York." Green eyes sparkled above cheeks that were indented with adorable dimples, and I was having a hard time reconciling the youthful face with that of a nun. The ones I'd encountered had always been old, and terrifying. "But I've lived here in Rome for the last seven years."

Her hand felt tiny and fragile in mine, but she gave us all overly enthusiastic handshakes. I even caught Sveta's eyes widening in surprise as the perky little nun showed absolutely no fear of our scary mercenary. Ivan chuckled, bowing over her hand to kiss it, and she blushed prettily, just like any other girl.

I was confused. "So, are you part of...?" I left it unfinished, I wasn't sure how secret Cameron's order of champions was, within the Church.

She and Cameron exchanged looks, but it was Cam who answered, somewhat sheepishly. "The Order of St. Silvius doesn't allow women. Sister Mary Alice is...a helper?"

The nun smirked a little. "What he means to say is that they can't seem to get me to go away. And since I've proven useful to them, they don't try so hard, anymore."

"Useful how?"   Sveta's question was perhaps a bit blunt, and nosy, but the perky nun didn't seem to mind.

"Computers.   I run their systems, their

catalogue, generally keep their lives from retreating back into the Dark Ages."

A light bulb clicked on in my head. "You're their Viljo!"

Cameron nodded. "Yes! Exactly. Though, I've sparred against her, and she's fiercer than she looks. She would be a formidable knight, if they'd allow it."

Sveta gave the smaller woman a speculative look then, perhaps sensing a kindred spirit. Personally, I thought the two women should get along famously, both having made places for themselves in male-dominated arenas. Lots to talk about, right there.

"So, where do we want to go first?" The amount of energy pouring off the tiny nun made me wonder just how much good Italian espresso she'd had, already.

"Show us things the tourists usually miss, but within walking distance. We need to be available if we get called."

Mary Alice – Sister Mary Alice? Sister Alice? I wasn't sure what was proper – pursed her lips thoughtfully. "I'm guessing that trying out the mock gladiator training is probably not something you're interested in, then." Sveta snorted, and I had to chuckle a little. Yeah, that wasn't going to end terribly or anything. "All right, let's start with a visit to Campo de'Fiori. It's this amazing market. We can eat samples until we get sick."

"Isn't gluttony a sin?" Cameron's smile at her was fond, and I got the impression they'd played this game before.

"If I'm sharing, it isn't gluttony." And she stuck her tongue out at him. Weirdest nun ever, I decided, but I kinda liked her.

We set out with the tiny nun in the lead, marching into oncoming traffic with little regard for our own personal safety. A horn blared, and Sister Mary Alice yelled something in Italian, which was answered loudly, and I seemed to be the only one who thought this was strange. Several blocks later, when the process had repeated itself several times, I finally had to ask.

"Okay, is no one going to talk about why the nun is cussing at people?"

The sister held up a finger, never breaking stride. "First, I'm not cussing. I'm wishing them a blessed day in a very aggressive manner. Second," she added another finger, "as small as I am, if I wasn't loud, no one would see me and I'd have been run over years ago."

"Well, okay then." What else could I say to that? Cameron shot me a grin over his shoulder. He'd been dying to introduce this strange, fiery woman into my life, I could just tell.

Our walk took us over the Tiber River, and we paused on the bridge for a few minutes to watch the small boats trundle up and down the waterway.

Sister Mary Alice sighed happily. "I just love this river. It has its own moods, its own temperament, and it changes as the light does. I could sit here for hours and just watch." Next, she pointed out several buildings that were visible from our vantage point.   "There are so many little museums and shops that we can duck into, after the market. If you see something that looks interesting, just give a shout out and we'll stop."

Sveta muttered something under her breath, and Ivan chuckled softly, answering her in Ukrainian. I was really starting to get annoyed with being left out of the conversations around me. I mean, I'd busted my ass to learn Spanish, and now they go and speak something else. How was I supposed to keep up?

"Just gonna start talking to myself in my own made up language," I grumbled, and Cameron rolled his eyes at me.

"Italian isn't very different from Spanish. I bet you could pick some up, if you tried."

"I have enough problems with my brain, no point in trying to cram additional languages into it just now."

Despite my grumbling – which was really mostly for my own amusement anyway – the morning turned out rather pleasant. Getting to the market quickly became low priority as Alice kept darting into this or that small doorway, always introducing us to a unique merchant or eclectic museum of some obscure notable. To my surprise, Sveta seemed to be getting into the whole tourist bit, even purchasing a few small things that she tucked away in a bag thrown over one shoulder.

I kept an eye on Ivan as we meandered, but the old man seemed to be keeping up rather well. Our pace was too stop-and-go for him to truly get winded, and once that thought occurred to me, I started watching Mary Alice closer, as well. Sure enough, she would glance toward Ivan before her next tangent had us investigating some famous cobblestone or bike rack, and I realized that Cameron must have said something to her about the old man's health. She was very carefully staging our tour with Ivan's illness in mind. Yeah, that settled it. I liked her.

The Campo de'Fiori was everything she promised, once we reached it. Vendor tents were strewn about the square, surrounding a statue of a hooded figure, head bowed and a book clasped in his hands.

"That is Giordano Bruno," Alice explained when I asked. "He was a philosopher who was burnt as a heretic on that very spot."

"Oh, that's right. I remember him." At one time in my life, I'd thought getting a degree in philosophy was going to mean something to my future career path. I hadn't been very sure what that path *was* exactly, but to a young, foolish man, it had seemed intellectual and romantic. Yeah, lookit me use my degree now.

If my memory of my very-distant education served, Bruno had been burned for contradicting the Catholic Church on some of their major tenets, as well as a then-scandalous view of astronomy and the makeup of the universe. Which had, in time since, proven to be true.

I shook my head as we passed the statue, giving the silent observer a small salute. "Guess you can say you told them so, now."

The market was just crowded enough to make you real friendly with your neighbor, and I smirked to myself when my eye caught the furtive gesture of a pickpocket, lifting the wallet of a tourist about ten yards ahead of us. That thief melted back into the crowd, but once I knew what to look for, I could pick out the stealthy movements of at least four more in our vicinity. None of them came near us, however, and the only time that one found himself in our path, he took one look at Sveta and literally turned on his heel and ran the other way.

The Ukrainian woman chuckled under her breath, proving that she'd been watching the pickpocket crew the same as I was. Mary Alice must have picked up on it too, because she glanced back at us with a look of embarrassment. "Sorry. It's a thing that happens."

"Not to us, apparently." Was I okay with a bunch of thieves working the crowd? No, not really. But there were only three of us that I trusted to be able to fight, and that wasn't a battle I wanted to pick just now.

"Do these tents remain here all of the time?" Sveta asked, munching on a piece of bread that she'd dipped in olive oil from one of the sample trays lining the walkway.

Sister Mary Alice shook her head. "No, they'll pack up soon and make way for other things. Footy games, sometimes, and then the little cafes will put tables out for people to sit and eat. At night, it turns into a kind of night-club type atmosphere. We wouldn't want to come here, then. It's kind of dangerous. Lots of bad elements come out with the dark."

Sveta grinned at that, and I pointed a stern finger at her. "No. Bad Sveta."

She gave me her best innocent eyes, which still sent a shiver down my back. "I have done nothing wrong."

"You were thinking about it." She didn't disagree with me.

No matter what the feisty little nun said about the dangers of the evening crowds, the pre-lunch set seemed harmless enough. We were surrounded by tourists and locals, church groups and mothers with five kids in tow. I picked out the accents and languages of at least four different nations, and everyone seemed extraordinarily happy to be there. That's why the tingle up the back of my neck caught me by surprise. It couldn't be the pickpockets, who hadn't set off so much as a glimmer of notice from my passengers. It had to be something else. Something worse.

I stopped in my tracks, forcing Ivan to stop short as well or bounce off of me. Sveta, one stride ahead now, turned back with a frown. "What is it?"

"I don't know." My danger sense, the little extra warning I'd come to rely on so heavily, had gone haywire when I became keeper of the souls. But what I couldn't see, my passengers often did. Right now, I knew that the white tattoos on my shoulders were slowly creeping up the back of my neck, spreading into my hair invisibly. They were preparing for something. "Keep an eye out, something's up."

Instantly, the two Ukrainians went on hard alert. Sveta's hand rested at her right hip, and I had no doubt she could produce some kind of weapon there at a second's notice. Ivan's white brows drew together as he did a slow turn, surveying the crowd around us.

Cam and Alice, now yards ahead of us, turned when they realized we weren't following. "Jesse?"

I didn't answer, my own gaze sweeping through the horde of unfamiliar faces that surrounded us. Suddenly, it didn't seem so cheerful anymore. I felt Sveta's hand come to rest at the small of my back, subtle pressure prompting me to turn. She kept her eyes on me, but tilted her head ever so slightly to my left, and I fake-casually let my eyes drift in that direction.

There was no reason to notice the man. He had his back to us, the hood of his sweatshirt drawn up so that I couldn't even see his hair. He stood alone in the throng, no friends with him that I could see, his shoulders hunched like he was maybe doing something with his phone. Just a lone figure creating an island in the sea of people. A dude, just like any other dude.

But the longer we watched, the stranger it got. He didn't move. I mean, at all. Never raised his head to glance around, never checked his watch, never scratched an itch. The crowd moved around him, jostling him from time to time, and he resolutely held his place as if that was the last cobblestone on the planet. Either that, or he knew we were watching him. With his back turned, the only way he could know that was if he had a friend somewhere else in the crowd telling him.

The souls sent pin pricks of discomfort across my shoulders and down my arms, my torso tingling like mild electric shock. "We need to go."

Sveta and Ivan didn't question it, and we all spun in unison to start marching our way out of the now-confining horde of innocent bystanders.

"What's going on?" We brushed past Cameron, who at least followed along behind, towing a very puzzled nun with him.

The street was less crowded, and we took a hard left without even talking about it, Sveta leading now. Ivan's long coat flapped around his legs as we took long strides, just shy of actually running.

"Is he following?" Sveta wouldn't turn to look, so I passed the question back to Cameron.

"Cam, glance behind and see if you see a guy in a dark gray hoodie with the hood up. But don't look like you're looking."

"Um…okay?" I heard a scuffle of shoes, as Cam pretended to trip, and when he spoke again, his voice was lower. "Yeah, he's back there. I think he has a friend, about half a block behind him. Didn't get a look at the face, they've both got hoods up."

Sveta grunted in response, then took a darting right turn, leading us across a busy street to the tune of blaring car horns. "Four now."

Daring a glance back myself, I saw two more hoodie-wearers fall in behind us, too carefully spaced between the first pair to actually be coincidence.

"Two more ahead. Left." At Ivan's quiet orders, we changed direction again, and we weren't even pretending we weren't running anymore.

"Cam, get her out of here." Sister Mary

Alice didn't deserve to get caught up in whatever this was about to be, and I had hopes that whoever the mystery men were, they wouldn't follow if the priest and nun broke off the other way.

"Wait, don't go down—" Mary Alice's warning came too late, as our next corner took us into a dead end alleyway, surrounded on three sides by windowless brick walls of the neighboring buildings.

"Son of a bitch." We'd been herded, clear as day. With that certain knowledge, the affirmation that we truly were being targeted, the full force of the power inside me surged forth, and beneath my long sleeves, I could feel my skin blazing with intricate white sigils. They spiraled over my palms, the backs of my hands, up to cover my scalp beneath my hair, and spreading down my thighs under my jeans. Without even looking, I knew I was shining like a floodlight to heaven. I heard Alice gasp "Oh!" and knew that she was one who could see the extraordinary amount of life force currently covering every inch of my skin. That would require explaining, when we got out of this. If we got out of this.

"Backs to the walls," Sveta growled, and her hand sprouted a vicious looking K-bar knife, the blade black and ominous.

The Ukrainian woman took up a stance on my left, Ivan on my right, and I only hoped that Cameron had the good sense to protect Alice behind us. I took two deep breaths, then dropped into an easy fighting stance. I may not be armed, but that didn't mean that I couldn't make a few of them pay for whatever they were about to do. A "snick" sound beside me revealed that Ivan had an asp in his own fist, and I had to wonder why I was the only one who didn't have *some* sort of weapon on me.

"You guys gotta learn to share your toys." A dark figure appeared at the entrance to the tiny box we were cornered in, followed by two more. I stilled my mind, pushed aside all thought, and relaxed my gaze to take in everything at once. My weight balanced on the balls of my feet, ready to leap in response to whoever moved first.

And because I learned a long time ago on a mountain in Colorado, that danger comes from above, I looked up. Sure enough, two of our shadows were coming over the lower roof just behind us. "Cam!"

The priest turned just as one of our assailants did some kind of parkour jump down the side of the building. Without hesitation, Cam threw out one hand and shouted "*Detorqueo!*" With the souls all up in my vision, I could see the copper-colored shield of power leave the priest's body and slam into his attacker, tossing the black hooded man into the wall like he weighed nothing.

The second man had waited, however, and he hit the ground on light feet, tucking into a roll and coming up between Cameron and the feisty little nun. And then Sveta barked "Incoming!" and I couldn't watch anymore.

The number blocking our exit had grown to four, and two of them had advanced to engage the Ukrainian duo. I saw one of them attempt a flying kick to Ivan's chest, which landed, forcing a pained grunt of out of the old man. Instead of crumbling beneath it, though, Ivan caught the man by the ankle and wrenched violently. The wet sound of the knee popping was loud in the close quarters, and immediately drowned out by the man's agonized scream. Ivan dropped him on the cobblestones like a blob of wet paper towels, then swung the asp backhand to take out the other knee. The old man didn't play.

Sveta, in the meantime, was toying with her opponent. Her face was split by the most feral grin I'd ever seen, and she tossed her knife back and forth between her hands, daring him to come close enough to snatch it away from her. Whoever the man was, and they'd all donned bandana masks under their nondescript hoods, he was already sporting a couple of blood slashes along his arms, proving that he'd learned the penalty for dancing with the cold-eyed mercenary already.

The other two strangers shifted forward, moving to join the fray, and Ivan snapped something at Sveta in their native language. I couldn't speak it, but I understood the sound of "quit fucking around and drop his ass" well enough. The woman only snarled, whether at the command or her opponent I couldn't tell.

Well, time for me to earn my keep. One of the men went for Ivan again, who had proven that sick or not, he could take care of himself. But two-on-one was bad odds for Sveta, I don't care how good you are, so I moved in to eliminate the other unoccupied fellow.

Apparently, they hadn't expected me to join

in the fight, because the second I lunged toward the hooded man, he nearly fell on his ass to reverse direction. Either that, or I looked really scary. "If you make me chase you, I'm just gonna get pissed!"

While he didn't go into full on retreat, he ducked every swing I sent his way and never returned a single strike. We must have danced all over that alleyway, and I used every trick I could think of to get close enough to actually have a decent fight. He was fast, I had to give him that. As fast as me, and that's saying a lot. But I had something he didn't, and he hadn't realized it yet. I had friends, and his were all unconscious or screaming on the ground.

Sveta had dropped her assailant the moment that I'd stepped into the brawl, proving that she could have at any moment before that, and with my target concentrating so hard on *not* hitting me, it was easy to maneuver him around until his back was to her. One blow to the back of the head with some brass knuckles she'd produced from somewhere, and it was nighty-night for the men in black.

Ivan's second opponent was down too, a dark bruise blossoming nicely across his temple before it disappeared under his bandana and hood. The old man had a hand braced against the wall, rubbing at his chest with a grimace, but when he caught me looking, he straightened immediately and gave me a cold glare.

Only then did I remember to check on Cameron and Mary Alice. Cam was down. That much I'd expected. He had a bad penchant of using magic first, and punching later, and it was going to get him killed someday. Sister Mary Alice currently had his head resting on her knee, examining the dilation of his pupils, and the two wall-crawlers were heaped in a corner like yesterday's garbage. I couldn't tell what had happened, but the nun's knuckles were bloody on her right hand.

"How is he?" I asked, at the same time that Sveta said "We must go." We could all hear the distinctive sound of Italian police sirens closing in from blocks away.

"…can walk…" His words were slurred, but with help, we got Cameron on his feet. Sveta took one arm and I took the other, and we mostly dragged the priest out of the alley, the last of us vanishing around the corner just as the blue cars with "polizia" on the side pulled up.

9

With Mary Alice's directions, we made our way through side streets, back across the Tiber. We forced laughter and chitchat as we walked, pretending to be a bunch of American tourists escorting their inebriated friend back home, but all the while I kept an eye on Cameron's vitals.

The pulse under my fingers was erratic, beating wildly one moment, then dropping so low that I was certain we'd lost him on at least two occasions. He responded to only one out of every four questions, and the answers had very little to do with reality. When I called him an asshole under my breath, though, that he heard, and he chided me with fuzzy words. "Bad Jesse… Very bad…"

"Just stay with us…we're almost home…" I'd nearly broken my fist saving his life once, after a bad spell reaction. I wasn't going to let him go now.

Home, unfortunately, was going to be as elusive as all the poets ever claimed. My soul-sight had eased back a little, once we were clear of the alley, but any magic user could have spotted the new wards overlaying our own on the front door of the bed and breakfast.

"Can you tell what it's for?" We eyed the strange spell work from across the street, propping Cameron up against a wall to give Sveta and I a rest. Slender the man may be, but light he was not.

"An alarm, I think. They will know we are here." Sveta's blue eyes swept the streets around us, watching for any sign of our pursuers. "The windows are warded also."

The only choice was to go check out the garden gate, but none of us were surprised to find it trapped as well, a thin line of burnt orange magic lying over Sveta's intricate icy blue web and the simpler, but stronger, copper threads of Cameron's spells. We obviously couldn't go to ground here.

"We need our gear." Both Sveta and I were reluctant to leave our weapons behind. "Do we break the seal and then run like hell?"

Mary Alice stepped up to the garden wall, running her hands over the old bricks, her slim fingers prodding at the gaps between the old stones. "No. We go over." And just like that, she scrambled up the ten foot wall like it was a ladder, and disappeared over the top.

"Did anyone else see that, or was it just me?"

Cameron, practically draped over Ivan at the moment, made some kind of affirmative noise, but I didn't think his testimony was going to be worth much in his condition.

After a moment, the nun's head, veil and all, popped back up over the top of the wall. "No one's here, and the inner doors aren't warded. Where are your things? I can pass them out to you."

Though I was certain there was more to the good sister than met the eye, none of us believed she could get the heavy weapon crates up over the wall by herself. Wiry as I was, I was elected to go over next, and managed it by planting my boot in Sveta's laced fingers for her to heave me upward.

There was a bit more scrambling on my part than the nun had displayed, but I made it over without injury to myself or others. Win.

On the ground again, thanks to the patio table Mary Alice had pushed over, I gave her an appraising look. "You look different without your costume, Spider-Woman. The nun thing is probably good for a secret identity, though."

She chuckled at me and rolled her eyes. "I free climb, when I have time."

"As a nun does."

"Of course!"

We retrieved our belongings, handing the weapon cases back over the wall with Mary Alice perched precariously on top. Cam was looking better by the time my feet were on the outside again, and he was at least leaning under his own power. While Sveta went to retrieve our van, I asked the all-important question, "So, where do we go now?"

"Perhaps we can to be finding shelter with the Order—" Ivan began, when Cam ground out "No!" We all turned to look at the priest, color slowly returning to his ashen cheeks.

His head still swayed drunkenly as he shook it emphatically to the negative, but his eyes were clearing by the second. "Can't go there. It was Frank." His energy expended, he slid down the wall, all the while mumbling, "It was Frank."

I crouched at his side, keeping him from keeling over entirely. "Who was Frank, Cam?"

It took him a few deep breaths to find the strength to talk again, but finally he managed, "Man from the roof. Saw his face. Was Frank."

Mary Alice knelt beside me, peering closely into Cam's dazed eyes. "Brother Francis? You're sure?" Cam nodded, then forgot to lift his head back up, just leaving it flopping there at the end of his neck. The nun frowned, an odd expression on her usually cheerful face. "Brother Francis is part of the Order. Why would the Order attack you, Jesse?"

The fight had been replaying in my head, and I knew the answer to that question. "No one attacked me. In fact, they went out of their way to come nowhere near me. They were after all of you."

"But why?"

I shrugged. "Same reason as everyone else in the world. You saw what I'm carrying around in me. Everybody wants it, and they needed to remove my protection to get it."

Before we could discuss it any further, our van pulled up at the end of the street, and I hauled Cameron bodily up over my shoulder. "I'll get him stowed, then we can get our gear."

We had our stuff, and transport, but we still had no idea where we were going. Once I informed Sveta about our assailants' identities, she looked sternly at the little nun. "You cannot return to your home. They know you. They know you were with us. They will look for you, and us, there."

Mary Alice nodded. "I'm apartment-sitting for a friend, across the city. I don't think anyone knows. We can stop there, at least long enough for Brother Cameron to recover."

"Tell me the way."

"Wait a second." I hopped out of the van, leaving the door open. "May as well let our friends chase their tails for a bit, right?" Walking back to the garden door, I eyed the locking mechanism, then stepped back to get the distance right. With a mental apology to our lovely hostess Lorena and a savage front snap kick, I splintered the jamb and sent the old door careening on its hinges to smack against the wall. The second my boot crossed the threshold, I felt the thin thread of burnt orange magic snap, sending out whatever signal it had been programmed to send.

Dashing back to the vehicle, I jumped in and slammed the door. "This has just become a good place to be *from*." Sveta, for her part, didn't quite squall the tires as we pulled out into the neighborhood.

Watching out the back window, I caught a brief glimpse of two identical black cars converging on the bed and breakfast, and then they were out of sight. I hoped Lorena was going to be all right.

I don't know who Sister Mary Alice's friend was, but their apartment was to die for. Cameron was deposited on the nicest leather couch I'd ever seen, and Ivan and I took turns watching out the windows for any unwanted guests while Sveta again laid down painstaking wards on the doors and windows. When she started to look a little gray around the edges, Mary Alice appeared at her side with a bar of dark chocolate and a small smile. Surprisingly, Sveta took it without arguing, munching on the candy like her life depended on it.

Jokingly, I asked for a bite, and that got me a snarl worthy of Gollum himself.

"All right, first. Aside from Cam, is anyone hurt?" I'd gotten the easy side of the alley brawl, and I knew it. Ivan had taken at least one hit that I'd seen, and I wasn't sure what exactly had taken place between the nun and the men from the roof.

"M'not hurt," Cam mumbled into the couch cushion.

Mary Alice sat down at his feet, pulling them into her lap to make room. "No, but you are a very stupid man sometimes. You know better than to throw spells around like that in combat."

She was right. The powerful spells, the flashy ones with all the pyrotechnics and laser lights, could effectively stop an enemy, it was true. But the toll it took on the caster meant that the user was going to faceplant in pretty short order after that, which was always bad in a fight. This wasn't the first time I'd seen Cam resort to magic – and I mean *big* magic – first, and damn the consequences. And they said I was reckless.

Cameron waved a hand around as best he could, dismissing her concern. Slowly, he managed to roll over, so he was a least not talking into the leather sofa. "We have to get to the Cardinal."

"Uh...how about no? Did you forget the part where your own people just tried to take your head off?" That's it, the spell sickness had scrambled his brain.

"I don't think they did." Using Mary Alice's arm for leverage, he managed to prop himself upright. "I think that was just those men, those few. The Cardinal wouldn't have had to send men after us. We were coming to him anyway. All he'd have to do is wait."

Ivan, seated in a plush leather arm chair, leaned forward with his elbows on his knees. "You are thinking they are to being…rogue agents. Corrupted."

"Yes. Someone got to them. Using them to come after Jesse and the souls."

We all knew who that someone likely was. *Reina.* If anyone could corrupt a church knight, it was her. "So we don't know who to trust."

Mary Alice reached out and took Cameron's hand, squeezing gently. "You can trust me. You know that."

He offered her a weak smile, but it faded quickly. "I think he may know there is some kind of problem. The orders I was given yesterday make more sense, now."

"What orders?" Sveta's cold voice could have cut through glass.

Cameron's eyes fixed on me. "I was supposed to keep you away from Vatican City. More specifically, keep you away from the chapel. He knew, you see? He knew that you weren't safe there."

"The Sistine Chapel? What's that got to do with anything?" I tucked the minor fact of Cameron's split loyalties away in my brain to hash out with him later. *Still don't know who to trust.*

The priest shook his head. "I'm not sure you'd believe me even if I told you. But we need to get you there. It may be the answer to everything.

We can't wait to be summoned to the Cardinal now, and we can't trust any summons we *do* receive. We'll have to get in on our own."

"They will to be watching for you. No doubt, your faces are to being known." Ivan made a good point.

"Woohoo! Disguises!" No one else seemed to be as excited as I was by that prospect. "Oh come on. None of you ever wanted to try to sneak into somewhere in disguise?" I got blank looks from the rest of the group. "You guys are no fun."

At least Mary Alice looked slightly amused. "Your best bet is to try to get inside with a large tourist group, but we'll be limited by what kind of disguise you can use. There's a dress code."

"Seriously?" She and Cameron both nodded. "Like, how dressy?"

"Men have to wear nice jeans or pants, and a shirt with at least short sleeves. Women can wear pants, but any skirts have to be longer than knee length and the shoulders have to be covered."

I eyed Sveta. I knew she owned at least one dress. I'd seen it. "Do you have nice clothes with you?"

She gave me a scathing look in return. "I prepared for this trip, even if you did not."

"Well, none of my t-shirts are church-appropriate." I wracked my brain, trying to think of the least offensive one I might have with me. The best I could come up with was the one that said "I'm why my guardian angel drinks.".

"You can borrow one of my polos," Cam offered. "It'll be a little big on you, but no one should notice."

I glanced down at myself, and frowned at the priest. "I'm not *that* skinny." Okay, I probably was, but it was bad form to point it out.

"I think we should all rest, then. The tour lines form very early in the morning." Mary Alice stood up, pushing Cameron to lie back down on the couch. "Sveta and I can take one of the bedrooms, if you don't mind, and Ivan the other. I'll see if I can find some extra blankets and pillows for you, Jesse." Which meant I was getting the chair. Great. Oh well, I'd slept in worse places. Way worse.

We all went about the motions of settling in to the strange apartment. Cameron was out like a light the moment he stopped speaking, and the two women vanished into the bedroom with Sveta's suitcase, presumably to figure out what she had that would pass the dress code check tomorrow.

Ivan took up a post near the balcony door, his ice blue eyes fixed on the street two stories below us. I moved to stand against the other side, just watching Rome go about life outside our little sanctuary. Finally, when the silence was about to drive me mad, I asked, "You okay?"

"I am to being well." As he said it, though, one hand rubbed over his chest where I knew he'd been kicked earlier.

"Don't lie. There's a priest right there." Cam was dead to the world and couldn't care less.

Ivan managed a ghost of a smile. "I am to being an old man, Dawson. Street fighting is to be causing aches and pains. You will know this, when you are to being older."

If aches and pains was the signal of being older, I'd been older for years now. "You don't have to come with us tomorrow, if you want. You can stay here and chill out for a few hours."

"I will to be making that decision in the morning." That seemed to be the end of that conversation, so I went to raid the refrigerator.

It was pretty much empty, of course, since the owner was presumably out of town. My forlorn sigh at the sight of the barren shelves got Mary Alice's attention, and after quickly assembling a grocery list, she ducked out to the local market to keep us from starving. Ivan vanished into his assigned bedroom, which left Sveta and me the only conscious beings within the walls. Though she still seemed a little shaky from her casting efforts, she settled in the middle of what was probably a very expensive rug to begin cleaning her cache of weapons. With nothing else to do, I plopped down next to her.

"The guy in the alley. Did you kill him?" I knew that Ivan's first victim, the one with the shattered knees, had been very much alive when we'd fled, but I hadn't truly seen what had happened to the rest of our attackers.

Sveta's eyes focused on the whetstone in her hand, calmly dragging the edge of one of her blades over the surface in smooth motions. "Which one?"

"Either. Both." The guy that took the brass knuckles to the head…well, that could have been a killing blow, I supposed, but I really hoped it hadn't been. Killing demons was one thing. When it came to killing people, I got all squicky.

"Why does it matter?" I placed my hands over hers, forcing her to look up at me, which she did with a dark frown.

"It matters, Sveta. Taking a life always matters." I could tell she didn't quite agree with me, her icy blue eyes searching mine for long moments. Finally, she sighed.

"I believe that they will both live. I did not see any of them take wounds that would be fatal." She pursed her lips for a moment, then amended, "Except for the one who was thrown into the wall. That looked…forceful. I do not know what injuries he took."

"What about the other guy who attacked Cam and the sister? Did you see what happened to him?" The mystery of Mary Alice's bloody knuckles was poking at my brain.

Sveta chuckled, moving my hands off her whetstone so she could continue. "For a nun, Sister Mary Alice has an interesting skill set." And that was all she would say on the subject.

I lounged back on one elbow, watching her sure hands move over her assorted tools of destruction. "Ivan sure kicked some ass out there. Pretty damn spry, for an old guy."

"Mmf."

"You think we'll be that able, when we're that old?"

"Mmf."

"Why don't you like him?"

At that, at least, she raised her eyes to look at me. "Why do you think I do not like him?"

"Pretty sure I've never heard a civil word

pass between the two of you. Even when I don't understand the language, it's clear your conversations aren't pleasant."

"The language often sounds angry, even when it is not."

"Bullshit."

Perhaps realizing I wasn't going to quit prodding at the issue, she laid her whetstone and knife down on the carpet between us, giving me a flat look with her cold blue eyes. "I have no feelings about Ivan Zelenko. None at all."

"I think you're lying."

"I do not care." With that, she rose to her feet and disappeared back into the bedroom, leaving me alone with a snoring Cameron.

Dinner, once Mary Alice returned, was what we'll call "subdued." Cam roused, looking a hundred times better, and Ivan and Sveta both emerged from their retreats. There wasn't enough room at the tiny kitchen table for all of us, so we sat picnic style around the living room floor, each of us stuffing our mouths with food rather than try to make small talk that no one really wanted.

Well, most of us were stuffing our mouths. I noticed that Ivan ate maybe two bites, the rest of the time just pushing his pasta around the plate with his fork. The rise and fall of his chest seemed stilted, and I saw the muscles in his face tense as he bit back grimaces when he breathed too deeply. Mary Alice and Cam noticed too, and I caught several meaningful glances passing between the two , Cam shaking his head slightly. Sveta, if she caught the interplay, didn't say anything, which I was coming to expect.

Ivan finally pushed his plate away, having eaten barely enough to keep a bird alive, and rose to his feet with an audible hiss of pain. I looked at the other three, waiting for someone, *any*one to call the old man on his injuries, but it quickly became apparent that they were waiting for me to be that guy. Well, fine.

"Okay, enough. You can't go on like this." I stood up too, because even ill, Ivan towered over me and I needed all the advantage I could get.

He turned, raising one white brow. "What are you to be speaking of?"

"Don't give me that shit. You're not well in the first place, and then you took a solid kick to the chest earlier today. We all saw it, and you're hurt, and you're pretending you're not."

He frowned, his pale eyes darkening like thunder clouds. "I am to being well enough."

"You're not. You're really not." Even as I said it, his shoulders shook with a wet cough that he forcefully bit back. "See? You may have broken ribs, you could put an end through a lung. You need medical attention. Real medical attention, not just me slapping a Hello Kitty bandage on it."

"This is not to being your concern," he managed, then had to stop as another cough snuck up on him. He pressed his fist to his mouth, but I caught the faint hint of red on his lips before he wiped it away with the back of his hand.

"It is my concern. We're all," I gestured widely, including Sveta in that whether she liked it or not, "concerned. You're our friend. We're worried.”

Another cough shook him, and he glared at me until he could get his breathing under control. “I did not ask you for to being worried.”

“You don’t ask friends. We just do. That’s what ‘friends’ means.”

He had more to tell me, I could see that much, but the force of his coughing bent him double at the waist. He braced his hands on his knees, and blood splattered brightly across the expensive rug. Alarmed, Cam got to his feet, taking one elbow as I took the other, trying to urge the old man to sit. Stubborn to a fault, he struggled against us as best he could, trying to yank his arms out of our grasps, but he just couldn’t seem to get enough air to function correctly. I felt the moment that his knees started to buckle.

“Cam!” Together, we lowered the white-haired man to the floor.

Ivan’s eyes were glassy, staring, and we could all hear the wet gurgling inside his chest. His lips had lost all color and his entire body heaved with the force of his coughing. There wasn’t enough time between bouts for him to even draw in a full breath.

“Ivan? Ivan, can you hear me?” The priest cradled the old man’s head, trying to get him to respond to anything at all. Those blue eyes remained unfocused, his breath coming shallower by the moment, and I made the decision I’d promised him I would.

“Call an ambulance.” When Ivan didn’t rise up off the floor to protest, that’s when I knew things were bad. Things were so very bad, I couldn't even fathom the level of the badness.

Mary Alice talked on the phone in rapid Italian, while Cameron and I tried to keep Ivan conscious. Every time he breathed out, we held our own until he gasped weakly again. Sveta stood back, watching the proceedings with an oddly blank look on her face, and the sound of a strange siren coming up the street was the sweetest thing I'd heard in a long time.

10

I have always hated hospitals. I'd spent more than my fair share in them, for starters, in varying degrees of "near death." I keenly remembered shaking with a cold no blanket could warm, staring up at a ceiling that never changed no matter how many different facilities I visited. The smell of antiseptic stung my nostrils, but couldn't smother the underlying reek of death and illness that permeated the very walls. In some of my more delirious states, I could swear I saw the ghosts of the dead passing through the walls.

Not even the birth of my children could make a hospital tolerable for me, and walking out those automated sliding doors was usually the best moment of my life. So understand that huddling in the waiting room for three hours, waiting for word on Ivan's condition, was an act of supreme loyalty on my part.

We weren't alone, by any means. There were several other families there, also awaiting an update from some doctor in a white coat. Cam and Sister Mary Alice, still wearing their holy garb, had spent a good portion of their time sitting with those people, quietly praying with them. It kept them occupied, made them feel useful in a situation where there was truly nothing to be done. I watched one woman, tears streaming down her face, press a grateful kiss to Cameron's cheek, blessing him in musical Italian.

The tension in the room, palpable and

prickly up my spine, eased a tad with every prayer the priest and nun shared. The anxious relatives obviously found peace in the practice, and I envied them a bit. I wasn't feeling particularly peaceful myself. They'd taken Ivan back hours ago. It had been too long. Way too long.

The last member of our group had stationed herself at the windows, watching out into the dark night, and hadn't budged an inch. Sveta's blue eyes were focused on something beyond the glass, and the stiff set of her shoulders gave off a very clear "leave me alone" vibe. Even Mary Alice, persistent as she was, had been turned away with a very terse grunt. Sveta hadn't said a word since the paramedics came, not even in response to direct questions.

The waiting room door opened, and every head in the place turned, waiting to see if this was the moment for them. A tall doctor entered, his dark eyes scanning the room with a slight crease between his brows. Finally, his gaze settled on me, my blond hair and beginnings of a reddish beard making me stand out like a sore thumb. "Are you with Mr. Zelenko?"

Immediately, Cameron and Mary Alice were at my side, and I stood, trying not to hold my breath for the verdict. "We are."

The doctor glanced between the three of us, his puzzlement obvious now. "Are you his family?"

"No, we're friends."

The man frowned. "I really should not be giving this information to anyone but family. Is anyone else expected?"

I opened my mouth, ready to launch into an argument I'd given many times before – Hospital bureaucracy was one of my top pet peeves – when a voice sounded from across the room.

"I am his daughter." We all turned to see Sveta leave her post at the window, her boots leaving black scuffs on the white tile floor as she moved to join us.

Somehow, I didn't think she was lying just for the sake of getting Ivan's medical information. It was the blue eyes. Sveta's eyes, Ivan's eyes. They were the same, and I realized I wasn't nearly as surprised by this revelation as I should have been. It was like something I'd always known, really, but never thought about at length.

The doctor's smile held obvious relief. He hadn't wanted to fight with us over giving out information either. "Your father is stable. We've given him some pain killers to help him rest, and he's receiving oxygen. The bruise to his chest is really quite minor and shouldn't cause him more than discomfort for a few days. However, I must strongly advise you to take him home as soon as he is able to leave here. I am surprised his doctors gave him clearance to travel, in his condition."

"What exactly *is* his condition?" The doctor glanced between Sveta and me, waiting for her nod before he continued.

"It doesn't surprise me that he hasn't told you. In my brief conversations with him, he has proven less than cooperative." The doctor flipped open the chart in his hands and offered it to Sveta.

"Your father has stage IV lung cancer. We didn't do any tests beyond a chest x-ray, but from what I can see there, as well as things that Mr. Zelenko has said, it is pervasive, and terminal."

Sveta examined the chart like she was committing it to memory, so I took it upon myself to quiz the doc further. "How long does he have?"

"I really couldn't say. That is a question for his regular doctors. I know that he has been receiving some treatment, so there must be records somewhere." The doctor paused, his lips pursed as he weighed his next words, then he sighed. "I can tell you that if he were a patient of mine, I would recommend hospice care. He should be made comfortable, for what time he has remaining."

"So, he is dying." The Ukrainian woman finally looked up from the file.

The doctor returned that cold blue gaze unflinchingly, and I had to admit a certain respect for the man. "Yes. And sooner, rather than later." Sveta nodded and handed the chart back to him, then turned on her heel and marched back to her window, staring out into the night again.

"When will we be allowed to see him?" Sister Mary Alice's voice was soft, gentle, the kind of tone you couldn't say no to.

"We are moving him to a room in the next few minutes. Normally, you would have to wait for visiting hours, but under the circumstances, I will leave instructions for you to all go up for ten minutes." He held up one finger in warning. "No more than that. Mr. Zelenko needs rest more than anything else, and so do all of you. After you are certain that he is settled, go home. Come back in the morning."

Cam and Mary Alice made nice "thank you" noises at the doctor, and I followed in Sveta's footsteps, stopping just far enough back that she couldn't reach me with a backhand swing.

"They're going to let us go up to see him, for a little bit." She didn't answer me. "Look, I don't know what this thing is between the two of you, but if it's like the doctor says, you have no time left to sort it out. You'd best be thinking of whatever it is you need to say to him."

"There is nothing to say to him that I have not already said." Finally, she turned her head just enough to meet my eyes in the window reflection. "I will wait in the van."

When I caught up to Cameron and Sister Mary Alice, the priest gave me a raised brow and I just shrugged. "She wouldn't come."

"Do you think she's telling the truth? About being his daughter?"

"Yup. You ever looked at their eyes? Really looked?" I'd have chided myself for missing it before, but again, it felt like something I'd known all along. "Besides, you've seen the level of angst going on there. That's totally a dad-kid thing."

"I didn't know my father," Cam offered.

"Well, trust me. She's his."

We rode the slowest elevator in the world up a few floors, following the helpful arrows on the signs to Ivan's room. On the way, I pondered my relationship with my own father. I hadn't been a good kid. In fact, I'd been a bad kid in just about every way possible. I lied, I stole, I did drugs. And that was just what I'd admit to now. I'd cleaned myself up eventually, but it wasn't until I became a father myself that I truly understood the hell I must have put my own through. How many nights had he laid awake, listening for me to sneak back into the house, scared to death that I wouldn't show up at all? How many times had a ringing phone, late at night, stopped his heart, certain that it was going to be *that* call about me?

A very wise woman, who was way cooler than me, once said that once you have a child, you always walk around with your heart outside your chest. I knew what that was like, now, knew the anguish my parents must have felt. I had to wonder, did Ivan feel that way about Sveta? Every time she went up against a demon, fighting for someone else's soul, did the big man's heart stop beating until he knew the outcome?

Just once, in all the years I'd known him, had Ivan mentioned his personal life. He'd had a wife, and a daughter. That was the extent of what he'd shared with me. Sveta had been even more tight-lipped, and I knew no more than that her mother had passed some time ago. There was an entire encyclopedic set of volumes of unspoken words between the two of them, and no time left to sort through them all. I couldn't force Sveta to talk to Ivan. But I knew it was always going to haunt me if she didn't.

Ivan's room was as generic as a hospital room can get. It gave me a weird sense of déjà vu, and I half expected to see my wife sitting in the far corner, her head bowed over a book. The old man himself looked shrunken against the stark white sheets, his face still lacking the hale and hearty color it normally held. One finger sported a pulse-ox monitor, the red light assuring us that it was working as intended. An oxygen tube ran across his face, and an IV stand on his left made very soft dripping noises, only audible because the rest of the room was so quiet. For a moment, I couldn't even hear him breathing, and I caught my own breath, waiting until his chest rose and fell again. When I let it out in a relieved whoosh, he opened his eyes.

"Dawson."

"Hey. How you feeling?" I hated myself the minute the words were out of my mouth. It's such a crappy thing to ask someone who's in the hospital. Of course they feel like garbage. That's generally why they were there. And yet, that always seemed to be the first words out of a visitor's mouth. We latched onto them, because it was something to fill the silence when we had no idea what else to say.

Ivan grimaced a little. "The bed is to being hard."

"That's to make sure you don't want to stay." I gave him a smile I didn't really feel, but already his eyes were drifting back over my shoulder, looking for a face I knew he wasn't going to see.

The blue gaze came back to me once he verified that I'd only brought Cam and Mary Alice. "Svetlana?"

"She's bringing the van around. Making

sure there're no bad guys waiting to jump us when we come out." Okay, so it wasn't precisely true, but it wasn't exactly a lie, either. I could tell by his nod that he knew exactly how much truth that statement was lacking, but we both let it pass.

"The doc's only going to let us stay a few minutes. You want us to bring you anything from your suitcase when we come back in the morning?"

"No." When I went to move away, give someone else a turn at the bedside, his hand shot out and gripped my wrist painfully tight. "The doctor. He told you?"

"Yeah. He told us." His hand dropped back to the blanket as if he'd exhausted all his strength with that one move. "You should have been the one to tell us."

"It was not to being important."

"We'll just have to agree to disagree on that, I guess." Because I couldn't seem to stop myself, I patted his hand before I stepped away from the bed. His skin felt dry and papery, like it was so thin he might blow away in a strong breeze. "Rest. We'll discuss it in the morning."

"No. You are to be going to the chapel. You will not to be worrying about me."

I sighed, mentally asking anyone who was listening for patience. "We really gonna have to have this talk again about who is worrying about whom?"

"Look, we all need rest, so nothing's going to be happening until morning anyway." Cameron intervened, smoothly sliding into my place next to Ivan's bedside. "Sister Mary Alice can't come with us anyway, she's too well known. So she can come here to sit with you for a while, keep you from being bored, and the rest of us will go on to the chapel."

Ivan seemed to consider this for a moment, then gave one terse nod. "This is to being acceptable."

On our way out of the hospital, Cam observed, "He's going to go to his grave giving you orders." I was inclined to agree with him, and truthfully, I was going to dearly miss that gravelly voice on the day it fell silent forever. Which was, apparently, much closer than I had ever realized.

Back at our borrowed apartment, no one seemed willing to take the bedroom that was supposed to be Ivan's. Sveta disappeared into the room she was sharing with the nun, Cam was going to bunk on the couch, and Mary Alice found me a heaping pile of blankets and pillows for my spot on the living room floor (after we scrubbed Ivan's blood out of the ornate rug).

While everyone else bedded down, I stepped out onto the balcony and clicked through the Grapevine app. I didn't know what time it was in Colorado, but Viljo's owlish face blinked at me from the small screen almost immediately.

"Did you know?" I jumped in before he could even start speaking.

The hacker paused a moment, then sighed. "About the cancer? Yes, I knew. He told me months ago, when he started transferring everything over to you."

"You should have told me." Hell, I should

have known. Men like Ivan don't start picking successors just for giggles.

"It was not mine to tell." Viljo pulled his glasses off and ran his hand over his face. "He is gone, then?"

"No, not yet. He collapsed, though. The doc says he needs to be put on hospice."

"He should have done that weeks ago. But he will not. You know that."

"Oh yeah, that's pretty damn clear." Below me, the dark streets were quiet, broken only by the occasional sounds of distant traffic. I found light in a window, blocks away, and fixed my eyes there. The moisture gathering on my lashes was just from the breeze.

I hadn't known Ivan when I first wagered my soul against a demon. I had two fights, one of which was nearly the end of me, under my belt before the white-haired Ukrainian had come knocking on my door, but it seemed like he'd always been there. He gathered us all, champions of every race and creed, kept us organized, kept us in decent gear and highly illegal permits and travel documents. I didn't know how he bankrolled it all, or even why he'd started it in the first place. He offered advice, counsel, and lessons when we needed it, and sometimes a decent ass-kicking when called for.

"What are we going to do without him, Vil?"

"That is why we have you, Jesse."

I snorted at that. "Shit. I don't even know half the people I'm supposed to be taking care of."

"You will." The keys of Viljo's keyboard clacked audibly. "Since it looks like things are…close. You should know that there are bank accounts that will transfer to your name upon his death. The money you are to use for air travel, arranging permits and identities, things like that. The things that Ivan does for all of you now. There will be some other legal mumbo jumbo, a few emails that will go out to some of his contacts, introducing you. Things like that."

"And Sveta?"

"What about her?"

"What's he leaving for her?"

Viljo paused so long that I thought the app had frozen, and only when I saw him swallow hard, his Adam's apple bobbing in his skinny throat, did I realize he was just trying to figure out what to say. "He told you about that too?"

"No. She did. There are arrangements made for her, too, right?"

The dark-haired geek nodded. "Yes, but she does not know. Nor does he want her to."

"Secrets. Always with the damn secrets. I'm telling you, Vil, when I'm running this show, we're gonna do this differently." Belatedly, I heard the words coming out of my mouth, but it was too late to bite them back. I grimaced, and muttered some very impolite words.

There was a highly suspicious wrinkle at the corner of Viljo's mouth, and I glared at him through my phone screen. "Don't you dare smile at that."

"Sober as a judge, that is me."

"Look, some guys from the Knights

Stuckupidus made a run at us today." Jesus, was it just today? So much had happened. "Send out an all-call, warning everyone to be on the lookout. Pretty sure they were after me, but just in case."

"Will do, boss." I didn't even bother to correct him.

"Anyone missing check-in?"

"Nope."

"Goodnight, Viljo."

"Later."

I stood out on the balcony until Cameron poked his head out with a concerned frown, then allowed myself to be ushered inside. Sleep wasn't going to come easily, and I could all but feel the nightmares nipping at the edges of my brain even fully awake.

Lying on the floor in my cocoon of blankets, I could tell that Cam wasn't sleeping either. It was justified, I suppose. His world had been turned on its ear every bit as much as mine had, albeit for different reasons.

"Quit thinking already, I can hear your brain curdling." That earned me a chuckle from the priest's direction.

"Sorry. You're one to talk, you're not asleep either."

"No. We're gonna feel it in the morning, if we don't, though."

Cameron chuckled again. "It *is* morning."

Damned if he wasn't right. The sun had yet to crest the horizon, but we were closer to dawn than to midnight. "Later in the morning."

We were silent for a few minutes, both of us

hoping against hope that slumber would sneak up on us when we weren't looking, and then I heard the leather sofa creak as Cameron turned to face my direction.

"Can I ask you something, Jesse?"

"Still a free country."

He was quiet again, and I started to think that maybe he really had fallen asleep mid-conversation, but it wasn't to be. "I saw your wrist."

A chill ran down my spine, and even though he couldn't see me in the dark, I tucked my left hand under the blankets. "That wasn't a question."

"You pushed your sleeves up when the paramedics got here, helping get Ivan on the gurney. I saw the mark on your left wrist."

"Still not a question." Part of my brain, the part that was still a teenage criminal, spun frantically trying to come up with a plausible lie, a story that would be believed. The rest of me, the grown-up part of me, knew that ship had already sailed, and sunk.

After another long silence, he sighed. "I guess I don't have a question. I just…wanted you to know that I'd seen it. I don't think Svetlana or Sister Mary Alice did. I wanted you to know that you could talk to me about it, if you wanted."

It was my turn to leave us in awkward silence again. Finally, I sighed. "I don't want to talk about it. You know I didn't sell my soul, or any of the ones I'm carrying. You'd be able to tell."

"This is true."

"So just…take it on faith that I haven't done anything terminally stupid, and let it go."

"If that's what you want." The couch squeaked again as he shifted his weight. "Was it him? The one from the cabin?" Cam was acquainted with Axel. They weren't friends.

"No."

"I'm not sure if that makes me feel better, or worse."

"Go to sleep, Cam."

My usual nightmares took the evening off, perhaps deciding that they too needed sleep this close to dawn. I know that when I finally slept, I dreamed, but I couldn't recall anything beyond being very cold and alone in a dark place. When I woke, I'd kicked my way out of my blanket burrito, so maybe that explained it.

11

Daylight came all too soon, and we rose and dressed in a semi-conscious state, ushered along by Sister Mary Alice's insistence that if we wanted to lose ourselves in the tourist lines, we had to get there early.

My dress clothes consisted of one fairly new pair of black jeans, which were just going to have to do because there was no way Cam's khakis were going to stay on my narrow hips, no matter how tight we belted them. I eyed one of his short-sleeved polo shirts with trepidation, knowing it would leave the demon contract tattoo visible for all eyes to see, but ultimately decided screw it. Cam knew already, and if either of the two women noticed, they didn't say anything. The shirt was bright red, which wasn't a color I usually chose, but it was either that, or lavender. And lavender just doesn't go with my eyes.

I pulled my hair back into a neat tail at the base of my skull, noting that the end now hit me just below the shoulder blades. It would be time to cut it again soon. After a quick shave, I was deemed presentable.

Cameron had forgone his priest's collar in favor of a navy polo and his khakis, looking every bit the fine and upstanding citizen I knew him to be. Clean shaven, hair gelled into fashionable spikes, we just had to hope that they'd be looking for a priest, not a civilian.

Sveta produced a pair of dove gray slacks

from somewhere, coupling it with a very nice white silk blouse. It had ruffles, even, around the collar and cuffs. She left her dark hair loose around her shoulders, one of the very few times I'd ever seen it down, and dabbed very subtle makeup on her face. Any other time, I'd have teased her about her fluffy shirt, but I could tell already that this was not the time for it. She made very little effort at conversation, getting through breakfast with the bare minimum words required.

"We'll meet you back at the hospital when we get done," I told Sister Mary Alice as we parted ways in front of the building. "I don't know what time that will be."

"It's fine. Brother Cameron has my number." She smiled, taking my hand and squeezing it gently. The hitchhiking souls in my skin fluttered a little, but in a pleasant way. They liked her. "Don't worry. I'll look after him. You go do what you have to do."

While I thought we were being absurdly early to just go stand in line, when we arrived at Vatican City, there were already at least fifty people ahead of us. The three of us slipped into the back of the line and were soon surrounded by more tourists, all of them entirely too cheerful for this obscene time of morning. All around us, they chattered and gushed and snapped selfies. There were college-age kids, middle-aged businessmen, elderly women with excited gleams in their eyes. For a few minutes, I envied them. I wished I could have been the one on vacation, touring amazing places and seeing amazing sights. I wanted to be able to appreciate the stunning architecture around us, to marvel at the history the place represented. Maybe even try to feel a bit awed at the sheer amount of faith and magic that I could feel in the stones under my boots. So many people passing through, for so many years, and their beliefs had soaked into the very bricks that built the place until it had its own kind of heartbeat, pulsing slowly but steadily. I wondered if life was easier, having faith that strong.

Instead of gawking at our surroundings, we three took turns scanning the growing crowds, seeing if anyone was paying inordinate attention to us.

There was a pair of Swiss guards nearby, their polearms held with an ease that said they actually knew how to use the archaic weapon. Cameron has assured me that they were actually formidable combatants, and I'd decided he must be right. Only total badasses could get away with wearing those gaudy uniforms with poofy pants. Luckily, neither of them spared us a second glance.

With Cam and Sveta doing the hawkeyed bit, I turned my attention inward, focusing on the souls under my skin. I believed they would sense danger before we could see it, but thus far, they had stirred only a little, feeling almost drowsy. I hoped they'd wake up, if I needed them.

I felt better, once the line started moving. It was easier to hide in a moving, seething mass of humanity than it was to just stand still like sitting ducks. By that time, the line behind us stretched halfway around the square, and the voices of that many people had become a very quiet roar.

Sveta, her eyes peering ahead of us with all the softness of a razor-studded block of ice, had dropped into a loose fighting stance that didn't match her outward appearance of fashionable thirty-something. I nudged her with my elbow, and her head snapped around, a glare on her face. "What?"

"You look like you're going to bite someone, or start snapping necks. You stand out. Smile. Put your arm around Cameron like you're his girl."

She almost balked, her jaw tensing visibly, but then her gaze swept over the crowd once again, and I think she realized that I was right. We weren't moving correctly, the three of us, and our tiny island of tension stood out like a beacon even in the throng. The dark-haired woman pasted a smile on her face, and slipped her arm around Cameron's waist.

Cam, for his part, looked like he had just been hugged by a viper – and he may have – but he draped his arm over her shoulders with a casualness none of us felt. "Not much farther. We don't actually need tickets for the chapel, we just need to get inside without being spotted. We can skip the museum and head straight there. After that, I think I can get us into the Cardinal's quarters."

"So…what happens if you get arrested, in Vatican City?" Because really, we were going to be lucky if we didn't wind up with the Swiss Guard pointing a bunch of pikes at us.

"They have a prosecutor here, and there is no jury. Most minor crimes end up in fines."

"And bigger crimes?"

Cam shook his head grimly, his eyes watching the long line of people behind us. "Normally, they turn serious cases over to the Italian courts. I think for us, they'd make an exception. But I guess that depends on how our conversation with the Cardinal goes."

After more time spent slowly shuffling our way toward the front of the line, I spotted something ahead of us that might cause us problems. "Metal detectors. We got anything that's going to be noticed?" I was specifically looking at Sveta, but she just rolled her eyes at me.

"You act as though I have not done this before."

"Hey, just covering all the bases." I took a moment to look her over – not in a pervy way, geez – taking guesses at where she had weapons concealed. Both sleeves, surely, since those were loose and flowing. Nothing on her thighs, her slacks were too form-fitting, but maybe something around her left ankle. The cuff on that side wasn't hanging quite right, but it could have just been wrinkled from the suitcase. Her hair, I finally decided. If she had to leave her hair down, which we both knew was a liability in a fight, she'd have something concealed in those thick tresses, too.

"Hey, she's supposed to be my girl, remember?" Cameron poked me in the side with a smirk, and I just shrugged at him. Sveta muttered something under her breath in Ukrainian, and while I don't speak the language, I'm pretty sure she was plotting our deaths.

Mentally acknowledging the fact that we

were probably the most inept covert operatives *ever*, we still managed to make it through the metal detectors without incident. Once past the entrance, the crowd dispersed more, the majority of the tourists heading toward what Cameron assured me were the museums.

"Come on, before it gets too crowded in there." The priest hurried us a different direction, rushing us past what I'm sure were historic treasures that would probably be very offended to find we'd just skipped over them.

He halted just outside an ornate wooden door, and gave me a hard look. "Whatever you do, don't make too much noise. You'll want to, but… Most people can't see what you're going to see and we don't want to draw attention."

"Pretty sure I can handle it."

I couldn't.

Now, I'm sure the Sistine Chapel is lovely. It was smaller than I'd expected, from the pictures I'd seen. I'm sure the artwork looked pretty awesome and I can appreciate all of the work it took to paint such a masterpiece. But I couldn't see any of it.

We stepped through that doorway, and my entire field of vision was dazzled by the light from overhead. All I could do was crane my neck as I stared up at the ceiling, vaguely aware that Cameron was guiding me out of the way of the other tourists behind us. No matter where I looked, streamers of blinding white light intertwined across the structure, winding down the columns, threading around every beam. It was a never-ending dance, swirling and frolicking above us.

Souls. Thousands and thousands of souls, encased within the ceiling of the Sistine Chapel. I could see every one of them, pick each one out distinctly, and the souls in my skin rose in answer, trapping me in my soul-sighted state whether I wanted or not.

"Holy shit!" Dimly, I was aware of gasps and disapproving noises from somewhere in my vicinity, but I couldn't be bothered to care.

"Shh." Cameron's grip on my arm tightened in warning. "People are starting to look. Get a grip."

"You get a grip." I did manage to lower my voice, at least. "I can't even... I... Why didn't you tell me?" There was a faint pressure just behind my ears, and I thought that if I closed my eyes for just a moment, I might be able to hear them singing, that beautiful host dancing to its own music inside the ceiling.

"It's not broadcast, for obvious reasons. Very few can see it, even those of us who are trained. I was taking a gamble that you'd be able to."

"Yeah. Yeah, I see it." Everywhere. They were everywhere, covering every inch and in every crevice. The area just over our heads grew brighter, the curious souls coming to check us out as if we were the oddities here. "They're happy. I can feel that they're happy here."

"What about...yours?"

Concentrating, I could pick out the thread of my passengers' existence from the sheer overwhelming life force around me. "They're calm. Peaceful."

"But they don't show any sign of wanting to join the ceiling?"

"No. How do we make them do that?"

Cameron sighed. "No one knows. That secret has been lost for a very long time."

Someone jostled us from behind, and I heard Sveta growl in response, but my eyes were glued to the ceiling above us, sorting out the intricate weave of souls, one elegant thread at a time. "How do you get them out of there?"

"We don't know that either. They're trapped there, and have been as long as the Order has existed."

"Not trapped," I corrected him instantly. "They're not trapped. They're safe." I couldn't have explained how I knew that. Perhaps it was just the simple sense of tranquility that radiated down on us. Maybe it was the fact that my own ethereal hitchhikers weren't losing their collective shit over any kind of perceived danger. This was a good place. A safe place.

"That's my hope. If we can remove yours from you, and store them here, they'll be safe and you'll be free."

I had the sudden realization that my eyes felt dry, and I wondered when I blinked last. At that thought, my vision blurred, and I forced my eyes shut, bending over to firmly remove the ceiling from my sight. "Gah...that's...ugh."

"You okay?"

"Fine. Just...gimme a second." Inside my

own head, I forcefully commanded my passengers to calm. They forgot, sometimes, that they were many, housed inside just one little me, and sometimes their reactions overwhelmed my very ordinary senses. A human body was not meant to contain more than one soul, after all.

Slowly, the glow outside my closed eyelids receded, and when I finally opened my eyes, the floor beneath my boots looked almost normal. Daring to glance up again, I could still see the white lacework of souls in the ceiling, but the harsh brilliance was bearable.

Sveta pressed close to my side, her voice hushed. "We need to go. Security is watching us."

"Keep me moving." I didn't trust my own feet not to get distracted by the spectacular display above. "Shove me if you have to."

Sveta linked her arm through mine, just a normal girl out sightseeing with her guy, but her nails dug into my bicep. The pain helped focus me, and between her and Cameron, they got me out of the chapel. Once outside, I lifted my face up to the sun, letting the perfectly ordinary light dazzle through my closed eyelids. It was different than the soul light, more solid, more real. It helped.

After a few minutes, Cam asked, "You good?"

"Yeah." I opened my eyes, happy to see that the world was once again just the world. "Yeah, I'm good."

"Okay, well here comes the fun part. Now we get to visit the Cardinal."

I straightened my shoulders, shrugging off

Sveta's grip as unnecessary now. "The first rule is, walk like you know where you're going, and no one will stop you."

Though Cam gave me a skeptical look, we headed off through the square at a brisk pace. About a hundred yards in, I started humming the Mission Impossible theme, and the priest gave me a dirty look. I just grinned.

You would think, with horrific things in the world like terrorism, and just flat out crazy people, security around the private quarters in Vatican City would be better. But it seemed like everyone was concentrating on making sure the tourists didn't get rowdy in their appointed tourist areas, and we were able to slip off the beaten path pretty easily. I was privately celebrating our good fortune, but Cameron's frown only grew deeper.

"This isn't right. There should be more people back here. Staff, clergy, just…people."

"So what's that mean?"

He sighed. "It's possible that I just don't know the patterns here well enough. Maybe I'm reading it all wrong."

"Or?"

"Or they already know we're here, and they've cleared a path for us." He glanced at me. "We can still turn around and try to get out of the city."

I thought about it for a moment, then shook my head. "No. We need answers, and we're not going to find them out there, just waiting for them to come after us again. Sveta?"

Her answer was terse. "I am bad at waiting."

"Then on we go." Cam's posture screamed reluctance, but I had to wonder if it was for our imminent peril, or because he was afraid to find out the answers we'd come for.

Finding the Cardinal's office was, as Cameron had noted, way easier than I'd expected. We passed several people in a long hallway that took no notice of us at all, which was probably odd, I agree, and Cam led us straight to a lovely wooden door that gave way immediately upon turning the doorknob.

Cardinal Giordano acted surprised, I will give him that, but there was something practiced about his movements that said he'd been expecting us. As he stood up from his desk, my eyes searched him for weapons, but found none. "Can I help you?"

He was younger than I expected. For some reason, I'd been picturing a doddering old man, gray-haired and wrinkled. Instead, the man before us was only in his fifties, his blond hair a few shades of gold darker than mine, but with a smattering of white at the temples. His face was weathered in the way a long-time gardener's would get, and he wore plain black slacks and a dark gray collared shirt. Beneath that, his body was lean and rangy, like mine might be someday if I lived that long, and he had immediately balanced himself on the balls of his feet upon rising, prepared to move quickly in any direction. He was a fighter, this one, or had been in the very recent past.

"Stop!" Sveta's voice cracked like a whip, and even I flinched a little. The Cardinal, however, froze in place instantly, one hand hovering near the edge of his desk. "You will not press the panic button." She had no visible weapons, but the older man nodded and took a step back from his desk, raising his hands to show his good intentions.

Cameron gave us both a glare – I had no idea what I'd done – and stepped forward. "Your Eminence, please forgive the manner of our intrusion. I am Brother Cameron of—"

"I know who you are, Brother." The Cardinal smiled faintly. "And I recognize Mr. Dawson's predicament, if not his face. I am not, however, familiar with the lovely young lady."

"Svetlana." She gave it over grudgingly, and offered no more.

"I am Cardinal Salvatore Giordano. Please, be welcome." He gestured for us to take a trio of seats in the corner of the plushly furnished office, but none of us moved. Finally, he nodded a little. "As you wish. Why have you come to visit me in so clandestine a manner?"

"We weren't sure who we could trust, Eminence."

While Cam made with the niceties, I let my gaze wander the room. Wards on the windows, the same lines drawn over and over in many different colors, all in varying degrees of brightness, proving that they'd been laid down over many years. Decades, maybe even. A bookshelf full of tomes, ranging from last year's bestselling spy thriller, to things that had no names and only the faintest hint of gilt left on the cracked leather spines. One of the chairs in the corner was more worn than the other two, and I guessed that it was the Cardinal's favorite.

Turning my attention to the man himself, I could barely make out the glimmer around him, the slight shimmer that told me he was a magic user. It wasn't an aura so much as just a slight wavering in the air around his shoulders, like heat off the asphalt. Easier to feel, than see.

Speaking of, there were three more magic-bearing presences just on the other side of the door behind us, and the souls in my skin fluttered enough to make my borrowed shirt ripple in a nonexistent breeze. "Company," I murmured to Sveta, and we each stepped to the sides, now flanking the doorway. If they came through, they were in for a nasty surprise.

The Cardinal caught the movement, glancing past Cameron to survey the scene, and I saw that he was correctly assessing the situation. "They will not come inside, unless I call for them. You must understand that in these dark days, a security force is unfortunately necessary." He must have caught something in Sveta's cold eyes, because he gave her a gentle smile. "I did not press the button, as you instructed, but there are additional safeguards on this room. Your presence could not go unremarked."

He spoke English very well, I realized, only the faintest hint of an accent slipping around through certain vowels. I couldn't place it. "Please, everyone. There is no need for…whatever this is. What is the source of this distrust?"

"We were attacked, Eminence. Yesterday,

in broad daylight, by several men. One of whom I positively identified as a member of the order."

I'd hoped he'd at least feign surprise, pretend like he hadn't known about it. Instead, the Cardinal sighed and shook his head sadly. "I had feared as much. I owe you an apology, Brother Cameron. You should have been warned."

"So wait, you knew about this?" Biting my tongue has never been a talent of mine.

The Cardinal again glanced over Cameron's shoulder to meet my eyes. "Unfortunately, yes. We have suspected for some time that there was…an unsavory faction within the order. I have put men that I trust to investigating, but we have been unable to pin down anything concrete."

"Add that to the list of shit we should have known sooner," I grumbled. Sveta snorted, which for her might as well have been a guffaw, but if Cameron could have killed me with a glare, he would have. "Were you just going to let us wander around the city as bait while you took your sweet time seeing us?"

"It was not my intention, no." Slowly, moving like he thought we were feral beasts, easily spooked (and he may have been right, in Sveta's case), he came around his desk to lean against it. "My intention was to keep you as far from Vatican City as possible, for your own safety. I didn't dream that they would be so bold as to actually strike at you."

"It was Brother Francis. Francis Laird."

Giordano grimaced. "Well, that explains that. Brother Francis' body was found in the river this morning, a victim of an apparently heinous mugging. It would seem now that his compatriots knew that he could be identified, and they removed him."

Cameron's face clouded darkly. "With all due respect, sir, what the hell is going on here?"

"That is something I would very much like to know myself." The older man ran a hand over his close-cropped hair with a sigh. "The world has become a very dangerous place over the last decade or so. The world is awash in new and greater evil, and I fear that I did not prepare you and your brothers adequately for what is to come. If a few of them have succumbed to temptation, I take full responsibility. I should have been ready."

"Why was Cameron told to keep me away from the chapel?"

Cardinal Giordano looked at me for a moment before answering. "You saw?"

"I did."

A gleam of keen interest sparked in his eyes. "What happened?"

"Nothing."

The holy man muttered "damn" under his breath, then immediately apologized. "It was too much to hope that they might have gone into the ceiling on their own. And to answer your question, I gave the order to keep you out of the chapel because we were not certain what would happen. Some had theorized that the souls would be absorbed into the receptacle automatically, and others worried that it might take your proper soul with it as well. Obviously, unfounded fears, but not ones I was willing to dismiss lightly."

"How did it happen? The ceiling, I mean?"

The Cardinal shrugged. "No one knows. All written records were destroyed by my predecessors, and we are left with only theories. The recent restoration of the ceiling was undertaken in an attempt to determine what Michelangelo had done with his paints to make such a feat possible, but we learned nothing. The thousands of souls have been there for centuries, and will remain so until they are called home at the end of days." He sighed again. "Which may be sooner than we know."

Cameron tilted his head. "You truly believe that? That we are facing the end times?"

The older man gestured toward one of his windows. "Can you look out there and say with certainty that we are not? The floods and famines, earthquakes and typhoons…war…" He turned back to us again, fixing his eyes on me. "And a great power returned to this world at the beginning of summer, an event for which you were responsible, I believe."

"Witnessing it is not the same thing as causing it." *Reina.* I should have known that the Knights Stuckupidus would know about her. "Totally not my fault."

"Regardless. It was felt around the globe, by those who are sensitive to such things. It cannot bode well for us."

"But can you help him?" Trust Cam to get us back on track. "They've come for him twice now, because of what he's carrying. Can you get them out?"

The older man pursed his lips. "Getting them out, as you say, has never been the difficult part.   I believe that Mr. Dawson knows this already."

"I would just have to pass them on to another person, the same way they came to me."

He nodded.   "And I fully understand why this is not a choice you would wish to make. However, it is still one choice, and in the end, may be the only one you have."

"I'm not going to do that to someone else." First off, there was no one in the world that I trusted that much.   Not even Cameron, pious and noble as he was.   Everyone had their breaking point, and sooner or later, some big bad would come to slurp up the souls like ramen noodles.

Second, I wouldn't have wished this burden on my worst enemy.   Aside from the fact that it made me a walking target, there was also the very real possibility that I was going to lose every single marble I had rolling around inside my head.   A fate worse than death, if you ask me, my body wasting away as my mind went walkabout.

Giordano seemed to debate something with himself, then stood up.   "Come with me.   I have something to show you that you may find interesting.   A…slightly less hard place to go with your rock."

12

Giordano led us out of his office, past the three bodyguards whose grim faces could have rivalled Sveta's at her coldest. They fell in behind us, which caused Sveta to drop back and walk behind them in return. There was some awkward shuffling as all the trained killers did a little dance, trying to keep each other in sight, and by the end, Sveta was smirking a little, having made fools out of them by simply doing nothing. The tallest of the men, apparently the leader, finally signaled one of his cronies to walk beside Sveta at the rear of our group, and we were able to proceed.

We were taken to an elevator, not precisely hidden, but tucked around a corner unobtrusively. There were no numbers on the buttons, a total of six blank yellow lights, but when the Cardinal selected a certain one, Cameron flinched.

"Your Eminence?"

The older man gave the priest a smile. "I am certain, Brother Cameron. I believe that Mr. Dawson and Miss Svetlana will have an appreciation for certain necessities we face in this line of work."

Cam didn't look happy with that answer, and I raised a brow at him. "If they're taking us to a torture chamber, I'm going to be really pissed at you." He didn't answer me, not even to chide me for my language, and that's when I got a bit worried.

The elevator took us down the three floors I

knew the building had, and then continued, the indicator above the door still insisting we were at the ground floor. Just because it was too damn quiet, I crossed my fingers and whispered loudly, "Please be Batman, please be Batman." Cameron looked like he might have a stroke, but the Cardinal laughed.

The elevator shuddered gently as it came to a stop, and the doors slid open. At Cardinal Giordano's gesture, we stepped out first, finding ourselves in a stone hallway. The low ceiling barely cleared my head, so Cam had to hunch a little or break his cranium. There was barely room for two of us abreast, and the souls in my skin gave an uneasy ripple. It was a good place to ambush someone, and all the potential bad guys were behind us.

"I'm afraid that you will find no caped crusaders down here, Mr. Dawson. And our Batmobile is in the shop." The Cardinal gave me a grin as he stepped from the elevator last.

I sternly bit my own tongue, and managed to keep my next question to myself. *Did it break a wheel, and did the Joker get away?* No one appreciated my jokes.

Awkwardly, in the cramped passageway, the Cardinal worked his way to the front of our group, squeezing between Cameron and me to take the lead. As his arm brushed against my chest, the souls in my skin went haywire, and I could swear I heard my back sizzling with the force of their agitation. Through sheer will, I held myself very still, pressing my shoulders firmly against the stone wall. I forced myself to breathe very calmly through my nose. *Stay there, just stay under the shirt…* My mental conversations with my passengers were never answered, but no telltale scrawls of white writhed their way down my arms, so I counted it as a win. The painful tingling, like pins and needles on steroids, subsided.

Magic. I could taste it at the back of my tongue, something like a cross of black licorice and molasses. Thick, and dark, and so very strong. There was so much magic in the holy man's person that the barest touch of his clothed arm nearly short-circuited my brain. That was something to remember for later. No matter what, never let the Cardinal get his hands on me.

My "episode" had been noticed. Cameron gave me a sidelong questioning glance, and I subtly shook my head. It was a story to tell later. Much later.

The narrow hall thankfully gave way to a much wider, and taller, passage within a few yards. The Cardinal paused there turning to look at Sveta and me.

"What you are about to see is…not public knowledge, for reasons which will become obvious. While I do not mind if you share this information with Mr. Zelenko, I would expect discretion in all other situations."

We gave him nods, of course, but inside I was thinking, *Yeah, but if I find aliens down here, I'm damn sure telling somebody.*

While the entryway had been old brick, the subsequent hallways were more modern, nondescript white paint over cinder block on the walls, very boring fluorescent lighting in tracks above us. The floor beneath our feet was institutional tile, and air smelled filtered, sterile. There was a faint hint of dampness, but I could hear the soft hum of dehumidifiers as they worked to keep the wet from seeping into everything.

We passed several doorways, again so generically normal they almost screamed "secret lair here!", before I asked "What is this place?"

"This is the lowest level of our headquarters. On the floors above us, we have training areas, armories, libraries, research rooms and the like." The Cardinal halted our procession in front of a large double door, one that had a numerical keypad. "Through here, however, you will find our holding cells and our infirmary."

"Holding cells. For prisoners."

"Yes."

I glanced at Cameron, but he wouldn't meet my gaze. He'd known, then. "And just who do you keep prisoner?"

"Come and see." Cardinal Giordano punched in a seven digit code – I only got the first, third and last two numbers, dammit – and the door opened silently.

A trio of men greeted us in the first room, their Kevlar vests and holstered sidearms looking strange in contrast with the white priest collars they all wore. Each of them sported the same cropped hair cut, one that I'd seen on Cameron too, when he'd first joined us, their shoulders and arms broad with muscles that spoke of use, not of trips to the weight room. The uniformity between them, and the three that followed us, was creepy, if I stopped to think about it.

My guard-souls did little flip-flops, uneasy but not alarmed. It'd be six on three now…seven, if Giordano fought. I didn't like our odds if this all went tits-up. (I had to give myself a little smirk and a high five for that thought, though, because really, I'm like twelve years old in my head and thinking that word in the presence of multiple priests seemed like the perfect form of rebellion.)

Though I could swear she'd been at the back of the line the whole time, I suddenly found Sveta beside me, and her fingers brushed against mine like she was seeking comfort. Since I highly doubted that, I let her take my hand, and palmed the tiny blade she pressed into it. I raised a brow at her, but her gaze was only for the six men surrounding us. I could almost see the calculations ticking off inside her head. Which one to take down first, where the weapons were, what cover we could find if we had to.

The room itself wasn't going to offer much in the way of shelter. Most of it was taken up by three banks of video monitors, obviously set to observe the building above, in addition to the cells within. It must have been laughably easy for them to spot us coming in, and I heard Sveta grumble under her breath as she realized the same thing. A barred gate on the far wall separated us from the deeper recesses of the building, and I recognized the retinal scanner on the left side only because I'd seen them in movies from time to time.

Giordano stepped up to let the machine read his eyeball, and the metal locked clicked softly as it disengaged.

"Gentlemen, if you would remain here. I will escort our guests." The blond man nodded to the small cadre of guards he'd suddenly assembled, and gestured for us to follow him down the hall.

Cameron halted at the door, catching it when it would have closed and locked behind us. Realizing that not all of us were following, the Cardinal turned to look. "I've seen it. I'll stay here."

"As you wish." When the older man turned away, Cam gave Sveta a small nod, his face serious. I wasn't sure if I felt better that he was watching our backs, or worse that he felt the need to.

While Giordano wasn't looking, I slipped Sveta's small knife into the front pocket of my jeans, making sure the hilt was tucked down out of sight. I wasn't sure what I was going to do with a blade that little – maybe clean someone's teeth until they begged for mercy – but it did make me feel better to have it.

"So." My voice bounced off the smooth walls, punctuated by the sounds of our shoes on the linoleum. "Who do you have down here that requires this much security?"

"I'm certain that you know, Mr. Dawson. Or have at least guessed. I understand that you had a run-in with a blood sorcerer earlier this year."

Magic came from the soul. It was the first thing Ivan had impressed upon me, even knowing that I didn't seem to possess that talent myself. A caster sliced away pieces of their very life force for their magic. Little pieces resulted in little wounds, ones that would heal over with time and rest. Bigger pieces could cause permanent harm, and in the most extreme cases, death. Magic had limits, unless you were willing to risk your life for it.

For those who were not content with the finite amount of power within their own bodies, there were ways to access more. It usually started with small sacrifices, I was told. A few drops of blood here, a deeper cut the next time, and so on. Eventually, the magic user's own blood was not sufficient, and that's when they'd move on to bigger things. Mice, maybe. Chickens. Cats. Goats. And when that failed to suffice… Well, that's when they would start sacrificing the lives of even bigger things. They could power their magic with the blood of other humans, and a death was the most powerful jump start of all.

Those that took that last leap were not redeemable. All the research I'd done since the encounter in Mexico told me that. Blood sorcerers couldn't be saved, couldn't be rehabilitated. There was only one way to deal with them, beheading usually being the recommended cure. The one time I'd seriously questioned Ivan about it, he had been quiet for a very long time. Finally, he said "Sometimes, the choice is to being made for you."

I didn't like to think about Ivan running around lopping people's heads off. I wasn't sure I'd be able to do it, if confronted. I hoped I'd never find out.

Perhaps Sveta's thoughts had gone along the

same lines. "How do you confine them? Prevent them from casting?"

"Heavy sedation, mostly." We paused next to a door with a single, narrow window, and he gestured for us to look inside. "Restraints, when necessary. Extreme wardings on every surface within the room."

The room beyond the window was white and bare, the large hospital-size bed appearing to be the only furniture. The occupant of that bed had their face turned toward the wall, so all we could see was the wild tangle of matted black hair crowning the head. A woman, I decided, judging by the general size and shape. She was painfully thin, almost emaciated, her bony wrists looking like sticks bound down by heavy leather restraints. A strap went across her thin chest, and two more cuffs trapped her ankles. The buckles on all of the restraints bore industrial looking padlocks.

"Is that really necessary? She's tiny."

"The day she was captured, she killed four men. And in the three years she's been here, she killed another two, and permanently crippled a third. Do not judge her power based on her physical size."

As we turned to move on, I saw the woman's head swivel toward the door, and a pair of dark black eyes locked with mine. She was young, I realized, maybe in her early twenties if that. Her dark brows stood out against her pale skin, and her lips were a strangely bright red, dainty like a doll's painted face. Marring that look, though, was the thick mouth guard, and I saw her jaw muscles work as she clamped her teeth against it.

"Why the mouthpiece?"

"Her teeth are filed to points. Without the guard, she slices her tongue and lips open for her spell casting."

As if she knew she was being spoken of, she blinked once, slowly, her lashes making brief shadows on her white cheeks, and then she smiled around the bite guard. For all that her features were delicate, fragile even, there was a malevolence in that gaze that chilled me to the very core. The souls in my skin rose up, coiling around my neck and down my arms, and I let them, suddenly needing the warmth they provided.

"We are currently housing fifteen blood sorcerers who have been deemed too dangerous to return to the world. All but one of them require around-the-clock monitoring, medication, and confinement."

I glanced into two more rooms as we passed. In one, the occupant sat in a chair with their back to the door, looking oddly like someone had put them in the corner for being naughty. I could see no more than the repetitive pattern of a hospital gown, and a large nasty scar down the back of the person's shaved head.

In the second room, there was furniture, a bookshelf, a television. The man inside glanced up and nodded a greeting, putting a thumb in the book he was reading to mark his place. He seemed sorely out of place, dressed in neat tweed with wire glasses perched on the end of his pointed nose. His graying hair was cropped short, and his mustache neatly trimmed. He could have been a college professor anywhere. Hardly the picture of a psychopath.

"Allen is one of our well-behaved guests," the Cardinal explained, when I asked. "I have always felt like he finds his confinement here a relief, safe from pursuing his unclean addictions."

"So you trust him."

"No. As I said, they are all closely monitored."

Sveta peered into a door on the opposite side of the hallway, and wrinkled her nose in distaste at whatever she saw. I didn't go check. "How long have they been here?"

"It varies. Our newest has only been here a few months. And I am about to introduce you to our oldest resident. He has been here for nearly fifteen years."

The oldest resident, it turned out, had a room to himself all the way at the end of the hallway. The long line of cells gave way to an open medical bay, and we followed the sounds of softly beeping machinery to the curtained alcove on the far side. The Cardinal drew the curtain aside with a rattle.

"This is Jeremy. He has been with us for a very long time."

Jeremy, if that was his actual name, was a still, pale figure on the hospital bed. Wires and tubes attached to him everywhere, like tentacles, and it was easy to see that he had been immobile in that bed for…I couldn't tell how long. Long enough that his muscles had wasted away, and his skin hung sallow on his frame.

"Is he…conscious?"

"No." Giordano picked up a file folder from the bedside table and offered it to us. "He has been in a persistent vegetative state for fourteen years."

I ignored the chart, but Sveta took it, flipping through it idly. "How did he get this way?"

The older man leaned against the table, clasping his hands in front of him. "Jeremy was an interesting case. Not only was he a blood sorcerer, but he actually went so far as to invite demonic possession."

That got a surprised snort, even out of Sveta. I knew it could be done. Axel had told me as much. But I'd never heard of it actually happening.

"He actually had a demon inside him?"

"Unfortunately, yes. We didn't know this until after his capture, and there were casualties before we determined the cause. After that, it was decided that he should be exorcised."

"Like…really exorcised? Rotating head and pea soup and all that?" What? My frame of reference was limited.

The Cardinal only nodded, however. "More or less. I was part of the team that attempted it. I did not become head of the Order until a few months after that."

"Attempted it. You did not succeed?" Sveta handed the folder back to him, and he examined it again like he'd never seen it.

"We succeeded in removing the demon, if that is what you mean."

"But?" The older man gave me a questioning look. "I heard a big 'but' in there."

He sighed, and nodded. "But. We were

unaware that he was possessed. He showed no adverse reaction to holy artifacts, had no problem crossing warded thresholds, nothing that would give us an indication that he was anything other than human. It was only when he was already inside our protections did the thing within him expose itself. When the demon came to the fore, it imbued Jeremy's body with extraordinary strength and speed, and a resistance to injuries that would have incapacitated a normal human. What began as a religious ceremony devolved into a battle for all of our lives. We succeeded, at the loss of four men, including the then-leader of the Order. In the process, Jeremy's mind was irretrievably damaged. He has been as you see him here ever since. Enough brain activity that we cannot truly call him brain dead, but he will never wake or be a functioning individual again."

I shuddered a little, and my skin crawled in a way that had nothing to do with my passengers. A fate worse than death, this. Locked inside a broken body, with no way of knowing if he could still hear, or feel. Horrific. "Does he not have family? Someone who is looking for him?"

"There are generally two outcomes, when a person chooses this path in life. The first is that their demeanor becomes so repugnant that their families cut all ties."

"And the second?" I knew the answer already. I'd seen Estéban's cousin Paulo start down that path. My protégé would have been his first human sacrifice.

"The families are often their first victims.

To my knowledge, Jeremy has no living kin."

The antiseptic smell was starting to irritate my nose, and the sterile white walls pressed ominously on every side. This wasn't exactly the best tour I'd ever been on. "So why did you bring us down here?"

"I believe that Jeremy offers a unique opportunity, one that I would encourage you to consider. It is not ideal, by any means, but it may be all you have." He gestured toward the sad, pitiful form on the bed. "Here is a vessel into which you could deposit your souls. He would not be able to use them for his own ends, obviously, and his body is well protected here. The souls would be safe, and more importantly they would be out of the hands of those who would use them for evil."

Instantly, my brain rebelled at that. Stuffing two hundred and seventy-five souls into that living shell, keeping them there while the body wasted away around them. The very idea was abhorrent, and I felt bile rise up in my throat, only to be swallowed down again.

But, that little voice in my head whispered, *they would be out of you. It would be the Church's problem, then. Mira and the kids would be safe…*

"You don't even know that it would work." My voice sounded a little raspy, and I cleared it loudly. "To pass the souls that way would require a contract, and a contract requires consent. He can't give it."

"I believe that we could maneuver around it, working within the mandates of the original contract governing possession of those souls.

Brother Cameron did send us details at the time, and I have had men researching it."

The original contract had belonged to Gretchen Keene, a genuine Hollywood starlet who had paid for her rise in fame with her soul. The collection riding under my skin had been hers once, collected from an astounding variety of lovers in her brief years. A loophole in her contract had allowed her to pass the souls to me, effective upon her death.

"The previous owner had to die. I'll pass, thanks."

"I don't believe it would come to something so extreme, Mr. Dawson." He offered me a smile that I'm sure was supposed to be encouraging, or fatherly, or wise or some shit. I just wasn't feeling it. "As I said, this would not be an *ideal* solution, but it would be *a* solution. And you seem to have those in fairly short supply."

"I'd rather put them in the chapel." The sense of peace I'd gotten there, the feeling that those souls were content, rather than imprisoned, I wanted that for the ones riding in my back. I mean sure, I wasn't really fond of them, and they were currently making my life a royal pain in the ass, but I wanted good stuff for them. After everything they'd been through, they deserved that.

The Cardinal nodded. "I agree, that would be a better course of action if we only knew how. That knowledge has been lost for centuries. I highly doubt we are suddenly going to rediscover it just in time to save you, Mr. Dawson."

"Weirder things have happened."

"At least consider it. Before the choice is

taken from you."

I made some vague noise that might have been assent, or might have been "fuck off" – Only I knew for sure, and I wasn't telling. – and we began our long trek back out of the creepy ass dungeon. About the time we got back to the guard station, someone back in the cells started screaming, a high breathy wail that spoke of horrors that could not be unwitnessed.

"Brother Seamus, if you would call Dr. Arlotti. It sounds like Piotr is awake again." Giordano gave us all nods. "I should probably remain here until the doctor arrives. I will have Brother James and Brother Thomas to escort you back to your hotel."

"No, that's all right. Cam knows the way out of here." There was no way I was letting anyone follow us back to the apartment.

The older man frowned. "It would be safer if you would allow some of my men to accompany you. For protection."

"We got it handled, thanks."

Giordano looked toward Cam like he expected to get some backup there, and frowned when the priest remained silent. "As you wish. At least take my card, in case you need to contact me. This is my direct line."

I took the offered card and tucked it into my pocket next to Sveta's knife, then grabbed an elbow of each of my companions and steered them back toward the elevator, muttering "Move with purpose, folk" under my breath.

When we finally made it out of the building

and back into the autumn sunshine, that's when I started to feel a little better. Cameron raised a brow at me. "You don't trust him."

"I trust him about as far as Anna could throw him. One-handed, even." I couldn't help but glance down at the paving stones under my feet, and for just a moment I felt like the pale girl with the mouthguard must surely be looking right at me, even through all the layers of earth and rock between us. "Let's get the hell out of here."

13

After taking the most circuitous route that we could, to prevent tails, our first stop was the hospital, where we were greeted with an empty room and a very disapproving doctor.

"Mr. Zelenko has checked himself out, against my medical advice. I highly suggest that you take him home, and get his affairs in order."

Sveta said some things in Ukrainian, which were perfectly understandable just by the tone. And probably because I was thinking the same thing. "Son of a bitch."

Cameron shook his head. "Do you think he at least got a ride back to the apartment, or is he out wandering the streets somewhere?"

"We'll know soon enough."

Back at our borrowed sanctuary, the first thing Sister Mary Alice said when we opened the door was, "I am *so* sorry!"

I smirked a little. "He's here, then."

The little nun did everything but wring her hands in her agitation. "I tried to talk him out of it. He wouldn't listen to a thing I said, and it was either bring him back here, or he'd have gone off on his own."

Cameron patted her shoulder gently. "It's all right. No one is blaming you."

"Where is he now?" Sveta's icy eyes swept the living room, noting a distinct lack of Ivan.

"Sleeping. And yes, I checked to be sure he hadn't climbed out the window or anything." Mary

Alice's forehead wrinkled. "He wouldn't, would he? I mean, I was only kinda half kidding when I looked in on him, but…would he?"

"Never say never." I clapped her on the shoulder too, and went to poke my head into Ivan's bedroom myself, just in case.

The old man was lying on top of the bedspread, his back toward the door. I suppose he could have been faking sleep, but the labored whistle of his breathing seemed too steady, too even for someone pretending. Quietly, I closed the door again. Sveta glanced at me once, as I rejoined the group, and I said "He's still there." That seemed to be enough for her.

We all changed back into clothes we were more suited for – my black T-shirt said "Non-Flammable? Challenge accepted." – and settled around the living room with hastily assembled sandwiches, where we filled the good sister in on what we'd learned at the Vatican. Her eyes went wide when she heard we'd been given the grand tour.

"You got to see the cells?" She looked at Sveta. "Even I'm only allowed at the guard station, and that's just because I keep the tech running. You're probably the first woman to ever walk those halls, as anything other than a guest."

I rolled my eyes. "Call them guests all you want, but those people are prisoners. I've seen mass murderers treated better. What gives you the right to keep them like that?"

"Some of those people *are* mass murderers, Jesse," Cam pointed out. "What else would you have us do with them? Execute them? If we don't have the right to confine them, I don't see how we have the right to end their lives, either."

I stuffed my mouth full of food so I didn't have to answer. There was no better solution, even as badly as I disliked the one they'd settled on. It just...felt wrong, somehow.

"You should take his offer." Sveta finally spoke up. "Transferring the souls to the comatose man. It would be best."

That felt wrong, too. "I don't know. Something feels squicky about it."

Cameron leaned back against the couch, tilting his head at me. "What bothers you more? Leaving the souls in that shell of a man, or leaving them with the Order?"

"Yes?" It all bothered me. Like, an army of ants crawling up and down my spine and a knot of nausea settling deep in my stomach. "I know you think he's going to be the one to help, Cam, but something isn't right. That whole conversation today was just too..." I wrinkled my nose, trying to come up with the correct word.

"Too ordinary." I glanced at Sveta, and she nodded. "He is too accommodating. Too helpful."

Cam threw up his hands. "You're both impossible to please."

"Hey, the only reason I'm still alive is because I *listen* when my heebie jeebie alarm goes off."

It was Mary Alice who stepped in to mediate. "Regardless of the Cardinal's intentions, you are still no closer to finding a way to remove the souls.

"That too." I ran my hand through my hair, with a frustrated sigh. "Are you sure you guys checked everything? Like, every little scrap of ancient paper and stuff?"

"Do you really think, after centuries of looking, they've left any stone unturned, Jesse?" Cameron was right, and I knew it. Just like the Cardinal said, there was slim to no chance that a heretofore unknown tidbit of information was going to surface in time to help me with my dilemma.

"How can stuff like this just vanish? I mean, everyone knows about the ceiling being painted. It was documented in the records of the time. And who the hell was Michelangelo, anyway? Some ancient spell-caster that no one talks about?"

"In every record we have, there is no mention of him having any magical ability at all. We literally have no idea how he did it."

"Following someone else's design, then?" Sveta offered, and Cameron shrugged.

"Possibly. I doubt we'll ever know. All those involved were dead and dust centuries ago. Even for those outside the Church who truly know the chapel's secret, it's a mystery. There are theories, to be sure, but no concrete—"

"What theories?" Yes, I was grasping at straws, but when you're neck-deep in quicksand, you'll take what you can get.

Cameron made a face. "Crackpot conspiracy stuff. Right up there with alien abductions and the Illuminati."

"Crackpots are only crackpots up until they're proven right, and then they're whistle-blowers and visionaries. Where do you find these theories? Google me something."

The priest and nun exchanged looks, and Mary Alice wrinkled her nose a little. "The best source is here in Rome, actually. If you want a complete compilation of every outlandish possibility in one place. Nothing on the internet, he doesn't trust it."

Cameron frowned. "We're not doing that. He's crazy."

"Don't know if you've noticed, but I'm not exactly sane." I pushed up to my feet. "We have two choices. Crackpot, or someone who might have actually been there. You handle the one, I'll get the other."

I heard Mary Alice questioning the other two about my cryptic statement as I went out the door, but I closed it before I could hear what explanation they were going to offer. I doubted they could say anything that was going to endear me to her, not with what I was planning.

Cameron's statement about everyone involved being dead already had caught my attention. Sure, any human who was hanging around back then was toast by now. With a few (one, actually) exceptions, I couldn't imagine any way for a person to live that long. However, humans weren't the only thing walking around down here, and we definitely weren't the most long-lived.

My feet took me down the block, around a

random corner, around another, just putting space between myself and the apartment. They didn't need to see this, and I didn't want Ivan put in danger in his condition.

When I finally found a nice, quiet little alleyway, I stopped, listening to the sounds around me for a moment so that I'd be able to tell when they changed. Quietly, barely raising my voice above speaking volume, I said, "Axel."

Life went on. I could hear cars puttering up and down the streets, people calling to each other, bird chirping from their nearby perches. Somewhere, a horn honked, and voices were raised in anger. A child laughed. An insect hummed in my ear, and I swatted it away absently.

Then, like someone hit the mute button on the remote, it all stopped. I was suddenly left in a cone of silence, and a chill crept over my arms. The sunlight, so bright and warm only seconds before became pale and washed out, a thin echo of itself. My passengers rolled themselves awake, watchful just beneath my skin, but not alarmed. The stink of sulfur teased my nostrils and was gone. "It's rude to creep up behind someone."

Behind me, my own voice chuckled. "But it's fun."

Turning, I found Axel in the alley, his arms crossed over his chest as he leaned against the wall in artfully posed nonchalance. His blond mohawk stood up stiffly, and the piercings in his face and ears glittered in the afternoon sunlight. The white t-shirt he always wore was pristine, his heavy black boots were never scuffed, and I could swear his blue jeans had been ironed and starched. I hated him a little bit, for always looking so fresh. Did demons even feel stress?

"It's going to get you hurt, one day."

"Maybe." The lanky man-demon pushed off the wall and hooked his thumbs in his belt loops. "What do you want? You don't call me up just to chat anymore. A lesser fellow might be offended."

I didn't have time to trade barbs with him, as entertaining as it might be. "What do you know about the Sistine Chapel?"

He pursed his lips, pretending to think it over. "Built in the late fourteen hundreds, by your calendar. Has some pretty artwork on the ceiling. Usually where a bunch of stuffy old men in robes hold super-secret meetings to determine who is the oldest and stuffiest."

I bit my tongue to keep from laughing at that. It wouldn't do to encourage him, but it sounded very much like something I myself might have said. Especially when he used my voice to say it. "More than that."

He raised a pierced brow at me. "Why do you ask?"

"Were you there, when the ceiling was painted?"

A faint smirk danced across his face, but he inclined his head. "I was."

"Then how did he do it? How did Michelangelo get the souls into the ceiling?"

Axel examined his fingernails idly. "You seem to be making a very large assumption there. What makes you think the artist had anything to do with it at all?"

"Are you saying he didn't?"

"I'm saying nothing, without being paid for what I know." His eyes flashed red for a moment, as if I needed the reminder. "I am merely pointing out that your questions are stemming from some leaps of logic that may or may not be supported by actual facts."

Of course he wanted payment. Ally or not – and that was still in serious question – he was a demon first. And demons get paid. "Not sure I'm willing to pay you when I don't know if you actually have the information I need."

He nodded a little, being entirely too amicable for my comfort. "For free, I will tell you that I was here when the ceiling was painted. I was here when the souls were delivered into their holding place, safe and sound. I was here when the Church tried valiantly to get them out, and failed. I have seen that ceiling besieged by every magic known to man *and* demon, with no success."

"That was people trying to get them out. How about putting more up there?"

The man-demon's mouth curved up at the corner, just a little. "That is not on the list of things I am willing to tell you for free."

"You're a dick, you know that?"

"And you're throwing a tantrum because you are not getting your way." The quirk of his lips became a full-fledged smirk. "Besides, if I told you the answer, would you believe me?"

"Yes." My answer was automatic, and I could tell that it took the demon by surprise.

"You've never lied to me. You may not tell me what I think I'm hearing, but you've never lied."

Axel pressed his lips together like he was pondering that, and for a split second, he looked troubled. "I didn't think you'd noticed."

"I'm human, Axel. Not brain dead."

He seemed to debate with himself for a moment, then gave a quick nod. "Then understand this. There are things I am unwilling to tell you, and things I am unable to tell you. There are certain rules by which even I must abide."

"Even if everyone around you threw the rule book out the window?"

"Especially if. You, I think, can appreciate that."

I hated him, not least of all because he was right. The rules were what separated us from the bad guys. Without the rules, we were all just apes, running around beating each other with sticks and scratching ourselves inappropriately. "What are you *willing* to tell me?"

"At this moment? Nothing." He looked over my shoulder, jerking his chin toward the street behind me. "You have guests."

Time moves funny when there's a demon present. It feels like it slows to a trickle, the light and sound moving through sticky syrup. I was pretty sure it took me like four years to turn around, and by then, the mouth of the alley was filled with hooded, masked men. Judging by how gingerly a few of them held themselves, we'd met before.

With an audible pop, the world lurched into motion again, the afternoon sun suddenly blazing down on us with the force of a plummeting anvil, and the noises of the world blaring into my ears like sirens. I counted seven heads, though there could have been more beyond my line of sight. There wasn't enough room for them to all come at me at one time, and it would be the only thing that saved me.

Hoodie #1 lunged forward, and I could smell the crackle of electricity from the black box in his hand before the sound of the stun gun could reach my ears and warn me. I had a brief second to be thankful it wasn't the kind with the projectile darts, and then I slapped the strike aside, using his own momentum to hip throw him over my shoulder to land at Axel's booted feet. The zapper went skittering out of his hand and down the alley, but I had no time to try to retrieve it. I had to settle for stomping hard on his midsection, and he curled into a gagging, choking ball.

The next pair came at me together, both of them sporting nasty, crackly zapping things. It was almost too easy to duck under the guard on the right, body checking him into his buddy who immediately collapsed with major voltage running through his body. Righty tripped over his downed friend, struggling to find his feet all caught up in thrashing limbs, and I used that opportunity to walk his head right into the side of the building. He dropped like a pole-axed mule, falling on his own stunner, which couldn't be healthy at all.

"Seriously, did you guys read the instructions before you handed those things out?" Four more. There were four left between me and the street. Two were hurt already, I could tell by the way they hung back, hugging their arms around their ribs. Even so, four on one was going to suck.

I glanced back down the alley, wondering if I could make it to the far end before they caught me. Axel, leaning against the brick wall again, shook his head. "You'll never make it. That one there looks fast." He pointed to Lead Hoodie. "And grumpy."

"You could help, you know."

The demon grinned, and cupped one hand to his mouth. "Help! Oh help!"

"Thanks." The rest of them didn't bother with stun guns. At some unspoken signal, they bum rushed me, one of them lowering his shoulder like a professional linebacker. There was no room for dodging in the narrow alley, and all I could do was brace myself, allowing the large man to scoop me up off my feet with the force of his charge.

There was no way around it, the landing was going to hurt. I managed two good elbow strikes to the side of his head before I hit the wall, knocking all the wind out of me and sending multicolored spots dancing across my vision. Still, muscle memory is a beautiful thing, and my body continued the fight without my direct input. While he helpfully pinned me about two feet off the ground, I managed to plant my foot firmly in his groin and grind my sharp pointy elbow down into a very nice little pressure point at the juncture of his neck and shoulder. There were advantages to being almost scrawny. With a bellow, he dropped me, staggering back enough that I could smash his face with my knee.

Something snared my left wrist, and a lance of pain shot through my shoulder as the arm was wrenched painfully in a direction it was never meant to go. I stumbled, off balance, and another restraint locked around my right wrist. Handcuffs, by the feel, locked down tight enough that I'd start to lose circulation in my fingers pretty damn quick. Stretched spread-eagle between two hooded men, the third swept my feet out from under me, my captors slamming my knees into the cobblestones with a loud crack. Someone's fingers laced through my long hair, forcing my head toward the pavement in a way that wrecked my shoulder joints again. More than that, with a grip on my hair like that, they could pretty much force me to do whatever the hell they wanted. Martial Arts 101: Control the head, and the body will follow.

The cry they wrung from my chest was more anger than injury, and I lurched against the restraining hands without much hope of breaking free, but I had to try. Bright pain did the samba around my extremities, and just when the darkness started oozing into the corners of my eyes, the souls in my back responded.

I felt them gathering themselves, heat and immense pressure pooling somewhere in the middle of my back. My vision was blinded by stars, the world around me reduced to streamers of color and light. One of the Hoodies said something, the voice garbled and unintelligible but the alarm plain through the high pitched bells in my ears. I didn't know what my passengers were about to do, but I was fairly certain I was going to burn to a cinder before they got around to it. I realized that I didn't really care.

"Bored now." It was Axel I heard clearly, my very own voice coated in a faint hint of other-worldly oiliness.

In my soul-dazzled senses, I could almost see him behind me, a looming form far larger than his actual size. I felt the moment that my captors recognized his presence, and the grip on my hair loosened just slightly. I threw my head about, trying to see, only to hear Axel yell "Head down!"

Even better than that, I managed to throw myself face first onto the cobblestones, just as a hot rush of air exploded over my back. It roared like a furnace, and when the sound died down, no one was holding my arms. Daring to look up, I saw four hooded forms lying at the foot of the wall, like dolls carelessly tossed aside. None of them seemed to be moving. "Uh…can I raise my head now?"

"Are they out of your eyes?"

I blinked a little, waiting for my vision to return to normal, then nodded. "They are now."

"Then go ahead."

I clambered to my feet, feeling the aches and pains that promised to become bruises and limping within a few hours. A set of handcuffs dangled off each wrist, and I flexed my fingers, trying to get some feeling back into them.

"Jesse!" From the street, Cameron's voice. "Jesse, can you hear us?"

"Here!" Even as I spoke, the Scooby gang skidded into view, Sveta not even bothering to conceal the wicked blades she held in each hand.

"I'm all right."

With a frown, Cameron knelt to examine the downed men, removing their masks and checking their pulses. "Edward. Peter. Raul." With a sigh, he ran his hands over his face. "All of them. I know all of them."

Sveta's knives disappeared, and she deftly unlocked the cuffs from around my wrists with a paperclip. I stuffed them in my back pocket, because who knew when you might need a pair. The marks around my wrists were angry and red, but I didn't think they were going to bruise too badly. "What I want to know is how they found me. And how did *you* find me, for that matter?"

Mary Alice, also tending to the rogue clergymen, tilted her head in puzzlement. "We heard you call for help."

"From blocks away?" I glanced over my shoulder, and much to my surprise, Axel was still there. He shrugged his lanky shoulders.

"You wanted me to do something." He wrinkled his nose, like a hound scenting, then pointed at me. "Check your front pocket."

I fished in my jeans pocket and produced the Cardinal's card. There was no magic on it. I would have been able to tell just by touching it. But upon close examination, I could feel a small raised place, barely thicker than the card stock itself. Ripping the card in half revealed a tiny black microchip, which I crushed under the heel of my boot. "Tracker." Why bother with magic, when technology was so much easier?

"I guess that settles whether or not the

Cardinal was involved." Cameron sounded glum, but not surprised. "We can't stay in Rome, Jesse. He controls everything here."

"I'm not leaving until I get my damn answers." Yeah, not my smartest decision, but now I was pissed.

Cam stood up, brushing his hands on his pants as if the touch of his former compatriots had contaminated him. "We don't even know if there are answers to be had. I mean, why is he doing this?"

I snorted. "For the same reason that everyone else is. They want what I have. It's the magical equivalent of a tac nuke. If they can get these things out of me, and into something they can use…" The very thought was staggering. Two hundred and seventy-five souls willing to sacrifice themselves under the right circumstances. I'd felt that amount of power, just once, and I knew what they were willing to do to destroy Reina. I was afraid of what they'd do if they were hosted inside someone with different allegiances.

"Giordano didn't want me near the chapel, because if the souls go into the ceiling, they're out of everyone's reach." It was the only place they'd be safe, I realized. The only place they couldn't be used for someone else's agenda.

"Who is this?" Mary Alice had finally noticed Axel.

The demon grinned and opened his mouth, and I stabbed my finger in his direction. "No. Do not."

"Aw…" Somehow, he even made his

mohawk wilt as he pouted. "But we could be such good friends."

Looking back to the little nun, she was frowning like she'd tasted something bad. When she didn't immediately point and scream "Demon!" at Axel, I realized she'd probably never heard one speak before. The oil-slick taint to their voices was unpleasant to be sure, but not easily identifiable if you didn't know the source.

Cameron moved to stand protectively in front of Mary Alice, giving the man-demon a death-glare. Axel was thoroughly unimpressed, and even went so far as to yawn.

"Okay, we can't just stand here with a bunch of unconscious bodies. Someone's gonna notice."

"Do we call the police?" Sveta snorted at the nun's question, and Mary Alice blushed faintly.

"This is beyond the reach of the police, I think." The Ukrainian eyed the downed men speculatively, and I touched her elbow to get her attention, then shook my head firmly.

"No. No killing."

"They will come again." She was disappointed in my decision, but I don't think it surprised her any.

"They will. But we're not murderers."

She snorted and rolled her icy eyes at me, but let it drop.

"I like her," Axel observed.

"Shut it."

The man-demon rolled his eyes too, but they stayed a normal color. I had to wonder what Mary Alice would have to say about his eyes flaring demon red. "You're no fun when you've had your ass kicked." I continued to glare at him, and he finally sighed, holding up his hands. "Fine. I know when I'm not wanted."

With a pop of imploding air, he vanished before our eyes, leaving only the hint of sulfur wafting around in his wake. I thought Mary Alice's eyes were going to fall out of her head.

"He…! What..? Who…?"

Ignoring her, Cameron spoke up. "We got in contact with our source. Let's at least go see him, then we can bail town. Find somewhere nearby, in case we need to get to the chapel, but further out of the Order's reach."

"Huzzah! We have a plan." No one seemed to share my enthusiasm.

14

I'm not sure what I expected to find when we dropped in on Cam and Mary Alice's "source." From their vague comments, I think I was hoping for a bespectacled loon with Doc Brown-style hair, wearing a tinfoil hat and surrounded by walls full of alien autopsy diagrams and I WANT TO BELIEVE posters. What I got was a lot more Scully, and much less Mulder. I admit, I was disappointed.

The man who opened the door to us could be politely called portly, his balding head ringed by a fringe of steel gray fuzz, which matched the walrus-style mustache that took up most of his face. He wore a tidy sweater vest, buttoned over his ample midsection, and his trousers were almost painful in their mundanity. Smiling behind his round spectacles, he ushered us inside. "Come in, come in!"

"Dear god, it's Wilford Brimley," I muttered. Sveta gave me a puzzled look, but Mary Alice elbowed me in the ribs, biting her lip to keep from laughing. Finally, someone got one of my jokes. I knew I liked her.

His name was Vernon, not Wilford, but it was close enough. He pumped all of our hands enthusiastically, his jolly cheeks glowing with his excitement. "I must say, it's an honor to have you here, Father, Sister. Sit, sit… May I offer you some coffee or tea?"

Cameron shook his head as he sat. "We are actually pressed for time, Mr. Rogers."

"Yes yes, of course. How can I help you? I'm afraid you were a bit vague on the phone." The large man hefted himself into a rickety office chair that groaned under protest.

I let Cam take the lead on this one, and spent my attention wandering around what was obviously an office. The walls were lined with shelf after shelf of books, floor to ceiling. Some of them were new, with shiny dust jackets and artfully designed titles. Others were too old to guess at their age, and the faint odor of mildewed paper hung in the air. Where the bookshelves wouldn't fit, the space had been taken up by file cabinets, each drawer labelled meticulously with some kind of personal code I couldn't even guess at deciphering.

The dark, wooden desk took up the smallest part of the room, actually, and it took me a moment to realize why it looked so strange to me. There was no computer. How long had it been since I'd seen a desk without a monitor and keyboard resting on it? Even the phone was old-school, being a rotary version with an actual cord on the handset. I couldn't remember the last time I'd seen one of those.

As I passed my hands over the rows of books, a few of them tingled under my fingers. Traces of magic, impossible to know how old or for what purpose. I wondered if I should say something to the man about the possible danger inherent in fading magic. It could spoil, go sour, and the effects could be unpredictable at best. At worst…well, suffice to say I still had nightmares.

"Hm, the Sistine Chapel legend? It's an

obscure one, that's for sure." Under Cameron's prompting, Vernon heaved to his feet again and went to one of the file cabinets, going directly to the file he wanted. Pulling it out, he offered it to the priest. "I don't have much, I'm afraid, and what I do have is based on single sources. No corroboration from that era."

Cameron took the file, examining the contents with Mary Alice leaning over his shoulder. "You've put a symbol next to this source's name. What does it mean?"

Vernon craned his neck to see, then nodded. "It means that person was burned as a heretic."

Lovely. I continued to explore the room, taking a closer look at the single bulletin board he had mounted on the wall. It was covered in note cards, each of them filled with tiny, cramped handwriting. Occasionally, a picture would be posted, each painstakingly labelled with the date, time, and source.

"Hunh." Sveta glanced over at my quiet outburst, and I pointed to a black-and-white picture of a ring of worn-down stones, nearly lost in a meadow of tall grass. "Look familiar?" *Mexico, 1937*, it said. I knew that in modern times, those stones looked just about the same, though the meadow in question was now cleaved in half by a deep chasm.

Sveta snorted a little and rolled her eyes.

Vernon's notes on the stones were sparse, and marked with more questions than answers. Again, I wondered if I should fill him in on some of the details, or just let it go. They were just rocks now, after all, the power that had been imprisoned there a millennium ago now out and wreaking havoc in the world.

The next photograph that caught my eye was a clipping from a newspaper, grainy at best and blurry at worst. Still, I recognized the woman, her jet black hair flowing loose around her face, just another body in a large crowd. *Chicago, 1954. Sept?* I'd seen her face much more recently, though I could swear she hadn't aged a day. "Well hello, Cindy."

The hand-crampingly tiny writing went on for four notecards, containing a list of dates that stretched back into the eighteen hundreds. Sorceress, he called her. Vampire, he wondered. Immortal? I doubted that. Just because she hadn't died didn't mean she couldn't. *"One day, you'll ask how it's done. And if you're very unlucky, I'll tell you."* I couldn't stop the shiver, and I took a moment to be grateful that I hadn't been in possession of the souls when my path last crossed hers. I wasn't sure my mind would survive seeing her as she truly was.

I wasn't sure just *what* Mystic Cindy was, in all honesty. When I'd encountered her, she'd been doing nothing more than translating some demonic text for me, on Ivan's recommendation. Dressed in a UCLA sweatshirt and blue jeans, she had looked like any college co-ed anywhere. But, as proven by Vernon's notes, she had looked like that for a very, *very* long time. No human lived that long, not naturally. At the time, she'd heavily implied that she was willing to tell me how it was done, and that

I wouldn't like the answer. Blood sorcerer, my instincts told me, using the life force of others to prolong her own. Those same instincts told me to stay far, far away from the tiny Korean woman, just in case I was right.

"Jess?" I glanced over my shoulder to see Cam giving me a worried look, and gave him a shake of the head. I wasn't down the rabbit hole again. "Come look at this, tell me what you think."

The file was made up of photographs of ancient documents, the ink on them nearly faded into illegibility. Each image was carefully notated with the source, date, time, and any other factoids that Vernon thought important. Cameron didn't even bother to let me look at the first one, simply flipping it over so I could see the translation on the back.

"They blaze like the sun. Only a man of pure faith can be rewarded with the gift of God's sight?" I raised a brow at Vernon.

"This was taken from a physicians' manual, published sometime following the painting of the chapel ceiling. It documents the case of a mad man who believed that he could see souls in the artwork."

Cameron pointed at the passage again, as if I just hadn't read it the first time. "He could see, Jesse. They thought him insane, of course, but…"

"And did they cure the poor man?"

Vernon checked some of his notes. "Erm…no. They attempted trepanning, and he died shortly after the procedure."

Sveta frowned, leaning over me to look at

the file. "What is 'trepanning'?"

The portly man cleared his throat a little. "Um…they drilled a hole in his skull to try to let the demons out. He died, of course. Medicine back then was not what it is today."

"Okay, so fine, he could see. That's not telling us much."

"He, the mad man, believed that he had been touched by God to allow such a gift, because he was a man of pure faith."

I couldn't help but snort. "Well, we know that's not true." My faith was anything but pure.

Cameron frowned, flipping a few more pages into the file. "Still, I feel like it's important."

"Wait, go back." Something caught my eye, and I pounced on the page when Cameron revealed it again. "There have been multiple reports of angel sightings in the chapel?" I glanced at Vernon to be certain I was interpreting his notes correctly.

"Oh yes. As recently as the nineteen sixties." He helpfully flipped to another page, obviously clipped out of a tabloid, yellowed with age. "Right here. Talk of a being of golden light, and the ceiling coming alive with swirls of color, moving in and out of the being's hands."

Sveta raised a brow at me. "This is important?"

"It could be…" I'd met an angel once. An honest-to-God, pun intended, angel. On top of almost frying what was left of my brain, he hadn't been the most helpful fellow. But, if I could get one to show up again, maybe that was the key we'd been looking for. "Not sure how to call one up, though. He didn't exactly give me his card."

At some point, I noticed that Vernon had a small notepad in his lap, and was hurriedly scribbling everything that we said. I stared at him until he noticed, and then he finished his sentence before he put the pen down, giving me a very bland look in return. There was a keen intelligence in those eyes, I realized, behind the jolly, befuddled show he put on. Here we were, confirming everything he'd ever suspected, just with our casual conversations, and he wasn't even going to be ashamed about documenting it.

"What do you think, Vernon?" I shifted to sit on the corner of the man's desk, tilting my head. "You think there's a sure-fire way to summon an angel? Got a hotline number in one of your files, maybe?"

He pursed his lips under his enormous mustache, pretending to think it over. "Well, no, not as such. Prayer seems to be the usual method, of course. Summoning is usually reserved for less savory creatures."

Less savory... "Son of a bitch." Cameron gave me a glare, but I ignored it. "Reina, Cam."

"What about her?"

"What is she? I mean, truly, at her core, what is she?"

I saw the color seep from his face as he realized. "A fallen angel."

Sveta cursed, and I nodded. "If it takes an angel to move souls in and out..."

Already, Mary Alice was shaking her head, though we hadn't precisely read her into the situation. "No, if someone had that power, the souls would have been taken already."

"She was locked up for about a thousand years, maybe she just hasn't made it over here yet." I couldn't believe that, though. Her minions had to have told her where that cache was. She'd been loose for months, surely she'd paid a visit already. "Maybe she can't get to it. Consecrated ground, and all."

Vernon snorted, sending his mustache fluttering in a most distracting manner. When all eyes turned to him, he shrugged his beefy shoulders. "That ground hasn't been consecrated in decades. Perhaps not ever. I found a fragment of a papal missive from the era, stating that they wished it to be unconsecrated so that all those who had been led astray could still visit, and find their way back to God."

"Cam?" I looked to him for confirmation, and he squirmed uncomfortably.

"There has been discussion that the original efforts have been…fading over time."

"So why hasn't it been renewed?" I'd seen Cameron, all by his lonesome, consecrate a good sized chunk of land. The spell had nearly killed him, and the protection had faded fairly quickly, but he'd done it. He'd told me then that it took multiple priests to make it a permanent effect.

"Bureaucracy. Like so many things."

"Jesus Christ," I muttered, and Mary Alice slapped my leg. I stuck my tongue out at her, and she returned the gesture, crossing her eyes for good measure.

"All right. So, for whatever reason, Reina can't get at those souls. Which is a good thing. And it seems like we can all agree that we need an angel, preferably one of the non-fallen variety." Cameron stood up from his chair, handing the file back to Vernon. "Thank you for your time, Mr. Rogers."

"Any time at all, Father. I am glad to be of assistance."

We lined up to shuffle out of the office, and I paused by the bulletin board full of notecards. Glancing back at Vernon, I tapped my finger on the picture of Mystic Cindy. "You need to steer clear of this one, Vern."

The portly man did a good job of feigning confusion, but there was a hungry light in his eyes. "Oh? How do you mean?"

"If you're a praying man, pray that you never find her. And that's all I'll say on it. She looks like a sweet young thing, but she's one of the few things in this world that terrifies me. Understand?"

"Wait…you've met her? You mean you've actually seen her?"

"Bye, Vern." I left with him still calling out questions behind me. Truthfully, all I'd probably done was stoke the man's curiosity, but I felt better that he'd at least been warned. What he did after that wasn't my business.

As we walked down the stairs, I pondered the fat lot of nothing we'd just learned. A crazy dude who could see souls, totally unrelated angel sightings, and a guy who very clearly had all the questions and none of the answers.

I mean, I totally get the grasping at straws and scrambling for any tiny shred of information you can get. When you have less than nothing to go on, you take what you can get. Even the idea that we were probably betting my life on it didn't really bother me. It's what I do. But betting the lives of the other two hundred and seventy-five people I was currently responsible for was less okay.

"So, we should go pick Ivan up and get the hell out of Dodge, right?" It wasn't running away, it was a strategic retreat. To my surprise, Cameron growled something that sounded suspiciously like a curse word. "Whoa, man. Language."

In response, he thumped his fist against the wood-paneled wall. "I just… I thought there would be more here. I thought we'd at least find *some*thing."

"Man, do you really think the Church just ignored this guy because everybody thinks he's nuts? I promise you, they vetted and double checked everything he had already. If there was an answer here, they'd have found it." The priest gave me a bleak look, and I actually found myself patting him on the shoulder. "Hey, it was worth a shot. At least we can say we tried."

"Jesse is right," Mary Alice chimed in. "The bit about the angel could be very important, if we can find a way to contact one."

I had to give the little nun credit, she was handling the weirdness rather well. "Not even fazing you, is it? The idea that there are angels and demons and souls just wandering around unsupervised."

She chuckled at me. "I have always believed that angels and demons walked among us, Jesse. It kinda goes with the job."

"I'm glad one of us believes in the job," Cam muttered, and the nun squeezed his hand. "If it turns out we need a man of faith for this, I think we're hosed. Not sure mine is up to the task anymore."

"We still have the sister," Sveta said. "There is no reason to believe it must actually be a man."

We all conceded that it was a good point. Hooray for equality in the demon slaying community.

"I don't know, maybe we need to go talk to Cardinal Giordano again," Cameron said as he pushed the apartment building door open. "There's still a chance that he himself is unaware of…"

Five men in black fatigues were waiting in the street outside, forming a lose semicircle around the door. A white van was parked just a few yards away, two more men standing guard at the rear door.

I poked Cam in the back. "You were saying?"

They hadn't bothered with hoods or masks this time, and they had night sticks to go with their Tasers No guns that I could see, but then they hardly wanted to kill us. Or at least me. Sveta cursed quietly under her breath, and I could feel her tense behind me, preparing to start the rumble herself. Mentally, I counted the odds, factoring Cam and Mary Alice in as unknown quantities. Seven visible opponents, and maybe more in the van. Four of us, provided that Cam didn't knock himself out of the fight with his spell casting.

"Brother Cameron." The one in the lead, a tall, swarthy man who looked like he'd last laughed during the Regan administration, focused on the priest at the front of our awkward line. "You have been ordered to report to headquarters."

"And if I say no?"

"That would be unadvisable."

Cameron shook his head. "What are you doing, Lorenzo? We're friends."

There was no hint of softening in the dark man's face. "One thing has nothing to do with the other."

Sveta's hand rested on my back, one finger gently tapping five times. I inclined my head just slightly, to indicate that I understood. On five, we'd go. My skin tingled under my shirt, my passengers gathering themselves for whatever happened next. I eyed the pair of men on my left, marking the nearer of the two as my first target. They both looked more like mercenaries than priests, and I had to wonder just what recruiting methods the good cardinal had been employing in recent years. At my back, Sveta's weight shifted slightly to the right. This was going to get ugly.

"Brother Cameron, I strongly advise you not to resist." Lorenzo flicked a hand toward the van, and the rear door opened from the inside.

We couldn't see any of the Knights of Doom that were surely in there, but the face that appeared in the dark opening was unfortunately familiar.

Ivan's jaw was clenched, his ice-blue eyes flashing angrily, but he held very still and remained silent as he was put on display for us. Something in the way he carried himself said that something uncomfortable was pressed against his ribs, just out of our sight. Sveta lurched forward, and I had to grab her around the waist to keep her from launching herself at the armed men. It said something about her mental state that she didn't just turn around and feed me my own arm.

"Shh…" I yanked her close, whispering in her ear. "They haven't hurt him. They've got a weapon on him, but they haven't hurt him."

"Jesse…" I could count on one hand the number of times that she'd ever said my name, but it was the tremulous tone in her voice that really chilled me to the bone. If Sveta broke, we were all screwed.

"I know. It's all right. I got this." I sure hoped I was right. Catching Mary Alice's eye, I firmly handed the distraught Ukrainian mercenary over to the much smaller nun, then stepped around Cameron with my hands raised. "Take me to your leader."

I always wanted to say that.

15

Our reputations had definitely preceded us. The instant we were all inside the van, we got jabbed with something in syringes, and we were out like lights. I fought it as long as I could, glaring at the one Cam had named Lorenzo up until the darkness claimed the last of my vision. I doubt he was impressed.

The sucky thing about being drugged is that you can't drag yourself out of your nightmares. I spent what felt like two or three years stepping out of that mysterious tunnel over and over again, struggling in vain to make out the features of the figure standing across the hard-packed field. Sometimes it was there, sometimes it wasn't, and I got to the point where I felt a bit lonely when the dark stranger was absent. He was at least someone I could see, unlike the quietly desperate pressure at my back that I could never turn to investigate.

I realized I was waking up when I glanced to the side and found Sveta there with me, her face set in a scowl. She didn't belong in this place, this dream of mine, but before I could point that out to her, she drew back her hand as if to slap me in the face. "Jesse! Wake up!"

I snapped awake, and just stopped myself from crushing the bones of Sveta's wrist in my grip where she had indeed tried to wallop me one. I relaxed my hold just a bit, but kept her trapped there for a moment, blinking my eyes until the rest of the room came into focus. Sveta herself had been victim of some bad wakings in her time, so she just held very still until I nodded and turned her loose.

"How long?" Long enough that my voice croaked when I said it, and I spent a few minutes trying to work the taste of something mossy out of my mouth.

"The sun is going down," Cameron announced, and I craned my head to find him peering out a window. His back was mostly to me, but I could read the line of tension in his shoulders, the hard clench to his jaw.

My head, I realized, was resting in Mary Alice's lap, and I felt myself blush as I heaved myself upright. "I'm the last one up, hunh?"

"We were starting to get worried." At some point, the little nun had removed her headpiece, revealing strawberry blond hair, cropped in a cute pixie cut around her face. It suited her.

I shook my head, but slowly, waiting to see how much residual dizziness I was dealing with. "I don't do well with sedatives. We're lucky I'm not puking." Immediately, both women scooted back, giving me identical looks of wary disgust. "So where are we?"

The room was just a room. It could have been someone's office or den, the hardwood floor covered with a rich looking rug. Someone had propped my feet up on an old throw pillow while I was unconscious. A desk was stationed in one corner, though it bore no signs of personal possessions, and the walls were covered with empty bookshelves, just waiting to be used. Cam's gaze was still all for whatever was happening outside, and from the angle of his head, I was guessing we were on at least the second floor.

"Vatican City," Mary Alice supplied. "In one of the unused offices, we think."

Leaning heavily on Sveta's shoulder, I shoved myself to my feet and teetered there, waiting to see if my body was going to rebel. When I stayed up, and my food stayed down, I counted it as a win. "Anybody try the door?"

"Locked and warded." Sveta displayed her left hand to me, showing a blistered sigil across the palm that conveniently matched the pattern on the doorknob.

"You all right?"

She nodded. "I used my left hand. I am not stupid."

"Guards?"

Mary Alice pointed at the bottom of the heavy door, where we could just see the light broken by a pair of feet. Maybe two. "They traded out about fifteen minutes ago. Right after I woke up."

It suddenly occurred to me that we were missing one. "Ivan?"

"He wasn't here when we woke." Cameron finally left his post and rejoined us. "I didn't see them inject him, in the van. I don't think they put him out."

"If they've harmed him..." Sveta snarled softly, and Mary Alice took her uninjured hand, squeezing it gently. To my amazement, Sveta allowed it.

"They can't hurt him. They need him to

control us." I took a few steps around the room, and was pleased to find myself steady and pretty much back to normal. "Any chance of getting out the windows?"

Cam shook his head. "Bars."

"Of course there are. Because who doesn't put bars on windows in the Vatican?" I glanced around the room, knowing that my companions had likely already searched it. "Weapons?"

"They found everything I had." I raised a brow at Sveta, knowing just what kind of thorough search that would have entailed. No wonder they'd knocked us out. Someone would have definitely died, if they'd have tried that on her while conscious. "And they have removed the chairs from this room."

Once she pointed it out, I could see the indentations in the rug where there had previously been furniture. "Guess they decided the desk was too heavy for us to throw."

I ran a hand through my hair, giving a sharp tug on the length like that might jump start my brain. "Wonder if I could unweave that ward…" I'd destroyed intricate spells before, using my borrowed power, but it had cost the life of one of the souls I now carried. I wasn't quite willing to go that far, just yet, but I knew it might still come to it.

"They'd know, the moment it broke. And we have no idea how many are actually out there." Mary Alice was right, but I desperately hated just waiting. Waiting made me feel useless, which made me antsy, which was probably going to lead to me doing something colossally stupid.

Fortunately for public safety, we didn't have long to wait. A low hum of voices on the far side of the door alerted us to incoming company, and without a word, the four of us spread ourselves in a semi-circle, ready to defend ourselves if necessary.

The knob turned and rattled just like an old horror movie, but as the door creaked open, the first person to step through was the one they knew we wouldn't attack. Ivan's ice-blue eyes swept the room, doing a mental headcount, and he held up one hand, silently telling us to stand down. I obeyed instantly. It took Sveta a moment to comply. She barked something at him in terse Ukrainian, which he answered in his gravelly voice, as quiet as I'd ever heard him. Reluctantly, she shifted her wait off her toes, relaxing out of her fighting stance.

Ivan looked all right. Still haggard, still pale, but he was standing upright and not moving like he was hurt. I was fairly certain that if he'd shown signs of damage, nothing would have held Sveta back. Just to be safe, I asked, "You okay?"

Ivan inclined his head a fraction of an inch, his eyes warning me to keep my big yap shut. Yeah, okay. Ixnay on the ancer-cray.

Immediately behind our venerable leader came the Cardinal, now dressed in more formal attire, which I'd always thought looked like a giant specter of death. I mean, really? A long black dress and blood red sash? How is this supposed to be comforting?

We cleared a path, allowing Giordano into the room, but when his attack dogs would have followed, Sveta stepped into their path. There was a moment of bristling and snarling, but Giordano motioned to his merc-priests and they reluctantly withdrew. The door boomed shut with some finality, and my skin tingled as the ward sealed again. There was going to be no quick exit, even if we managed to take the Cardinal hostage.

"Let me first apologize for the abrupt manner of your arrival." Cardinal Giordano seated himself on the edge of the desk. "I wish it had been done differently."

"Must be that nasty rogue faction. Pesky things." Hey, my first defense is always sarcasm. The old clergyman nodded his head in acknowledgement, while admitting to nothing.

"Why?" Cameron's voice was choked, and I couldn't tell if he was holding back tears, or rage. "Why have you done this?"

The older man sighed. "The treasure that Mr. Dawson bears within him is too precious to risk it falling into enemy hands. It has been decided that he will be placed in protective custody until such time as a solution can be found."

"Oh *hell* no." I didn't trust the Church any further than I trusted Reina and her flunkies. "I've seen your protective custody, and I'll pass."

"I am afraid this is not a discussion, Mr. Dawson." The Cardinal fixed me with an emotionless stare.

"You can't hold him here against his will! He's an American citizen!" Cam took two steps forward before Ivan caught him with one restraining hand and a stern look. "The media will have a field day with this."

Giordano nodded his agreement. "Which is why none of you will be allowed to depart. Information of this nature is too sensitive, too volatile to be released to the general public."

"You will have to kill me first." Man, there were just times when I wished Sveta knew when to keep quiet. It's probably how most other people feel about me.

The Cardinal inclined his head to her. "Regrettable, but if necessary."

"When I don't call home, they'll know." I hadn't even called Mira since we'd arrived. Hadn't been able to bring myself to. If I never spoke to her again, there were things I wasn't going to get to say, and that more than anything else was pissing me off.

"It is a sad truth of this world, Mr. Dawson, that Americans go missing in Europe all the time. I hardly think that your family and friends will be surprised." He offered me a small smile, and I wanted to punch it down his throat. "At the very least, they should be safer for your absence."

"I'm not giving you these souls." Even if I knew how, I wasn't about to give that smug bastard control of the two hundred and seventy-five lives living in my skin. Across my shoulder blades, I felt my tattoos grow warmer, my passengers supporting my decision whole-heartedly. "And they won't come to you willingly."

"That remains to be seen." He pushed himself up from his seat. "I will see that an evening meal is brought to you, while we arrange for more permanent accommodations for you."

"Hey, do me a favor." He raised a brow at me. "Hunch your shoulders over a little bit and go 'my preciousssss.'" No one laughed, but Mary Alice took in a quick breath behind me. "That's what this is really all about, isn't it? You don't give two shits about protecting these souls, or me. You just want the power. Do you know how much I'm lugging around? What I could do, if I wanted?" In response, my ghostly companions began winding their way down my arms, leaving the faint feeling of static electricity running across my skin.

Giordano frowned, truly frowned, for the first time. "This world is being plunged into chaos as we speak. Even before you unleashed the Adversary, the marks of it were everywhere. Natural disasters, wars, famine. All happening at once, all looking to push the human race to the end of their existence. The power that you hold could be the tipping point, the thing that saves us all, and you would squander it in a feeble attempt at your own freedom?"

"Dude, just watch me." I rolled my head on my neck, feeling the joints pop gently. The white tendrils of power crept out from under my sleeves, coiling over the backs of my hands, down to my very fingertips. The soul tattoos spun their way up my throat, up into my hair, stopping just short of washing over my eyes, like they understood that I would need my true vision for a fight. "They are more than willing to burn themselves up for me. Just ask them. And then what will you do?"

"You can't do this." He shifted his stance to the balls of his feet, and I felt Sveta and Cam go still on either side of me. If the Cardinal thought I wouldn't hit a holy man, he was sadly mistaken.

"I can. And I will." I desperately didn't want to. All these months, I'd gone out of my way to avoid putting myself in a position where I'd have to make this choice. But if the Cardinal was going to force the issue, I wasn't about to just go to my cell with my head bowed like a good little champion. "I will walk out of here, right over the top of you and all your little minions." I jabbed my finger at him for emphasis, and that's when things went all pear-shaped.

The Cardinal's eyes flicked to my wrist, where my sleeve had ridden up just slightly, revealing the stark black mark of my deal with Henry. His eyes went wide, and then they went blood red, and he bared his teeth in a snarl. "What have you done?!"

Before anyone could move, he had me by the throat, and I was slammed against the empty bookcases hard enough to drive the air from my lungs. My boots kicked at the air a good foot off the ground, and all I could do was stare down into the churchman's face, now drawn up in a horrible mockery of his usual features. Something rippled just beneath the skin, a foreign presence making itself known along the lines of his skull. His fingers dug into my throat, cutting off all air, and I knew I had about seven seconds before darkness would claim me.

"What have you *done*?!" His voice was not his anymore, at least not his alone. Erupting beneath the range of human vocalization was the thick, otherworldly oil taint of demon speech, and the red glow of demon eyes burned like old blood, forced through actual human eye tissue.

Two things happened at once. Cameron grabbed the Cardinal from behind at the same moment that I slapped both my palms against his face and began to squeeze. An explosion of light blinded me, all the more stunning for its absolute silence. The older man screamed with his demon-infected voice, and I was suddenly able to breathe, my boots hitting the floor with a thump.

When my eyes cleared, Cam was sprawled on his back at my feet, and Giordano was huddling in the farthest corner of the room, my handprints clearly visible as blistered, burned flesh on his cheeks. Sveta had her shoulders braced against the door, and the guards outside were slamming themselves against it with no thought for their own well-being. Mary Alice hurriedly helped Cameron regain his footing, and Ivan stood his ground between us and the newly revealed enemy.

"I had always suspected you to being corrupted, Salvatore." Ivan's gravelly voice was grim. "I did not expect this."

The black-robed man hissed, doing a pretty damn good Gollum impression after all. "You will all die for this. They will never find the pieces." Across the back of his hands, darkness appeared, vines and tendrils of black creeping their way out of his sleeves. At his collar, too, the network of ebony lace began to work its way up his neck, recoiling when it touched the burns on his face.

It wasn't hard to recognize that here was my

true opposite. Me, with my tattoos of white and my souls, and him with the darkness of blight etched on his skin. There was a demon in there, riding shotgun with the head of the greatest organization of demon hunters in human history.

"How could we not know," Mary Alice whispered. "The church, the holy objects…how?"

"Because it's inside him. Protected, until it shows itself. Just like he said." I flexed my fingers, feeling the tingle of power just under my skin. "It can't handle the touch of the souls, but so long as it stays down, the Cardinal still can." I smirked. "Looks like Coma Guy's demon didn't get very far, when you drove it out of him."

"Dawson," Sveta growled, and something heavy slammed against the door, shoving her boots two inches across the ornate rug. Cameron and Mary Alice hurriedly went to add their weight to hers, slamming the door shut again.

Our situation had changed drastically in the last few seconds. Giordano alone, he could have been reasoned with, appealed to. But the Cardinal wasn't calling the shots anymore, and a demon worked under entirely different motivations and rules. It probably said something about me that I suddenly liked our chances a lot more.

The rules that governed demonkind had become fluid in the last few years, dangerously so. Where once I would have bet my life (and had, come to think of it) on the fact that they couldn't harm a human being without permission, I'd been proven wrong. I'd seen them yank souls out of living creatures, leaving worse than a shell behind.

The rebellious faction was no longer content with taking what they'd been allotted. They wanted the world now, and the human race was just collateral damage. But there was one thing I'd never seen fail, the one thing that no demon could resist.

"Okay, tall dark and crispy. Let's make a deal."

"Jesse!" That from Cameron, but I ignored him.

The demon-cardinal focused his blood-red eyes on me, and sneered. "I see the mark, champion. You have already bargained away what I want."

"I haven't. That mark has nothing to do with the souls I'm carrying. Do you think they'd still be defending me, if I'd sold them for a pack of gum and two tickets to the ball game?" As if to prove my point, the white tattoos flared brighter, forcing the possessed man to drop his gaze. "You know I'm telling the truth."

Conflicting urges played across the older man's face, the demon's form rippling just beneath the skin in wholly nauseating ways. It was clear that the two weren't in agreement on what to do with me at all.

The pounding on the door ceased, and a voice called from the other side, muffled but audible. "At the count of five, we will fire on this door!"

"Better move quick, Crispy. Your boys are about to bust in here and mow us all down. And no one knows where these souls are going if I die." Giordano's eyes flared a muted scarlet, and the voices outside began their count. I tapped my non-existent watch. "Tick tock."

Finally, the black robed figure stood up straighter, and inclined his head just slightly. "I…accept."

"Call off your goons. Then we'll sit and negotiate how to kill each other like civilized fellows." Outside the door, they'd reached "three."

"Withdraw your power." It was costing him, I realized. Not the Cardinal, but the demon inside. It was costing him to face down the presence of two hundred and seventy-five souls.

Tone it down, guys. I was never sure if they heard my thoughts, or just happened to decide to obey at coincidental times, but the tattoos slowly receded back under my clothing. Unseen by anyone else, I felt them retreat to their customary places on my back.

The man in the hallway shouted "One!", and my three companions made dives to clear the frame. The massive oak door slammed open, cracking one of the bookshelves as it rebounded, and a five man tac-team burst into the room, small automatic weapons immediately coming to bear on those of us who were *not* wearing a long black dress.

"Halt!" At the Cardinal's command, all five men froze in place, but their guns never wavered. Let me tell you, the barrel end of a gun looks absolutely immense when it's pointed at your face. "Stand down, brothers. There has been a misunderstanding."

Sometime in the split second that my attention had been on the gunmen kicking in the door, Giordano's demon had managed to retreat from the surface. He looked and sounded just like an ordinary person, no trace of red to his eyes or oil in his voice. Perhaps feeling my gaze on him again, he straightened his garments with a sharp tug. "Brother Lorenzo, if you could see that an evening meal is brought up, I think I will be spending some time with our guests, talking. And chairs, for all of us."

The men holstered their weapons like they hadn't just been about to blow all our brains out, and the man in front nodded. I assumed that meant it was Lorenzo under the mask, but I couldn't have sworn to it. They all kinda looked the same, dressed up like dark Storm Troopers.

"Have them bring my gear." The Cardinal raised a brow at my demand. "Unharmed and untouched. And a pair of sharp scissors." After a moment, the old man jerked his chin toward his henchmen, and they departed, presumably to do what he'd said. The door no longer latched, but it was heavy enough to stay closed when we swung it to. "Don't worry, I'll work it into the deal. Don't want you giving away anything for free."

"I appreciate your integrity."

"There are just so many things wrong with that sentence."

Ivan tugged at my elbow, and I leaned closer to him, never taking my eyes off the blond man in the corner. "I should be the one to do this." Understand that Ivan whispering is still like a small avalanche, so of course everyone heard.

"*Ni!*" That was the only word I vaguely

understood as Sveta went off on a Ukrainian tirade. Whatever she was saying, she was really letting the old man have it. For Ivan's part, he just stood with a faint smile curling one corner of his mouth.

When she finished, or at least stopped to take a breath, I nodded my agreement. "What she said." Ivan's white brows drew together like he was going to argue, and I gripped his shoulder. "I'm the only one who can do this. I'm the only one who has what he wants. We all know this."

The white-haired man's jaw clenched, but he nodded and took a step back. Turning to face the demon-ridden cardinal again, I stood up straight, falling into an attention pose that I could hold for hours if need be.

"I am Jesse James Dawson. I will wager my soul, and the two hundred and seventy-five others that I currently carry with me."

16

Constructing a contract with a demon is (or should be, anyway) a long, labor intensive process. When you're dealing with an especially intelligent demon, it gets even worse. On top of that, add in the fact that Giordano himself had his own intelligence, his own wishes and desires, and the process got downright messy. The conversation itself made my head swim at times, as my opponent seemed to flip back and forth between his demonic passenger, and his own voice. It was hard to know which one I was talking to at any given time. My first term was that the contract bound both of them, not just one or the other, and he (they?) agreed to it without haggling.

We agreed to fight that night, after full dark when the sunlight couldn't aid me and the square would be emptied of onlookers and collateral damage. He allowed me the use of my sword, and when it came time for him to choose his own weapon, his lackeys produced a blade of his own. I was allowed to inspect it, finding it to be a very fine broadsword, and I tried not to show how shaken his choice left me. I'd hoped to be fighting the demon, not the man. A demon, in its true form, has no need of a sword. A demon doesn't bleed, not really. It doesn't die, even. It just gets banished back to the other side until it can gather the strength to cross over again. A man I could stab, maim, kill. He would bleed, and scream, and die. Despite our circumstances, it troubled me.

He agreed to let me keep the spells that currently wound around my body like invisible armor, the protections laid over my sword and chain mail. Mira's spells, most of them. Some of them Cameron's, some of them Estéban's. In return, he'd be free to use his own powers, whatever they were. Superior strength, the Cardinal had said, when describing Coma Guy's abilities. Speed. The ability to ignore severe injury. And then where was that whole "crossing the supernatural veil" trick that demons were so fond of.

Ivan caught my eye, and I knew he was thinking the same thing. It was entirely possible I'd have to defeat him twice. I could kill the man's physical body, and the demon could still rise up from the corpse to fight me again. He could build another body out of blight, as big and as stronger as his own power would allow. I was willing to bet that it wasn't some weakling Scuttle in there.

I could have quibbled over it, but ultimately let it pass. Sometimes, the best way to avoid a trap is to know where it is in the first place.

"No matter how this ends, they all go free." I knew what he'd say in response to that. I knew the loophole he would leave himself. I had to hope that my friends were skilled enough to fight their way to freedom after my death. I didn't for a moment believe the Cardinal would let them leave Vatican City alive.

"Agreed, so long as there is no retribution against the men of the Order after this day."

I raised a brow at the Cardinal. Altruism wasn't something I expected from a demon. "You actually care what happens to them?"

"They have been loyal and true. Their safety has long been one of the terms of my…arrangement." That from Giordano himself, no trace of the demon's foulness in his tone. "None of this is their fault."

"Do they know? About you?"

"They know…something. No one knows the entire truth, and so they cannot be held responsible for their actions."

It would have been easier to hate them, if they'd been totally complicit. Dammit. "So long as they raise no hand to us, we will do the same in return." Behind me, Sveta hissed, but I knew she'd obey. Violating the terms of a demon contract could have all sorts of unintended – usually disastrous – consequences.

With that term settled, another black slash burned itself into my left forearm. The marks had started at the knuckles and now coiled up toward my elbow. Much longer, and I'd have black coils and spirals all the way up my biceps. The older tattoo, Henry's tiny little mark, existed in a small circle of open flesh on my wrist, untouched by the darker, deeper sigils. I felt bad for Henry. If I died here, there would be no one to get him his treat for a job well done.

Oddly, the older man had the same black marks slowly creeping their way up his arm as well. I'd never seen that happen to a demon I'd challenged before, so I had to conclude that it was an effect of the human body it inhabited. The demon's eyes would look out of his host's from time to time, flashing brighter when the pain would hit, but for the most part, it stayed silently tucked away inside the human body it inhabited.

They fed us dinner, and I managed to resist making any "Last Supper" jokes. Even the Cardinal ate, though none of us felt like speaking beyond what was necessary for the upcoming duel. Our belongings, all of them, were delivered from the apartment we'd occupied, and a quick examination showed that everything was accounted for and unmolested. Sveta immediately started producing weapons from her luggage and strapping them on without even bothering to hide them. No one said a word or moved to stop her.

It was nearing midnight already when we finally decided that we'd covered everything we could humanly (or inhumanly) think of. The demon-possessed man rose from his seat, giving us all a small, courtly bow. "I will give you an hour to prepare. Then my men will bring you to the square. They will leave you in peace until that time."

Unspoken was the warning that should any of us attempt to escape, we'd be violating the terms of the contract and the fight would be over before it started. My soul, and all those that I carried, would be forfeit.

The door closed behind him, leaving the five of us in awkward silence. They all looked at me, all of them pretending that there was no fear behind their eyes.

"Can I banish the demon without hurting the host?" It was the only thing I truly needed to know.

Sveta and Ivan exchanged glances, then the

woman shook her head slowly at me. "You cannot force a demon out of a host that it has taken with permission."

"And if I kill him, the demon can still piece together a body and manifest here. Yes?"

"Most likely, yes."

"And then we go again." Two fights. I'd never managed to end even one fight in a condition where I was able to immediately fight again. Even if I won the first one, I'd lose the second in a heartbeat.

And of course, winning meant killing Giordano himself. I wasn't murdering a human, I kept telling myself. He'd be trying to kill me, and I was allowed to defend myself. But still, he'd be dead at my hand, if I was able, and then I'd have to fight the thing inside him, with zero idea of what it looked like, or what its abilities were.

"Jesse, you can't hesitate on this one." Cameron clutched at my sleeve. "If you lose, Reina will destroy the earth."

"No pressure there, Cam, thanks. But no, I don't think so." I'd done a lot of thinking, during our negotiations. Negotiating with demons always threw the strategic portion, the chess-playing portion, of my brain into high gear, and I thought I could see this move fairly clearly. "The Cardinal called her 'The Adversary.' Her minions don't name her like that. They call her master, but they don't say any name she might respond to, because they don't want to risk her attention falling on them, I think. I don't think he belongs to her."

"Then what is he doing?"

Sveta snorted. "He is covering his ass."

I pointed at her. "Exactly. I don't know who this demon is, but I don't think he's picked a side yet. He's trying to establish a power base so he doesn't get plowed over in whatever is coming. Or, at the very least, gain a big bargaining chip."

"This is not to be changing the fact that we do not wish him to be possessing these souls." Ivan gave me a stern look.

I sighed. "Look, I'll fight with all I have. You all know that. But…I'm not optimistic about this one." That was unusual for me. I normally went into a fight believing that I'd triumph, somehow. This time… I reached for that confidence, and I found it sorely lacking. *The way of the samurai is death.* Something was coming. Something not good, or bad, but big. Bigger than my brain could encompass, at the moment.

It was also possible that I was starting to lose my mind.

"God is to be having a purpose for you still, Dawson. He will not desert you now." The old man's voice was steady, and I wondered what it would be like to have that much certainty in the bank. I also wondered just how far I could get, riding on Ivan's faith alone.

"So…what are the scissors for?" Cameron picked them up from where they'd been placed on the desk, looking them over like I'd somehow managed to smuggle a secret weapon in under their very noses.

"To cut things," I informed him, taking them away from him before he hurt himself. "Most specifically, my hair." I offered the sharp implement to Sveta, handle first. "If you please."

My hair was nearly past my shoulder blades now. Even braided, it was still long enough to be used against me, and I'd been down that route once. Then, it had resulted in a wrenched neck and not much else. I'd been lucky. Now, I was pretty sure my luck had been all used up, and I wasn't about to take any chances that I didn't have to.

Sveta looked at the scissors like I'd just tried to hand her a ticking grenade, and blinked at me in total confusion. I had a small bit of satisfaction knowing that, after all this time, I'd finally flummoxed the unflappable champion. "I…don't…"

"Here. I used to cut my brothers' hair." Mary Alice took them from me, nudging me toward a chair so that she could begin the process.

"It doesn't have to be pretty. Just hack it off. And make sure you don't leave any of it lying around, after. I don't want them to have my hair." Magic could be done with leftover body parts, blood, things like that. Even if I intended to be dead, I didn't want my enemies to have that. The last thing I needed was for something to show up at my door, wearing my face and getting close to my family.

"Hush. Let me work." The little nun trimmed my long locks away with quiet efficiency, her gentle hands tipping my head to the side from time to time, making sure that she got the sides even and everything. Cameron and the Ukrainians watched in stoic silence, the only sound being the soft snip-snip of the scissors. Long coils of blond hair fell into my lap, and I rolled them between my fingers. Mira had never seen me with short hair. By the time we'd met in college, I was a card-carrying member of the hippy hair club. I was a little sad that she wouldn't get to see me like this. I wondered what she'd think.

"After." My voice bounced around the bare room, and Mary Alice swatted my shoulder for making her jump. "After, you have to see that Mira and the kids are protected."

"Jesse," Cam started, and I silenced him with a glare.

"Shut up, and let me talk." They'd given us back our phones. I could have called Mira, one last time. Said things to her that needed saying. I didn't. The four people around me would bear witness to my last will and testament, and I knew that they'd all see it carried out without fail. "I have a life insurance policy. Should be enough to pay off the house for her, with some left over."

Mira was strong. In fact, she was the strongest woman I'd ever met. She'd be all right without me. And she wouldn't be alone. My family was still there. My mom and dad adored her, and my brother Cole would always drop everything if she needed help. And my best friends, Will and Marty... Well, sure, Marty wasn't exactly speaking to me anymore, with good reason, but he'd never let Mira down. I was certain of that.

The kids, though. Annabelle would remember me. Billy would not. I wouldn't get to see them grow up, go to prom, learn to drive, get married, have their own kids. I'd never know if my daughter would play soccer or join cheerleading. I'd have no idea whether or not Billy would prefer science or art. I'd never get to explain to them how sorry I was for leaving them.

"Make sure my weapons and armor go to Estéban. Don't let him get any stupid ideas about avenging me. He has issues." That's how I'd met my young protégé, the half-trained heir to his champion bloodline pursuing the demon that killed his brother across international borders. He'd grown up since then, settled, but I still wanted one of them to tell him "no." He'd need to hear it.

"Take my paintball gear to Viljo. He'll know what to do with it." I was fond of the little computer geek. I wasn't sure if we were friends, per se, but we were comrades, which was the next best thing.

I fell silent, realizing that I didn't really have anything else that needed to be passed on. My normal things, clothes and the like, Mira would handle. My truck, she could sell, though honestly she'd probably have to pay someone to haul it off instead. I knew that Ivan and Cam would come up with some kind of cover story, something to tell the people who were better off not knowing about demons and wars in Hell. Terrorist attack, maybe. Choking on bad gelato. Hopefully nothing too humiliating.

"I'm done," Mary Alice said, brushing the last wisps of hair off my shoulders into her hands.

I stood, running my hands over my close-cropped hair, and felt a bit naked. I hadn't had hair that short since my mother was dictating my appearance at around age ten. Mary Alice had trimmed the sides and back as short as she could without electric clippers, and left the top a bit longer. It felt like it was standing straight up, as if it was startled to suddenly be so short.

In a weird way, I mourned my long locks. It had been a part of who I was, my very identity, for most of my life. But there wasn't time to deal with that now. Rolling my head on my shoulders, I nodded at the others. "Help me with my gear."

First, I donned a clean shirt and jeans, because it just seemed like I should meet this battle looking my best. Or at least, as good as I get. The two women turned their backs while I dressed, like modesty even meant something at this stage of the game. When that was done, Sveta and Cameron set about getting me into my padding, followed by the chainmail armor that went over it. They worked in silence, with the ease of people who have buckled a man into medieval safety equipment before.

It wasn't fancy, my armor, but Marty had made it strong and durable. The mail shirt slipped over my head with a jingle, and it felt strange to not get my hair caught in it. The sleeves hung to my elbows, and from there, my forearms were protected with heavy leather bracers, the insides of which were etched with Mira's protective runes. The lower half of me was covered with more chain from the waist to the knees, and from there to the ankle I'd taken to wearing heavy leather greaves, too. My steel-toed combat boots would do for my feet, leaving me as protected and mobile as I was going to get.

A thought occurred to me, about halfway through, and I snorted a soft laugh.

Cameron looked up from where he was buckling my metal chausses around my thighs. "What?"

"I'm wearing a shirt that says 'In my defense, I was left unsupervised.' I definitely do not meet the Vatican dress code."

"No, no you do not." Cameron shook his head, finally breaking into a hard-won laugh.

Sveta handed me my sword, and I slid The Way out of its scabbard a few inches, feeling the bone hilt warm at my touch.

"To be gathering around." We all looked over at Ivan, who had been quietly observing up to this point, and he motioned for the others to assemble around me. "He is allowed his protections. Therefore, we will pray."

Without question, all of them knelt, their joined hands forming a circle. I stood in the middle and felt the air pressure change in my ears as their collective wills completed the invisible magic barrier. With his white head bowed, Ivan murmured softly in his native language, joined a heartbeat later by his daughter's voice. Cameron and Mary Alice chimed in a moment after that, in English, but I knew from experience that their words would be the same. They were working the magic – sorry, saying the prayer – as a group, with Ivan taking the lead. I'd watched Estéban's mother, Carlotta, do something very similar when we were in Mexico, but this was the first time I'd ever been the target. Frankly, standing there with four grown adults kneeling at my feet was a little awkward.

My passengers roused at the feeling of magic being worked, but they weren't agitated. Instead, they seemed to roll over and over, basking in the glow of my friends' prayers. I could feel layers of spells settling on my skin like spider webs. It tickled.

Sveta's power was easy to pick out, her blue-white touch tingling like tiny ice crystals. Cameron's spells – prayers – tasted faintly of cinnamon at the back of my tongue, and other warm, bright things, and were the color of burnished copper. The smell of wet granite and steel gray magic most definitely originated with Ivan, and it occurred to me that I'd never seen him cast anything before. I wished that it wasn't going to be one of the last things that I got to experience. There was a wisp of light blue, airy and indistinct, that almost scampered as it wove between the other threads. Mary Alice's magic was smaller than theirs, somehow, but possessed a keen, precise edge. Ivan was an anvil, falling from a great height, while Sveta was a keen sword flashing through darkness. Cam was dynamite, explosive and abrupt, and Mary Alice was the sniper, wasting no effort for maximum results.

Somehow, they made it work. Their combined powers spun around me, a vortex at a glacier's pace, and I knew on some instinctual level that I would be faster, stronger, harder to injure. My body was still human, of course, and made of easily breakable stuff, but for as long as it would hold up, I would be damn hard to kill.

There was a small sigh, somewhere just outside my range of hearing, as they completed the spell and Ivan tied off the end, letting it drift down atop my head like a butterfly landing. The four released their hands, and the circle broke.

Mary Alice listed over onto her side, breathing heavily, and Cameron rested a hand on her shoulder. He looked pale himself, but didn't seem to be suffering from the spell sickness too badly. Sveta's lips were pressed firmly together, a faint hint of blue around them, and her breath misted when she breathed out.

"You all right?" Of all of them, I needed her at her best when the shit hit the fan. She would be the one to get them all out, if anyone could.

Slowly, she blinked, then nodded, the movement exaggerated and comical. Ivan draped his black coat around her shoulders, wrapping her in its warmth, and she didn't protest. Hypothermia was one of the possible reactions to using magic. We just had to hope she could recover quickly.

Of all of them, Ivan seemed to be the least affected. He got to his feet with no trouble. "We are having twenty minutes more, if his words are to being true."

Twenty minutes. Twenty minutes left to ponder the decisions that had lead me to this point. I didn't regret any of them, by any means. If I had each one to do over, I'd take the same exact path. But, there were things in the future that I'd regret. I regretted not being able to protect the two hundred and seventy-five souls that had been bequeathed to me. I regretted not being able to see my kids grow up. At that moment, I really regretted the fact that I would never know the meaning of that stupid damn tunnel dream.

"Clear me some room. I'll warm up." They scooted to the back of the office, propping Sveta and Mary Alice up together for warmth and support, and I used what little open floor there was to begin stretching out.

I could lose myself in the katas, given the opportunity. My brain could stop whirling around, and my body could just move in the ways I'd taught it over the years. Step, thrust, pivot, step back, block, disengage. Again. The Way flowed in my hands, like always, feeling almost like a living thing in my grasp. Moving in the armor got easier as I reacclimated to it, until it too was just an extension of myself. Under normal circumstances, the katas would tire me out, and I would never have gone through so many just before a fight. But today, with the life force of the people around me bolstering me, lifting me up, I felt like I could have run a marathon in my armor.

When the knock came at the door, I was ready.

17

It was Minion Lorenzo who had come to fetch us, with five of his very bestest friends. Apparently, he didn't get the memo that we weren't allowed to punch our way out of there. They marched us down the hallway to an elevator, Ivan supporting Sveta and Cam nearly carrying Mary Alice. The elevator was uncomfortably cramped, there being eleven of us in there, and none of the menfolk were small types. I was probably the skinniest guy there, but my armor and padding gave me bulk I wouldn't otherwise have, so we were packed in like sardines.

The streets were eerily empty as we walked through them, our footsteps echoing against the buildings that loomed over us. A few lights glimmered in some of the windows along our path, providing us with enough illumination to see, but it was obvious that there was no one lingering behind those glowing squares. No one was here. No one would see.

St. Peter's Square seemed impossibly large when we reached it, devoid of all human life. The only figure standing on the cobblestones was Giordano himself, and for just a moment I wondered if this was going to be the tunnel dream, forever stepping out into the open to see the Cardinal standing across the way. But no, the cobblestones under my feet were not the hard-packed earth from my dream, and the sense of the people behind me was not the quiet, painful desperation that plagued my nights. The Cardinal's back was to the giant Egyptian obelisk that crowned the square, and that too was missing from my dream. It wasn't yet time for the tunnel.

Giordano had traded his robes for black fatigue pants and a steel breastplate, his sword already bared and hanging loosely from one hand. The armor was going to limit my kill shots, which was the whole point of armor. Crippling blows, then. Get him on the ground, and go for the neck. Under my calm, analytical analysis of the situation, my stomach rolled with faint nausea. I was really going to do this.

Minion Lorenzo gave me a small shove out into the open area, then herded my crew to one side, his cadre of merc-priests keeping them surrounded at all times. Mary Alice was largely being supported by Cameron, and Sveta was still huddled in her father's oversized coat. Ivan kept his arm around her shoulders, and when his eyes met mine, he nodded very slightly.

Okay then. Here we go. I drew The Way from its scabbard and left the case lying on the ground, hopefully far enough back that it wouldn't become a footwork hazard. I strode out to the central circle of paving stones, stopping a few yards away from my opponent.

The older man inclined his head. "Shall we begin?"

Before I could answer him, time came to a stuttering halt, and what little ambient sound there had been became glaring, crushing silence. The scent of sulfur hit me like a slap in the face, and Giordano's attention was suddenly no longer on me.

Raising his sword, he pointed it at something over my left shoulder.

"You!"

"Indeed." It was my voice, but there was no mistaking the demonic oiliness underneath it. Axel stepped into my view, his thumbs tucked nonchalantly into the belt loops of his jeans.

The Cardinal's demon flashed a dull red behind his human eyes. "You are not welcome here, Architect!"

"I didn't ask." The blond demon's eyes flared bright red, lighting up the square like a crimson strobe for just a moment. His power wasn't trapped inside a human body, and he was flaunting that fact.

The demon-cardinal sneered, and I saw the ghostly image of another face moving beneath Giordano's skin. "Here to protect your pet champion? You cannot interfere, or his souls will be forfeit."

"I have no intention of interfering." Axel shrugged his lanky shoulders, never once looking in my direction. "I am well aware of the rules. I wrote them. I am merely here as an observer, insuring that the rules, *all* of the rules, are obeyed in this contest. Violating the terms would be…unwise." He glanced over at the tiny group of church knights surrounding my friends, and gave them a downright evil grin, the scarlet strobe issuing from his eyes again. "Very unwise indeed." There was an uncomfortable shuffle in that area of the square, and I wondered how far Axel could push the trigger-happy priests before one of them took a shot at him.

"If you are merely here to observe, then clear the field."

The punk-haired demon held up his hands, nodding his acquiescence. "Of course." He backed away, to the outer edge of the square, his glowing eyes giving a constant indication of his location. He didn't want the merc-priests to forget.

In a very strange way, I was glad to see him. Axel was nothing if not a stickler for the rules. He'd protect Ivan and the others if this all went south, simply because it was something that had been agreed to. A little of the tension went out of my shoulders, knowing that my own personal demon was watching over this little debacle.

I raised The Way in front of my face, a salute to the Cardinal. "I am Jesse James Dawson. Face me."

It took a moment for the older man to reassert his control over his own body, but he finally dragged his eyes away from Axel and back to me. "I am Cardinal Salvatore Giordano, of the Ordo Sancti Silvii." He sketched a similar salute with his own weapons. "Begin."

First, at no point in human history did katanas clash with broadswords on the battlefield. They are completely different weapons, for both being swords, requiring totally different fighting styles.

Second, my usual strategy when fighting a demon was a war of attrition. Slice a bit there, snip a chunk here, each tiny bit eating away at the creature's power. A demon bout could last upwards of an hour, if I was quick enough to stay out of its clutches.

This fight wasn't going to be like that. Sure, there was a demon walking around in that man suit, but the human mind was still there, and before he had been a demon-possessed cardinal, Giordano had been a champion.

I had a split second to admire his smooth footwork as he closed the distance between us, and then my attention had to be all for the fight. He was good. He was really good.

The broadsword was light and lithe for something of its ilk, and the Cardinal wielded it equally well with either hand. My plan had been to dart in and out, ducking under his reach to slice at his exposed legs, but I never got the chance. I was on my heels in a second, angling my sword to let his blows slide past, scared that a true strike from the heavier blade might shatter mine.

The cobblestones were just uneven enough to make me worry for my own footing as he backed me across the square, the sounds of metal on metal ringing out like a pealing bell. In the nick of time, I recognized a feint for what it was, and spun the opposite way instead of standing where the broadsword would have hacked into my right shoulder.

It gave me distance and a chance to strike back. I didn't aim for the body, encased in its protective steel shell, but instead snapped a strike at his hands. If I could get him to drop his weapon, I could end this quickly.

Of course, ending it meant killing him. I

wasn't under any illusions that I could get Giordano to surrender. Even if he would, his passenger would not.

And *damn* he was good. Giordano retreated, retracing the ground I'd just covered, but he did it in such a controlled manner that it looked like I was the flailing idiot chasing after him. Twice, my strikes missed by a hair, and the third time he caught my blade on his guard, attempting to wrench it out of my grasp with a deft flick of his wrist. I disengaged, spun left, and aimed a backhanded swipe across his ribcage. The sword clanged against his breastplate, but he grunted from the force and took a heartbeat longer to follow me.

We danced back and forth like that for what seemed like forever. Neither of us could land a decisive blow, but we were each too close for the other to relax. The tip of his sword caught my thigh in passing, ripping links out of the mail but leaving the padding beneath miraculously intact. I got one good shot across his lower back, where his armor gaped, but I came away with nothing more than a rent in his own gambeson. Both our chests were heaving, and despite the strengthening spells on me, my arms burned with my efforts. A katana wasn't meant for a protracted bludgeoning type of fighting. Eventually, he was going to beat through my defenses with sheer brute force.

Dimly, I became aware that people were shouting. I heard Cameron's voice, calling encouragement, maybe, and Ivan's gravelly bark with orders for me to focus, to center. They were slow words, stretched out in a bizarre fashion like a malfunctioning film reel, and only then did I realize how fast the Cardinal and I were moving. If the demon gave him super-speed, the spells that Ivan and crew had cast on me more than allowed me to keep up. The endless minutes we'd been fighting must have been seconds, the pair of us whirling through our maneuvers at speeds a human body was never meant to move, and I became increasingly certain that the only reason our bodies hadn't ripped themselves apart was the extra strength we had also gained from our benefactors.

Even with the words comically elongated in the hyper-fast world I briefly existed in, my muscles responded instantly to Ivan's command, and I brought The Way back to center just in time to catch the next overhand strike at my head, shoving it off and away in a move that left me all up in Giordano's personal space.

The look in his eyes when I head-butted him was priceless. Blood burst all over the both of us from his shattered nose, and before I could blink the goo out of my eyes, he clubbed me with his free hand hard enough to send me to my knees. Instinctively, I rolled, feeling the breeze as his kick just missed my stomach. He followed me, a snarl on his face as his boots tried to stomp down on any part of me that couldn't get out of the way. All I could do was keep scrambling, never getting enough space to find my feet again.

Finally, I picked my spot, planted my free hand and lashed out with my heavy boot, catching him in the side of the knee. The crack as it folded sideways was audible, but instead of buckling, falling, he snared my ankle with one hand, bringing his sword down in a vicious overhand. I had no leverage to jerk away, so I lunged forward instead, forcing him to drop my foot or lose his balance. I came up inside his guard, catching him in the gut with my shoulder, and we both went down in a tangle of limbs and blades.

A fist found my kidney, painful even through chain and padding, and my elbow found his already crushed nose, eliciting a hiss of pain, the first sound I'd heard him make since we started. A hand grabbed at my face, and I bit down out of reflex, tasting blood right before something caught me in the left temple and lights exploded behind my eyes. Before I could get clear, get myself some recovery space, he clouted me again with the heavy steel pommel of his sword, tumbling me across the stones as my passengers screamed alarms inside my pounding skull.

The Way was still in my hand, I thought with a sense of groggy triumph, at almost the same moment that a booted foot came down on my wrist. I felt the small bones snap and I screamed, my fingers instantly going numb. The bone hilt of my katana fell from my grasp, and my digits refused to obey my commands to pick it up again.

It happened in a heartbeat, a literal split second. I could feel the onrushing air as the broadsword came down at my unprotected neck. The souls burst forth, blazing hot with every intention of incinerating the Cardinal though it would cost them their very existence. Heat enveloped me, and then something cool and black moved over me, inserting itself between me and my certain death.

The broadsword struck home. I heard the meaty thunk as the heavy blade lodged in something solid, but oh so vulnerable.

Turning my head, I found Ivan standing over me, as tall and straight as he ever was despite the sword that had cleaved through one shoulder and halfway into his chest.

There was an instant of perfect stillness, the very rotation of the Earth shocked into immobility. The Cardinal stared at his unintended victim, mouth just beginning to gape open in surprise. Ivan's knees folded ever so slightly, the slow, inexorable fall of a mighty redwood. My left hand found the hilt of my sword, snatching it from the ground in the same motion that brought me to my feet, screaming things that had no words. Bright metal flashed, the spells twined around the metal burning themselves out in that moment of contact. Warmth sprayed over my face, soaking me in gore.

The Cardinal's head bounced twice as it hit the ground, the face still staring up at the sky with shock written on the dead features.

Time stuttered back into motion.

They were screaming. They were all screaming. People, souls, the choirs of heaven for all I knew. I caught Ivan as he pitched forward, but it was all dead weight. Somehow, I became aware of someone mumbling "nononononono" over and over again, and later I would realize it was me.

The piercing blue eyes were already clouding, and the old man's lips were free of blood, which meant that his breathing had stopped almost instantly. His neat white shirt was a sea of red, and no amount of pressure was going to stop the gushing from the grotesque wound, though I tried, covering myself in sticky blood. There would be no tender goodbyes, no last words of wisdom. Ivan was gone.

"Foooool...." Behind me, the headless body shuddered, and I thought for one horrific second that it was going to rise again, shambling at me like the zombies of my earliest nightmares. Instead, a black geyser erupted from the corpse, raining bits of Giordano down on us. Shards of the burst armor zinged past my face, one of them drawing a line of fire across my cheek. The seething ball of darkness heaved and pulsed, a massive thing no longer confined by its meat prison, gradually taking form. "His sacrifice means nothing. I will devour you whole!"

The Cardinal's demon loomed over me, a tidal wave at its peak before it crashed down and crushed all beneath it. I saw wings unfolding, bat-like things that spanned twice my height. Horns curled from within the seething mass of sentient darkness, and it just kept growing larger, forming its body from blight and sheer will. My sword was on the ground near my feet, but all I could do was hold Ivan's limp body in my arms and watch.

NO.

The word rang out with such force that the half-formed demon was flung back, scrabbling at the cobblestones with its shadowy talons, and every window facing the square shattered in a cacophony of broken glass. The demon's red eyes flashed out of the formless cloud as it shrieked, "You cannot! You cannot interfere!"

YOU HAVE VIOLATED THE TERMS. The voice came from everywhere and nowhere at once, and a few seconds later, I realized it sounded a little like me.

"Not I!" The tolling voice was painful to the demon, and it writhed in agony as it lodged its protests. "He! He violated! A fighter on the field who was not allowed!"

My brain knew that it was Axel who stepped into my bloodstained field of vision, but my eyes saw only golden light, the kind that could burn out your retinas and make you happy for the pain.

THE CHAMPION DID NOT FIGHT. HE WAS UNARMED. YOU STRUCK DOWN A LIFE THAT WAS NOT YOURS TO TAKE.

I'd seen a fallen angel before. You could see what she'd once been, the glory of her being now tarnished and tethered indelibly to the earth by the evil she'd become.

The angel before me was not fallen.

I'd been forced to turn my gaze away from an angel's true form the first time I'd seen one, my grip on sanity tenuous at best. My mind could conjure a memory of white-gold light, so bright it rang in my ears like church bells, and then it would shut down, protecting me from myself. Now, I couldn't have looked away if my life depended on it, and I could all but feel the contents of my skull coming to a boil.

YOU ARE FORFEIT. The angel that was Axel

raised one shining hand and whispered a word in a language I never wanted to understand, but felt like a punch that went right through my guts and maybe into the bedrock far beneath me.

The cloud of unformed demon screamed in a tone above the human range of hearing, folding and warping in on itself. What could have been wing spars snapped into fragments, and the gigantic horns flaked away like ash until the proto-demon was disintegrating faster than it could bring itself together. As if impossibly massive hands were wadding it up into a ball, it compressed tighter and tighter until it winked out of existence. The silence that followed was deafening.

The angel turned its gaze toward me without moving at all. "Close your eyes, Jesse." A normal voice. Axel's voice. My voice.

"Can't," I managed to choke out. It was all going fuzzy between my ears, liquefying into soup and I still couldn't tear my eyes away. I couldn't tell if my tears were burning hot streaks down my face, or if my eyes were pouring blood.

"You must, or you will die. Close your eyes. We will still be here when you open them again."

It took every ounce of strength in my body to slowly lower my eyelids, one excruciating millimeter at a time. Once closed, I could still see the angel, burned on the back of my corneas maybe, but it didn't make my brain slosh around inside my skull anymore. I only knew that I'd keeled over when my forehead met cobblestones with a resounding clunk.

Approximately four hundred and twelve years later, gentle hands cradled my skull – which was doing its best gong impression – and slowly lifted my head off the cobblestones.

"Get him on his feet."

Fuck you, Axel, I thought, but my mouth couldn't seem to get its act together enough to say it out loud.

It must have been Cameron who was holding me, because the voice came from right above me. "He's injured. He needs a hospital."

"If you do not get him on his feet, we will have two for the morgue instead of one." That elicited a hiss from nearby, and a scrape of metal as someone picked up one of the fallen swords. "You are welcome to try if you wish, Svetlana, but it will not change what has happened here tonight."

Christ, these idiots were going to get themselves killed if I didn't pull myself together. What I tried to say was, "I'm up." What came out was something like, "mmfffp," but it was enough to get their attention.

"Jesse? Jesse, can you hear me?" Cam had to have been leaning right down in my face, and I swatted at him with what little energy I had. Unfortunately, I'd forgotten my broken wrist, and the agony sent bright streamers through my head. My eyes snapped open, boggling at the pain, and I was belatedly relieved to see that Axel was just Axel again, his lean face frowning with concern over the heads of my friends.

Someone had taken Ivan's voluminous coat from Sveta, and laid it respectfully over his body.

As Cam helped me into a sitting position, I was grateful that I wouldn't have to look at Ivan again like that. I couldn't process that, not yet. Of course, Giordano's exploded corpse was also still nearby, his head tucked at his side with his mouth open like he was singing to the stars, and nausea rolled in my gut. I couldn't process that yet, either.

"Get up, Jesse. We are not finished."

"Mmrfglgle." Of course, everybody knew that what I meant was, "Why? The bad guy is dead."

"The entire world knows where I am now, and they will be coming. I have altered things to make it difficult for them to simply appear here, but it will not last, and it will not stop them from manifesting in the city and simply walking in. Get *up*!" Axel's eyes flashed crimson, and I shook a finger at him chidingly. That wasn't right, an angel walking around being all demon-y.

Once Cam figured out that I was going to obey, he helped me to my feet, supporting more of my weight than I was at the moment. I gave him a thumbs-up with my uninjured hand.

"Come. Quickly." Axel started toward the entrance to the chapel, walking backwards to make certain we were following.

Cameron and I hesitated until Mary Alice said, "Go. We'll stay with him." With Ivan, she meant, and I glanced that way to see Sveta kneeling at her father's side, face blank and eyes distant. "I will pray for him."

"Go." I nudged Cam, and congratulated myself on managing an actual word. Slowly, we tottered after the lanky blond demon-angel-whatever-he-was. It seemed like it took forever for us to cross St. Peter's Square, and it never occurred to me to wonder where we were going. Stepping through the doorway to Sistine Chapel, I realized too late that blood was dripping off my fingertips – *not my blood, his blood, Ivan's blood* – and felt a little bad that I was marring the holy site.

Once through the door, my passengers buzzed and fizzed under my skin, excited to once again be near the ceiling. Axel led the way to the center of the structure, pointing to a place on the floor for Cameron to stop.

"We must deliver the souls, before the Adversary arrives to take them."

I snorted, feeling just slightly drunk. Y'know, if being drunk felt like being run over by a steamroller. "Can't. Dunno how."

"But you know, don't you?" Cameron fixed Axel with a somber look. "You've always known."

A ghost of a smile crossed the punk demon's lips. "I am the Architect."

I found the strength to jerk my head up, focusing on his smug face. "It's not in the paint." He shook his head no. "It's in the building itself. Something in the way it's constructed." He nodded. "You…built this place. Like, you actually built it."

"I designed it. Human artisans did the actual construction. But yes." All this time, and I thought his moniker was more metaphorical. The one who wrote the rules, the one who orchestrated the game. But all along, he'd been an architect in truth, building a wonder of the world that no one knew about.

"You're the one that has been seen here, escorting the souls into the ceiling."

"Not alone. Never alone." I opened my mouth to ask another question, and the angel-demon's eyes flashed red. His patience had obviously run out. "I owe you explanations for many things, but we do not have *time*." He pointed at Cameron. "You are necessary for this."

"Why me?"

The blond demon smirked. "Because you are a man of faith. Repeat the words I will say to you."

I couldn't tell you what they said. I'm guessing it was Latin, since Cam was prone to casting his spells using that dead language. Axel would intone a phrase, to have Cameron dutifully repeat it back, and I felt the tingles of magic settle around my shoulders. Instead of their usual alarm, my passengers rose to meet it, doing an oddly frenetic skip and hop around my skin. I watched the white tattoos appear and disappear at random over what skin I could still see, each one alighting for only an instant before it was gone again. As Cam and Axel's game of Simon Says continued, the lights on my skin became lights in front of my eyes, and then lights dancing all around my head, filling the air with tiny little will-o-wisps that twirled in increasingly complex patterns.

Cam's shoulders, which had been so sturdily propping me up, trembled with the effort of whatever he was casting, and it was my turn to take his weight on me, doing my best not to wobble and throw off his concentration. Higher and higher, the teeming multitude of fireflies rose, until they reached the painted artwork above us. They flashed then, and my mind heard it as a shout of joy, as the two hundred and seventy-five souls merged into the structure, safe at last with their brethren. The spell ended with a single word that ended on some kind of pure, crystalline chime.

Suddenly, every injury I'd ever had in my entire life hurt again, and my skin felt like it was too large, draping over a scrawny, weak frame. I was empty, alone, for the first time in months. I felt like a shell that would blow away in the first strong breeze.

Above us, the souls swirled and pulsated for a moment, growing ever dimmer in my sight until it was once again simply paint on the ceiling. I knew the souls were there, but I could no longer see them. My magic sense was gone with the souls that had granted it to me.

"Can I lie down and die now?"

Cameron managed a drained snort. "Seconded."

"I would prefer it if you did not." Axel didn't smile, not quite, but it felt like he wanted to. "You have more to attend to."

He was right. Coming out of the chapel, we looked across the square to see the distant forms of Mary Alice and Sveta kneeling near Ivan's body. For a moment, for just a second, I swore there was someone else there, someone with coffee-colored skin and dreadlocks decorated with bits and scraps of colorful yarn. That other figure knelt between the two women, a hand on each of their heads, but when my eyes forced me to blink, it was gone. *Felix?*

"Freaking angels, just showing up when the party's all over…" It would be right, though, Felix being here. Ivan had encountered the angel before, still disguised as an eccentric, homeless sage. He'd like it if Felix came to comfort his daughter.

"He's safe, you know." I glanced at Axel, and the demon-angel refused to meet my gaze. "Your Ivan. His soul was spoken for long ago, and he is at peace."

After a moment, I nodded. "I'll tell Sveta. I think she'll appreciate knowing that. Not sure she'll appreciate knowing that you got him killed in the first place." Hey, when did I start managing complex sentences again? Go me.

Axel's eyes flared, but just for a heartbeat. "I didn't."

"Sure you did. That's what your little speech was all about, before the fight. All that going on about the rules? You were letting Ivan know what he could do to save me. Not to mention that there was no way he could have crossed the square fast enough to get between me and his holy demon-ness, not at the speed we were moving."

He was silent for long moments before answering. "He acted of his own free will. He chose. Do not take that away from him."

Cameron's voice was steady, for all that I could feel the tremors shuddering through his body as we took turns holding each other upright. "We have to get out of here. We're gonna wind up in jail if we don't move."

That reminded me that we hadn't been alone when this nightmare started. "Hey, where' are the minions?"

"They ran," Cameron informed me. "The second the demon came up out of the body, they bolted."

"Do not worry about the remains. They will be disposed of before they can be seen."

"No." Axel raised a brow at me. "Not Ivan. She gets to bury him, you understand?"

He pursed his lips, but nodded. "You will find him at the hospital morgue, then. He passed in his sleep, peacefully, from the growths that invaded his body." Without another word, he disappeared into thin air, leaving behind only a whiff of sulfur. A scream of denial and rage issued from across the square, Sveta knowing only that her father's body had vanished from under her very hands.

"Get her," I told Cameron, releasing my hold on him and folding down to the ground as gracefully as I could manage. "Explain. Tell her he wasn't taken."

It was the best I could do. I watched Cameron stagger his way to the two women, nearly hitting the ground himself as Sveta lashed out in her grief and rage. Whatever he said, he got her to hear him, and I saw him enfold her in his arms, Mary Alice petting the other woman's hair like she was a small child. Svetlana's sobs rang against the cobblestones, against the empty buildings that surrounded us.

My whole body was pain, crowned by the

throbbing in my brain and the high pitched whine in my wrist. Maybe, if I closed my eyes for just a second, I would be able to get up again. The darkness drifted in from the corners of my eyes, and it took me a moment to realize it wasn't just the fragments of my contract tattoo flaking off and wafting away. The blackness was soft, soothing, and I let it wrap me up and cradle me in a place where nothing hurt anymore. I didn't know anything after that.

18

They excommunicated Cameron, which sounds like it would be something really painful, but is really just the Church saying "you can't play in our sandbox anymore." Most of the merc-priests scattered like cockroaches in the aftermath, leaving behind the bewildered and shaken remains of the Order of St. Silvius to pick up the pieces. Somewhere in all the chaos, the blood sorcerers all disappeared from their cells beneath Vatican City, including the comatose guy. The Church had to find someone to take the blame, and they chose Cam.

He wasn't nearly as upset as I'd expected him to be.

I didn't get a chance to talk to him about it until we were already at the airport, heading for two different gates as our paths took us in different directions, at least temporarily. "What will you do now?"

The ex-priest shrugged, shifting his backpack on his shoulder. "I think maybe I'll go home and have sex with my girlfriend."

"Dude. TMI."

He gave me a wicked grin, and another shrug. "I still have a job. I'm still a librarian, officially. I still have Bridget, if she'll keep me after I go home and tell her the absolute truth. She's going to kill you, by the way." Man, didn't I know it. "I think… I think this is a good thing. God and I…we're good. I don't need the Church to tell me that."

"Well listen, if you're still keen on the whole champion gig, I know a guy who's hiring." It was a crappy joke, but they were the only ones I had left. I had no idea what was going to happen with our own very loosely organized group of miscreants. Recruiting seemed to be the least of my issues.

Cam got on a plane for the States, with Sister Mary Alice to see him off. The plucky little nun was determined to stick it out in Rome, helping the Order rebuild itself.

"Regardless of who and what Cardinal Giordano was, the Order has served a noble purpose. It can again."

I shook her hand – with my left, since my right was encased in a sturdy cast – as we parted ways at the airport. "Well, keep me posted on who they choose to replace him."

"Will do." She eyed our hands for a moment, then threw her arms around my neck to give me a tight hug, nearly leaving her feet to do so. "Be careful, Jesse. God be with you."

"We'll see about that." Theoretically, my life had gotten a lot safer, now that my burden had been lifted. No extra souls hanging around meant that no one was going to come kicking my door in to get at them. I could be out. I could just never accept another champion contract, and walk my happy ass away like I'd promised Mira.

Except we all knew I wasn't going to. Ivan had entrusted the lives of his champions to me. He could have chosen any of us. Estéban's mother,

Carlotta, maybe, or Terrence. Someone who had been at this longer, or actually had some magical ability of their own. But he'd picked me, for reasons I still couldn't fathom. Regardless, I couldn't let the old man down.

Sveta and I boarded a flight for Ukraine, Ivan's body in the cargo hold of the big jetliner. She hadn't talked much since the fight, making quiet phone calls in her native language that I wasn't privy to. I was tempted to nudge her a bit on the plane, to try to get some conversation going, but she spent most of it staring out the window and seeing nothing beyond what was going on in her own mind. I let her. I hadn't lost a parent yet, and she was about to bury her second one. What could I possibly say?

We laid Ivan to rest in a cemetery that had graves older than my country of origin. Ornate statues and heavy granite monuments looked down on us as we stood next to the casket and listened to a priest speak words I couldn't understand.

The day was bright and sunny, for all that winter was right around the corner, and there were a handful of people there who came to clasp Sveta's hands and say all the things you say at funerals. Through it all, she was dry-eyed and silent. Only after the other guests departed and the caretaker began the rather undignified process of filling in the grave with a backhoe did I tug at her elbow, guiding her out of the way a few yards. We watched the heavy machine do its work for probably half an hour before she said a word.

"My mother is buried a few yards that way,"

she said, pointing. "I was eleven years old when she died, and I went to live with him. I do not think he understood what to do with a girl child, and so he taught me the only thing he knew."

I stood and quietly listened. It's what friends do.

"If I could have, I would have put them nearer to each other. My mother was the one who ended things, but she never stopped loving him, I think. She would tell me stories of him, of his bravery and determination. She would tell me 'Sveta, you be just like your father, and you will be a good person.'" A faint smirk crossed her face. "I am not certain this is what she intended."

I recalled a conversation Ivan and I had had on a cold California beach what seemed like an eternity ago. "He loved her." She wouldn't take her eyes off the heaps of dirt, cascading into the open hole in the ground. "He loved you, too."

"That was never in question."

I felt like I should be saying more. Offering some kind of deep philosophical insight into death, or maybe just giving her a hug. The hug would probably get my other wrist broken, and the best I could manage on short notice was, "This sucks."

A hint of a smile ghosted across her face, and was gone. "Yes. It does."

"What are you going to do now?" We hadn't talked yet, about after. Everything had been focused on getting through this moment, discussions of "after" had seemed pretty inconsequential up to this point.

"I will see that you return to Kansas City

safely.”

"And then?”

"I…have not decided yet.”

"You’re welcome to stay, you know. Even if I don’t really need a bodyguard anymore.”

That earned me a sidelong smirk. "You will always need a bodyguard. You are a hazard to yourself and others.”

"You’re not wrong.”

I slept through most of the flight from Ukraine to the States, a combination of pain killers and exhaustion finally catching up to me. We changed planes in Chicago, and Sveta surprised me by collecting her luggage there. "Surely you can get the rest of the way home without causing yourself major bodily harm.”

"Stranger things have happened.” I offered her a fist to bump, which she returned with a roll of her eyes. "You gonna be okay?”

"We will see. I will keep in touch with Grapevine, if you need me. Do not hesitate to call.”

"Will do.” I wouldn’t. Unless the hordes of Hell were snapping at my heels, I would let her have her time, to do her grieving her way. I watched her walk away, wending through the crowds like a shadow until she simply disappeared from my view, and I wondered if I’d ever actually see her again.

It was another few hours before my feet hit the ground in Kansas City, and then, *only* then, did I call my wife.

I hadn’t spoken to Mira since we’d left, nearly two weeks ago. I knew that Cameron had spoken to her, assuring her that I wasn't dead, so she wasn't waiting at home fretting. I also knew that there were things that I had to say, decisions that I had come to, that were going to change things. They were going to change *every*thing, actually.

She picked up on the second ring, and we both sat in silence and listened to each other breathe for a few seconds. "Jesse."

"Hey."

"Where are you?"

"I'm at the airport. Back in KC."

"Oh. You didn't let me know. I could have come to pick you up, or sent Estéban or…"

"I know." I found a spot of empty wall and slid down it, taking shelter behind my luggage and weapons crate. "I thought we should probably talk first."

When she spoke again, her tone was wary, sensing whatever it was that I was about to drop on her. "Okay."

"Ivan's gone. Cam told you, right?"

"He did."

"You know that he wanted me to take over for him. He wanted me to take care of everyone, keep the group running, keep everyone safe."

"I remember."

"I think…" I sighed, running a hand over my close-cropped hair and finding the sensation frustratingly unsatisfactory. "I think that we can't keep going on like we are, just running around and reacting to the bad shit that happens. This war that's coming, whatever it is, I think they have to get through us to make it happen. If we sit around and wait for them, they'll pick us off a few at a time and there will be nothing left."

"So what will you do?"

I'd thought about it a lot, since the square. Scraps of conversation from here and there, things Axel had let slip, things I'd heard from Felix. Things that I'd deduced on my own. I'd asked an angel once why God hadn't sent help. His answer was, "What makes you think he hasn't?"

"I think we're the help, Mira. I think, whatever this demon war is, we're supposed to be the thing that stops it. If this happens, we're all – the human race, I mean – we're all going to get trampled. These armies are going to bowl right over us and never even look down to see what they're stepping on. It's not a matter of helping someone win, we have to stop it before it happens."

I could hear her swallow through the phone. "And?"

"And I'm going to go pick a fight." Not soon. I had at least six weeks of broken arm to heal, and then there was the matter of gathering up as many fighters as I could muster on my own. Not just my own champions, but whoever I could find. Cam's friends in the Order, Carlotta's family if they'd come. A few others. But soon. Soon, I would call Reina up, and we would end this, one way or another. It was the only thing I could think to do.

Mira's voice was thick with a sob that she refused to let out. "I can't let you come home. You can't bring this to our door, Jesse. I can't… I can't risk this, anymore. I'm done."

"I know." She had to. For the sake of her, for the sake of our children, she had to. I'd known that, going in. There was only one way this conversation could have ended, which is why I hadn't called her to come pick me up in the first place.

That didn't change the fact that my heart was cracking into two jagged halves.

"I'll let you know when I've found a place to stay. I'll probably call Will."

"Okay. We should…we should at least get together for you to see the kids. Anna misses you a lot."

"I miss her." There was no burning sensation in my eyes. I was resolutely *not* blinking back tears. "I'll call you soon."

"Okay." There was an awkward pause where she tried to decide whether or not to say "I love you." Finally, she settled on "Be safe."

"You too."

I sat there for probably half an hour, ignoring the looks I got from the travelers who passed me on their way to wherever they were going. It had to be this way. I knew it. Ivan, long separated from the woman he loved and the mother of his child, had known it. It was just the way the world worked. Finally, I called my buddy Will, in the hopes that he'd let me crash on his couch.

It was weird, settling into a bachelor's apartment. I'd never had one myself, having moved straight out of college dorms into the first apartment Mira and I had shared. I guess it wasn't as bad as sitcoms would have you think. There were no weird stains on the carpets, no laundry scattered in inappropriate places. The fridge actually had food, not just beer. I couldn't detect any funky smells, and Will was more than happy to cook for two instead of one. If it wasn't for the fact that my bed was a lumpy sofa that was too short for my six-foot-one frame, and that nothing in the place smelled like sage and strawberries, I could almost forget that I wasn't living at *my* home, with *my* wife, and *my* children.

A few nights after my return to Kansas City, if not to my actual home, something scratched at the balcony door around midnight. Henry's moon-shaped eyes peered in through the sheer curtains, reflecting the light of the TV I kept playing for noise. I did a quick glance around to make sure that Will wasn't within earshot and slipped outside, hugging my hoodie around me. The weather had taken a turn for the colder, promising an early winter.

"Hey, Henry."

"James Dawson! I have returned! I finded you!"

I couldn't help it. Demon or not, the little guy made me chuckle. "Yes, yes you did. Well done."

The small demon perched on the narrow railing, his clawed toes curling around it like a bird's talons. "I finded the information! Much danger, very brave is Henry!"

"I have no doubt of it." When he went to open his mouth to divulge what he'd discovered, I held up a finger. "The thing is, Henry, I don't care anymore." Whether Reina had been the one to make a run at my family, or if Axel himself had done it to get me off my ass, it was no longer important. What's done was done, and I had to go forward.

The demon's bat-ears visibly wilted. "But...I finded it."

"Yes, you did. And I'm going to pay you for it. I just...don't want to know what you found out." I fished a ping-pong ball out of my pocket and held it out to him. There was a faint tingle at my fingertips, but nothing like I'd felt before. My hyper-sensitivity to magic had gone with the souls, and I hadn't had time to decide if I missed it or not.

Henry's eyes lit up red for a heartbeat, and he snatched the plastic toy out of my hands with a coo. "Oh so pretty, oh so shiny..."

"Thank you for your hard work, Henry." The black mark on my wrist itched as it flaked off, the contract fulfilled. I scratched at it, and tried not to think about how much my other arm itched too, confined in its plaster prison.

He made over his treasure for a few moments, then looked up at me, tilting his bald head with a slight frown. "Is James Dawson well?"

That startled a laugh out of me. "You're asking me if I'm okay?" He nodded like a bobblehead, his ears flapping. "I'm...as okay as I'm gonna get, for right now."

"Does need anything more?"

"No, not at the moment. I'll call for you if I think of anything." I turned to go inside, then paused. "Hey, Henry?"

"Yes?"

"You wouldn't happen to know how to kill an angel, would you?" He pondered for a few seconds, then shook his head, slow and solemn. "Didn't figure you did. I'll see you later."

Part of my diabolical master plan to stop this demon war was going to center heavily on being able to kill Reina. Demons I could handle, no problem, but that wasn't what she actually was. I had a feeling that holy water and fast sword work wasn't going to cut it. Heh. "Cut it." My pun-fu was still strong.

I only had one person to go to, and I was truly dreading that conversation. He owed me explanations. He'd said that much, and I intended to hold him to it. But I didn't figure that angel murder was going to be something he was going to give up out of guilt. I mean, he kinda had a vested interest in people *not* knowing how to make him dead.

I went back to work, technically on light duty because of my arm. I called and talked to the kids every single night, while Mira and I awkwardly tried to figure out if we were actually separated or what. I joined up with the D&D game that Will ran on Wednesday nights. I met up with Estéban twice a week to spar, increasing in intensity after I got the cast off my arm. Most of all, I waited.

Axel came looking for me sometime before Thanksgiving. I was taking the trash out to the Dumpster behind work, leaving tracks in the faint dusting of snow that had fallen since sundown. I slammed the lid down, and turned to find the blond demon leaning on the corner of the building, still in only a t-shirt and jeans. We watched each other for a few moments, before I shrugged and crossed the distance between us.

"Was wondering when you'd turn up."

"I was…finishing some things." He wouldn't meet my eyes, his own trained firmly on the tips of his black boots. "Your arm has healed."

"Yup." I wiggled my fingers to demonstrate. "Almost back to a hundred percent."

"That's good." He fell silent, scuffing a pattern in the snow at his feet.

"Look, man. I appreciate the 'wracked with guilt' thing you've got going on here, but I'm freezing my balls off. Can we do this somewhere warmer?"

"I…" He frowned, changed what he'd been about to say. "Yes, we can. The coffee shop on the corner is open until midnight. Meet me there after you have finished?"

"Uh…sure." So, mark 'coffee date with a demon' off my bucket list.

No one was shopping, this time of night, not this close to Black Friday. Closing the store was quick and easy, and I shooed the pair of teenaged work minions toward the parking lot as I locked up, then turned my steps toward the warm glow from the coffee place down the block.

There were more customers there than I expected, one whole section taken up by what looked like a college study group, books and laptops scattered over every available surface. The barista served me a hot chocolate, 'cause that sounded like the best thing in the entire world at that moment, and I made my way into the farthest corner, where Axel was waiting at a secluded two-person table.

I nodded at his empty hands as I slid into the seat opposite.   "You should have ordered something. It's rude to take up a table and not buy anything."

He still wouldn't meet my gaze, keeping his eyes on his clasped hands on the tabletop. "I…was unaware. I will remember that next time."

"You're kinda creeping me out." That made him look up at least, surprised. "This whole meek and cowed thing… This isn't you. What gives?"

"Perhaps I have simply been doing some thinking, these past weeks."

"Yeah, haven't we all." I sipped at my hot chocolate, letting the heat seep into my fingers. I hadn't been able to get warm, since Rome. I'd become too accustomed to the extra life force, and now my body seemed reluctant to return to normal. I caught myself hesitating as I stepped through doorways, waiting for the familiar ripple in the souls as they warned me of lingering magic. My vision seemed dull now, and I'd debated whether or not I needed to go get my eyes checked. And it remained to be seen if my inherent danger sense would return, now that my extra guardians were gone.

"You have questions."

"No doubt."

"I will answer them." I quirked a brow at him and he nodded. "All of them. If they are answers that are in my possession."

I drank a little more, trying to put things into the right order in my head before I started. "First, what are you?"

"I am a demon," was the immediate answer.

"You're not. I saw you. I saw the real you, and you're not like them. You're not like *her,* either. You're not fallen."

He made a face. "It is slightly more complicated than mere appearances."

"Then give me the 'Angels for Dummies' course."

Axel sighed. "*She* is a fallen angel. You are correct. You have seen an angel in its pure form. You recognized how hers has become twisted and corrupt."

I nodded, motioning for him to go on.

"I…was an angel. Originally. Exactly like her. Exactly like the rest of the Host." He fidgeted with his hands, something I hadn't seen him do before. The conversation was truly uncomfortable for him. "I am a demon now. This is fact."

"Then why are you different?"

"Because…I was asked to become a demon. I did not fall. I did not rebel. I am following orders, and therefore despite being a demon, I still appear as an angel."

"Whose orders?" He gave me a flat look. "Seriously? God-with-the-big-G said 'hey, go be a bad guy'?"

"In so many words."

"Why would he do that?"

"Because free will without choice is

nothing." A glimmer of red flared behind his eyes, but in deference to our surroundings, he kept it low key. "Humans cannot choose to be good if there is no other choice available. I do my duty, providing that choice."

"Are you the devil, Axel?"

He snorted. "Your devil. Your Satan, your Lucifer. There is no such creature. It is a human fancy, created so that you can pretend that your acts of evil were not all your own." He shook his head. "I am only myself."

"The Architect."

"Hm." He pressed his palms flat against the table to stop his fidgeting. "What else do you wish to ask?"

"More like I have a few observations to make."

"As you wish."

I leaned back in the chair, stretching my legs out. "So if you're doing the big G's bidding, following all of the rules that he set out for this little ant farm down here, then *she* is one who has said 'take this job and shove it.'" He'd avoided saying her name, even just the name she'd given herself, so I'd do the same. I didn't need another guest at this party.

"Essentially."

"You will fight her, along with whoever else is on your side, because if she gets her way, she'll turn the world into a smoking crater and destroy life as we know it."

"More or less."

"And in the process, that war will probably

turn the world into a smoking crater and destroy life as we know it."

Axel grimaced, but nodded. "It is likely."

"So, here are my thoughts. Your arch-nemesis needs to die. And I don't mean get banished back to wherever it is you guys hang your hats, but truly and actually dead. I get the idea that her lackeys aren't the smartest of the bunch, so they'll likely fall apart without her." He watched me, an expectant gleam somewhere deep in his eyes. "How do you kill an angel, Axel?"

"*You* cannot do it."

"Can you?"

He paused for a long time, then finally shook his head. "No. We cannot harm our own kind."

"But you know how."

"I…." Again, he hesitated, and frustration flashed across his lean features. "No. I have suspicions. I have seen hints. Rumors. But this is one secret that even I was not entrusted with. But I have seen it happen. I have seen one of the Host destroyed before my very eyes. It can be done."

"So, someone knows. Be it demon, or angel, or maybe even human, somebody knows."

"Yes."

I nodded, draining the last of the chocolate from my cup. "Then point me in the right direction. We need to know."

"I can…give you a few places to start. Perhaps you can see something there that I cannot."

He gave me a list of names and texts that I could start my search on, and we parted ways, me walking to my truck in the snow and he just poofing into nothingness.

Back at Will's place, I lay on the couch in the darkness for a long time, pondering. My arm was healed. I had a general path now, if not an actual map to my destination. It was time to stop hesitating.

I logged into the Grapevine app for the first time since I'd returned from Rome. It loaded instantly, but the link to chat with Viljo in person was grayed out. He wasn't online, then. Before I could close out of the program, the link turned green, and I pressed on it instantly. The little window buffered for a moment, and then the hacker's bespectacled face appeared.

His dyed black hair was mussed, and I could tell he didn't have a shirt on as he adjusted his glasses. "Jesse? I thought that might be you. Is everything all right?"

"I'm fine, Viljo. Sorry I haven't been checking in."

"It is all right. Estéban did your check-ins for you." Of course he did. Viljo settled in his chair, reaching off screen and coming back with a can of energy drink. "What can I do for you tonight?"

"I need a list."

"Of?" Already his fingers were flying over his keyboard.

"I need a list of all the champions we have. I want it filtered down to the only the ones who have no family, or children."

The hacker's hands paused, and he peered at

the screen. "Why?"

"Because I asked for it, and I'm the boss now."

After a moment, he sighed and nodded. "That is still most of you. Families are the rarity, rather than the rule."

"Good." I was going to ask them to put their lives on the line in a way they'd never foreseen. If I could avoid destroying another family while I was at it, so much the better.

In the middle of his furious typing, Viljo glanced to his left, at something I couldn't see. There was no mistaking the faint blush that crept over his cheeks, though. "Um, can I get this to you in the morning?"

I grinned. "Do you have someone there, Viljo?"

"Um…I… Well, yes, but…"

A woman's bare arm reached into view, taking control of his mouse, and I heard a low voice say "Say goodnight, Viljo."

The hacker gave me an apologetic shrug and a totally unrepentant grin. "Goodnight, Viljo." The screen went black.

I stared at my dark phone for a few moments, then chuckled and dropped my head back on my pillow. *Good on you, man.* See, I'd recognized the unique pattern of scars on that woman's arm, and I would know that distinctive accent anywhere. *Good on you too, Sveta.*

Rolling up in Will's second best comforter like a burrito, I closed my eyes to sleep. Tomorrow, I'd start kicking over hornets' nests.

Chapter 1

The automaton was obviously malfunctioning. There was a lurching hitch in its gait as it moved, and even an untrained ear could hear the distinct click where the teeth on several gears had either broken or been ground off. The faint charred odor of long-stale grease followed the construction wherever it moved, and when something snapped like a gunshot, no one in the vicinity was surprised.

Well, no one save the draft horse attached to the coal cart, and that monstrous creature shied with a startled bellow, dragging the wagon halfway down the block and scattering pedestrians before it like a flock of pigeons. It barreled toward the busy cross-street, which would most surely cause a disaster, but a well-meaning passerby managed to snag its harness and bring the beast to a stop. Its dappled flanks heaved with the efforts of its sudden, if brief, flight.

The automaton staggered to an abrupt halt, frozen forever holding its load of coal, as its gears seized up and the snapping cables within its chest sent pulleys pinging around inside like bullets. Only the strong steel construction kept the mechanical parts from escaping and flying into the nearby pedestrians like shrapnel. A sad plume of smoke trickled from its auditory receivers, accompanied by the last plaintive whine of its mechanical voice box.

"Goddamn piece of tin-snip rubbish!" The coal master appeared, his bristling mustache broadcasting his irritation even if the stream of profanity had not been a clue. "Piece of scrapyard junk!" He kicked the automaton in the leg, eliciting no response at all from the metal creature – it was well and truly broken – but causing no small amount of damage to his own booted foot.

A small crowd gathered, drawn by the impending disaster with the cart horse, and entertained by the antics of the livid coal master. Chuckles passed amongst them as they watched him hop in circles on his uninjured foot, cursing fit to turn the air blue.

"You there!" The coal master pointed at another automaton, identical in all ways to the first except that the second was still functioning. "Take this coal to the cart, then haul this thing off to the shop. We'll break it down for spare parts."

A mechanical voice answered, "Yes sir" with a faint crackle of damaged wiring behind it. The second construct was not in much better condition than the first, and one could hear a slight ping with every step as an internal cable vibrated just a bit too hard. If one knew what to listen for, of course. That second machine would be inoperable within a month, in all likelihood. That was what became of poor maintenance practices.

The crowd dispersed after a few moments, everyone returning to wherever their lives were taking them. No doubt home to an evening meal, to stoke a nighttime fire to ward off the early autumn chill. Perhaps to curl up beneath a lantern and read to one's children, or beloved.

No one noticed the figure in the dark cloak, standing safely to the side of the hurried pedestrian traffic. She took refuge deep inside her hood, lest someone see, and stood so still that not one glance darted in her direction. Such was their way, the way of the humans. Always so frantic, always so preoccupied within themselves. It worked to her advantage.

When the throng had cleared somewhat, she stepped from the growing shadows, gliding along in a rustle of skirts just like anyone else around her. Certainly, under the cloak her gown was much too fine for this area of the city, but it was also decades behind the fashion with a faded band around the hem where the coal dust had been washed from it many, many times. It would not attract attention, not here. Just as she wanted it.

By the time she had walked eight blocks, there was a distinct change in atmosphere as she left behind the coalworks of the city and ventured into higher class districts. The clothing here was of better quality, more recent acquisition. With the cooler weather coming on, velvets were making their return, along with collared coats and heavier gloves, and fur wraps would soon replace summery parasols. These things she noted, making a mental note to adjust her own wardrobe accordingly.

Most went about in carriages, or the new horseless conveyances, the steam pistons hissing and popping as they sped down the street, scattering those still on foot from their path. Shopkeepers were shuttering their windows for the evening, dousing their lanterns, calling out farewells to their neighbors in commerce.

Here, she crossed the street quickly, vanishing

into the alleys before anyone could question why a woman would be doing such. This was not the area for doxies, and her presence would be noted and wondered at if she lingered too long.

In the alleys, with no eyes to see save vermin and inebriates, she moved faster, realizing that she would be late if she did not make up some time. The incident with the coalworks automaton had distracted her longer than she had intended, and she was behind schedule.

Four blocks north, and two east, and she found the grate just as she'd left it. The bolts into the sandstone colored brick had long since stripped smooth, and it took nothing for her to lift it away and duck into the passage within, replacing the barrier behind her with no sound at all of dragging metal. A human would never be able to lift that grate, she knew, stripped bolts or no. Only she used this entrance, even the city vagrants having long since given up the effort of moving the grate as futile.

Once inside, she only had to crouch for a few paces before the tunnel opened up into a t-shaped junction. A sewer once, long forgotten and paved over, the building atop it constructed decades after the tunnel's function was abandoned. A small trickle of water still meandered down the center of the paving stone floor, never deep enough to dampen her skirts, but enough to create an almost musical melody as it wended through the uneven stones.

Sometimes, when time permitted, she would pause here, locating a particular tone or note that was out of place, and then she would shift the stones in their beds, altering the water flow until it suited her. Tonight, there would be no such indulgence.

Taking care not to slip on the moss-covered stones beneath her boots, she traversed her own well-known path, taking her deep into the bowels of the building.

Already, she could feel the thrum at the back of her skull, the deep vibration caused by the sheer number of living beings above her. Hundreds and hundreds of voices, murmuring amongst themselves. Singly, they were nearly silent, but in multitudes, they roared at a frequency just below human hearing. Their feet, encased in polished shoes or high-buttoned boots, shifted restlessly on the wooden floor far above. In their hands, the paper of the programs rustled, crackled.

She heard the first low draw of a bow across a cello, and quickened her pace. She would miss the opening if she did not hurry. The orchestra was already warming up.

The strings and woodwinds were humming at a higher pitch just behind her jaw joints as she emerged from the sewer tunnel, shifting a large prop barrel to cover the opening as she did every time. The storeroom into which she entered was covered in the cobwebs of long disuse, but she still took care to lift her skirts, leaving only the faintest of tracks through the thick dust. Her oil can, kept near the door to lubricate its hinges into silence, was still there and untouched just as she expected. She inspected the hinges before deciding that more was unnecessary. Just as well, she didn't have time anyway.

The backstage area was largely clear, the hands already scattered through the riggings above the stage, either to watch or to adjust the scenery as needed. The performers were in the wings, waiting for their cues, knowing just how much time they had before curtain by what place the orchestra was in their warm-ups. The dancers had been corralled, slippers rosined and laced, and last minute adjustments to the costumes had been given up as lost causes. The show was about to begin.

She slipped through the darkness behind the stage with the ease of long practice, finding the servants' stair that would take her to the box level. Her box would be waiting, as always, the one nearest the stairway, allowing her to slip in and out unseen.

The muted roar of many voices was almost silent by the time she found her seat in the farthest back corner of box number seven, a corner that even the stage lights could not penetrate. She would be safe there, shrouded in her cloak, motionless. No one would ever glance at the dark box. No one ever had.

The timepiece pinned to her bodice whirred softly, marking the change of the hour, and on cue, the heavy burgundy velvet curtains parted, golden cords drawing them to the sides of the stage. Like the sunrise, she always thought, the world suddenly revealed in a sweep of all-encompassing light. Nothing else existed outside of that brilliance.

The music swelled from the orchestra pit

below, and she allowed herself to be lost in it, swept away on the tide of melody and harmony, each instrument strumming a different chord inside her head. It was flawless. Well, nearly so. The third bassoon was flat, though his compatriots largely drowned out his sad efforts, and the fourth viola was missing a string, which she nimbly fingered around in a display of inspired improvisation.

No one else in the audience would ever notice. In fact, only the maestro himself would be aware of the errors, and so long as the orchestra kept on beat, he'd be unlikely to say a word. He'd become complacent, in his advancing years. He'd been there nearly as long as she, and she knew that his joints pained him in the colder weather. The oncoming winter would swell his knuckles, stiffen his knees. It wasn't as if he could simply replace a bearing or oil a gear. Humans did not repair themselves well. He had earned a small measure of respite.

The chorus took the stage, setting the scene for the night's performance. She closed her eyes, noting which voices were new, which cracked with strain, picking out one or two that were sharp on the harmony. She would have to send a note. That would have to be corrected.

The lead soprano, a young woman named Caroline, treated the audience to the pure notes of her first aria, and the silent watcher was forced to move her jaw slightly to relieve the pressure. The high notes, while technically perfect, caused an odd vibration somewhere behind her left ear, one reason that she had never enjoyed the sopranos so much.

Perfect, yes, but piercing.

The next voice, though… Oh, that was the one she always came to hear. The lead tenor's melody rose above the rest, the chorus falling silent as all eyes went to the handsome, strapping young man at center stage.

Well, once he had been, at any rate. Simon LeClerc was advancing rapidly toward his mid-forties, and if he had to use a girdle to hold in his slight paunch, or use bootblack to conceal the gray in his dark hair, the audience was willing to suspend disbelief. However, while stage makeup could cover a myriad of physical ills, she could hear the hint of strain in his formerly vibrant voice. He was flat. Soundly, decidedly flat. It wasn't much, just a hairsbreadth off from his former perfection, but she could tell.

The audience was rapt, of course. Hanging on every note that tumbled from his lips. The human ear was not designed as finely as hers, would not be able to discern the tiny flaw that she detected so keenly, but it was only a matter of time.

She was sad, she realized. For decades, she had come to watch Simon, his beautiful tenor voice soothing in a way the higher pitches could never be. For years, she had chosen operas particularly suited for him, and she had basked in every bit of applause he had so rightly received. But now…

She'd noticed the faltering voice last summer, and had hoped that it was merely weariness. By the autumn production, his voice was once again all that it could be, all it had always been. But the Christmas choral was nearly a disaster by her standards, Simon deliberately hiding his own melodic line beneath that of the weaker tenors in the chorus, hoping that no one would notice he could no longer carry the lead. The spring fete had been much the same, and though the summer season had been cancelled for extensive remodeling to the opera house, the lengthy rest had alleviated none of his problem.

She was forced, finally, to admit that Simon was aging past his prime. Soon, he would have to depart, make way for someone younger, someone who could hold their pitch. Unfortunately, there was no one in the chorus who could easily take his place. Enthusiastic, yes, but none of them had the power or purity of Simon at his greatest. He would have to be allowed to finish this run, complete the fall season. Perhaps by Christmas, she would be able to locate a replacement.

She would have to send a note.

Departing from the opera house after a performance was never as easy as arriving. There were celebrations to wait out, patrons coming back stage for tours, or to bestow gifts upon their favorites. The stage crew had to reset for the next night's show, the costumers had to gather the garments dropped negligently by the dancers. The maids had to make their way through the entire building, gathering up programs, crumpled and forgotten. They swept the carpets, and the boxes, all save for box seven, because of course when no one used it, cleaning was not necessary.

And so she sat in utter stillness, waiting until the booming echo of the last closing door had faded away. Waiting until she was well and truly alone. Only then did she make her way down the servants' staircase, through the backstage area, into her forgotten storeroom and out through the sewer. The grate slid back into place easily, and she was once again in the open street.

She drew her hood up higher around her face, and kept to the shadows. This area of the city was empty at this time of night, all the merchants closed, all the opera-goers moved on to other diversions. She would be noticed, here, and so she passed through quickly, silently. Only once did she hear the clop of a horse's hooves, the creak of carriage springs, and then she froze into her unnatural motionless state, only her eyes moving as the conveyance trotted by and off into the darkness without marking her presence.

The coalworks, now those offered a different kind of threat. The coalworks never slept, men and automatons ceaselessly shoveling the black rocks into the furnaces, generating the steam that powered most of the city. Always brightly lit, always heavily travelled, passing through the streets of the coalworks promised almost certain discovery at every turn. A woman in the coalworks at this time of night was no lady, that was a given, and could not be expected to be treated as such. She always had to be careful, returning home by that path.

The sounds were the worst part. The constant grind and rattle of the machines, the clang of metal on metal. Voices, both human and automaton, raised to be heard over the volume, dissolving into a harsh cacophony, discordant, unintelligible. It made it impossible to hear anything with any precision, impossible to detect something coming up behind.

The street lights cast prying, orange orbs about themselves, a revealing gleam that she avoided through long practice. Not even the hem of her long skirts brushed their circles of light. With one hand, she kept her hood pulled down, shadowing her face even more, her head ducked to avoid making eye contact with any stray gazes. As such, with her eyes on the cobblestones beneath her boots, she did not see the man lurching out of the alley until it was too late. He barreled into her and bounced off so hard, he may as well have walked into a wall.

"Oof!" He staggered back against the wall, blinking bleary eyes in confusion for a few moments. "Hey there… Watch yourself, girly." Coal dust covered his face, leaving his eyes like two bright points in a mask of black. His clothing was rough spun, and oft patched, his boots were more hole than leather. A coal worker, then, and probably out of the building to sneak a belt of liquor in the back alley across the way.

"My apologies, sir." Two steps back, the shadows were deeper. She withdrew cautiously, keeping her hood tugged low.

"Here now, wait, that ain't no way to offer a proper apology." The man pursued her, and she caught the scent of bourbon strong on his breath as she'd expected. "Pretty thing like you, there oughta be something you could do to make up for almost runnin' a fella over." With a leer and a speed a man that drunk should not possess, he darted forward, grabbing at her wrist.

She could tell the moment he realized that there was no soft, yielding human flesh underneath the brushed silk of her sleeve. The confusion darted across his face, dulled with alcohol and idiocy. "What…?" He leaned forward, craning his neck at an angle almost enough to throw himself completely off balance, peering up into the recesses of her hood. His eyes went wide, shock chasing away some of the effects of the booze. "What the hell…?" His chest expanded as he gasped in a breath, surely to exclaim loudly, or to call for aid, or… Whatever his purpose, she could not allow it.

Her free hand shot out, grasped him around the throat, and his voice came out in a choked gurgle. His eyes bulged out, and his hand scrabbled at hers, grimy fingers tearing the lace trim from her glove. Lifted a few inches off the ground, his feet drummed against her legs, doing her no harm and offering him no aid. His face slowly turned purple, and the vessels in his eyes burst, staining the white red. After a few moments, he stopped struggling, hanging limply in her grip. She held on a few moments longer, then simply let go, the man falling into a heap at her feet.

She glanced around, but there was no one in sight. No one sounded alarm, there was no thunder of running boots and tweeting of police whistles. She remained unseen.

Carefully lifting her skirts, she stepped over the body on the cobblestones, and continued on her way.

About the Author

K.A. Stewart has a BA in English with an emphasis in Literature from William Jewell College. She lives in Missouri with her husband, daughter, two cats, and one small furry demon that thinks it's a cat.